NAUGHTY ALL NIGHT

JENNIFER BERNARD

CHAPTER ONE

Exactly one minute ago, Kate Robinson had been speeding merrily toward town; one curve in the rutted road later, she was stuck in the mud with her wheels spinning uselessly.

And if that wasn't a perfect metaphor for her entire life, she didn't know what was.

She was supposed to be in Los Angeles right now, winning over juries and having brunch with friends—not fetching fertilizer for her grandmother's peony farm in tiny Lost Harbor, Alaska.

Movement at the side of the road caught her attention. A porcupine trundled toward the trees, half its quills raised in defense mode. She must have startled it with her muddy disaster.

With a sigh, she pressed the accelerator again, just in case something had changed in the past ten seconds. *Whir. Spin.*

Nope. If anything, the car had sunk deeper into the mud.

Maybe she shouldn't have been dictating an email as she drove. It was a bad habit from her LA life. When you spent that much time stuck in traffic, you learned ways to use the time productively. Which was better, gridlock or a mud bath? At least with traffic, you knew you'd get moving eventually. On the other hand, the view from this particular mud bath was definitely better than a zillion brake lights.

Spruce trees loomed on one side of the road, and a view of Misty Bay on the other. Against the backdrop of a slate-gray April sky, snowy peaks shone like jagged white teeth. Even though the mountains across the bay still had plenty of snow, at this elevation things were starting to edge toward spring.

This was "break-up" season in Alaska, when the snow melted and the ground thawed, and mud swallowed up everything. Including the old Saab her grandmother Emma was letting her use.

Kate's phone beeped with an incoming text.

ARE YOU BACK?? How come I had to find out from Jess that you were in town?

The text came from Maya Badger, one of her closest friends. Even though they'd only spent time together during the summers, when Kate's parents had sent her to stay with her grandmother, they'd bonded immediately and been best friends ever since.

I'm in denial. Sorry. Can't wait to see you.

Lies. Why the denial?

Long story.

Also, it wasn't really a story she was ready to tell Maya, who was now the police chief of Lost Harbor, Alaska. She'd have to fudge it, a fact that depressed her. Her and Maya's friendship had lasted so long because they could tell each other things they didn't share with other people.

But not this.

Come out with me and Jess tonight. We're getting out of LH and seeing some live music at the Moose Is Loose.

I'll try. That did sound fun. Really fun. But she'd have to get airlifted out at this point. *Quick question. How do you get a car out of the mud?*

How stuck are you?

You know those dinosaurs who got stuck in the tar pits? Like that, except if they had cars.

Calling you.

But apparently she didn't have quite enough service here for a call to go through. And in the next second, the words "no service" appeared where there had been a measly one bar.

Great. Maybe with her vast police powers, Maya could figure out her location from the signal that had just dropped. She could send help—a tow truck or something.

Or maybe she should see if there was anything she could do herself. Maybe she could push the car out of the mud. She put her hand on the door handle, then remembered that she'd left her mud boots back at the farm. She'd been so excited about a drive to town that she'd put on her cute purple suede half-boots with the chunky heel.

Suede didn't like mud.

If she was going to free the car by pushing it, she'd have to do it barefoot.

But first—

She picked her phone up again.

Might as well complete that email she'd been dictating while she still remembered the point she was trying to make.

To DBoone@lhfd.org.

Subject. Your refusal to be reasonable.

Mr. Boone, my grandmother has unfortunately misled you. I am the owner of the property on Fairview Court. She signed it over to me two years ago when she thought she was at death's door. I mentioned the requirement about her chickens, and that I take care of them, only as a colorful and amusing detail. The fact that she's alive and I'm not taking care of her chickens doesn't change the fact that I am the legal owner of the property. It has no bearing on my right to ask you to vacate the premises.

Was she being too legalistic in her approach? That was an obvious occupational hazard. That was why she'd mentioned the chickens to begin with. But her efforts to be charming had fallen flat—at least for Mr. D. Boone.

She scanned the last email D. Boone sent, the one she was now responding to.

I have an agreement with Emma. I know her well, and I know for damn sure she wouldn't go back on her word. A deal is a deal. On that note, are you holding up your end of your deal? When's the last time you fed Emma's chickens?

She ground her teeth together. How dare this complete stranger lay some kind of chicken guilt trip on her? How could she feed the chickens when she lived three thousand miles away? Besides, Emma liked feeding her own chickens. She was a stubbornly self-reliant pain in the ass.

Kate hadn't mentioned Project Kick Boone Out to her grandmother because she feared that Boone was right. Emma would throw a fit about breaking an agreement. Her hope was that she could coax him to leave.

Or her. She didn't actually know D. Boone's first name. But the emails were so brusque and uncooperative that she'd jumped to the conclusion that they had to come from a man.

An extremely aggravating man.

But then again, weren't they all?

A sound caught her attention, the low rumble of a vehicle coming from behind her.

Potential rescue? Possible kidnapper? Since this was Lost Harbor, odds were on rescue, but she was taking no chances. She rummaged in her bag for the bear spray Emma had made her bring.

The vehicle slowed to a stop behind her. It was a large crew cab truck with so much clearance it could probably drive right over her little Saab. The man who jumped out of it was equally large. His long legs came first—clad in work pants and mud boots.

AKA what she *should* have been wearing.

Then came the rest of him—broad and tall and muscular and a little intimidating, considering that she was alone in this forgotten spot on the side of a remote Alaskan road. He wore a weathered work jacket unzipped over a gray Henley.

With easy strides, he made his way through the mud to her car. She kept her hand on the can of bear spray next to her on the seat. He noticed that move, and his lips quirked. They were very appealing lips, she noted. Firm and full, with a sensual curve to them.

"If I help you un-muck your car, will you promise not to mace me?" His deep voice fit the general oversize nature of his physique.

She relaxed enough to allow herself to smile at the stranger. "Do you think you can get me out of this? It's a mess. I swear, that mud came out of nowhere, Officer."

One corner of his mouth lifted, indicating that he'd gotten her joke. But he maintained his serious expression. "You have to pay attention this time of year. No cell phones while driving."

Ah, so he'd spotted her phone on the seat next to her bear spray. "Are you planning to help me or lecture me?"

"Maybe a lecture would help you." His reasonable tone made her teeth clench.

"I can guarantee that it wouldn't. No one likes to be lectured."

"I said it might help you, not please you." The word "please" in his deep, rumbling voice sparked a surprising little thrill deep in her belly.

Oh no. None of that now.

"If you want to please me, you could tell me what you recommend here. Do I need to call a tow truck?"

He took a step back and surveyed the muddy ruts that had claimed her tires. "What have you tried so far?"

"Not much. Just a little cursing and whining and regretting the fact that I didn't bring my mud boots. I tried powering out of it, but that made it worse."

"Yes, that would make it worse. The tires can't get any purchase on the mud, so they just dig the tracks deeper and deeper the more they spin. They need something solid to grip onto. I'm surprised you haven't encountered this situation before. It is break-up, after all."

"I'm not from here." She bit off each word as she spoke it. This was sounding suspiciously like that lecture she'd told him she didn't want. "I've never seen break-up before. Not this kind, anyway. But I'm sure you don't want to hear about my love life." She could practically hear the "ba-da-bum" after that lame joke.

He was watching her closely as she spoke. His eyes were two shades of blue south of gray, a surprisingly soft color in the midst of all that masculinity. They looked almost silvery in the misty light.

Heat came to her cheeks under his scrutiny. "Sorry, dumb joke."

"Eh, it was all right." He shrugged one massive shoulder. "A little obvious, but not bad."

For a murderous moment, she wondered how bad it would be if she used her bear spray on him right now. Surely someone else would come along to rescue her. "Can we get back to the main event here? Car. Mud. Stuck."

"Sure. As I was saying, you need something under the tires."

Then came a pause. A long pause, like he wasn't going to say anything more than that.

"And?" she said impatiently. "Has winter frozen your brain?"

"Oh sorry. I thought you didn't want a lecture. But I'm happy to explain the physics of it. It has to do with the force of friction and fluid dynamics, not to mention momentum. You see, when you hit a muddy patch, the last thing you want to do is slow down. Momentum will overpower the force of the friction—"

Oh my God. He wasn't lecturing her, he was *teasing* her. And honestly, she completely deserved it. She hadn't exactly been polite to this stranger. Sure, she was having a hell of a few months, but that didn't mean she had to take it out on him.

"Can we start over?" she interrupted in her sweetest possible voice. Witnesses melted when she used this tone. Juries fell in love. Judges ruled her way. "I would dearly love to hear everything you know about mud. Who wouldn't, really? I could listen to you all day long. But I hate to keep you from whatever you were doing before this. So for your sake, perhaps we could shift to the action part of the lesson?"

She gave the word "action" just a bit of flirtatious edge. She loved a good double-entendre.

He definitely picked up on it. She could see it in the gleam in his eyes and the ever-so-slight quirk of his lips. But he had impressive control. Clearly he had no intention of letting her get the upper hand.

"Yes, ma'am, I'll get right on that." he said. She detected a bit of a drawl. Maybe he wasn't from here either. "I'll be sure to write up my notes on driving in the mud for you. They could save a life. Possibly even yours, but most likely someone else's."

"That's a low blow. I'm a very skilled driver, I'll have you know."

"I'll have to take your word on that." He turned away to head for his truck. "I have some blocks in my truck. Lesson number one. This time of year, always bring blocks."

CHAPTER TWO

Darius swallowed back his grin as he went to retrieve his blocks from the bed of his truck. He always carried a selection of chunks of two-by-fours, four-by-sixes, one-by-sixes and other bits of lumber for emergencies like this. Most Alaskans did, but him especially. A rural fire chief was always on the job. Just this week, he'd helped a stranded motorist change a flat tire and pulled another rig out of a ditch.

He didn't always get to rescue such a live one, however. Ever since he'd pulled over, she'd been spitting fire at him.

And he'd done everything possible to goad her on, he had to admit. There was nothing like a woman who gave as good as she got.

He wondered what her name was and where she was from. *Definitely* not local. Even if she hadn't said as much, he would have known she wasn't from around here. She was too...fancy, for lack of a better word. Her dark hair fell in glossy waves past her shoulders. Her lightly tinted aviator sunglasses looked like something you might see on a billboard. They took up half her face, giving him the impression of catlike bone structure and a sexy full mouth.

The icing on the cake was the fitted shiny red leather jacket she was wearing. You didn't see a lot of red leather around here, and he hadn't known what a sad situation that was until he'd laid eyes on her.

He grabbed an armful of blocks—at least one for each tire—and carried them back to the Saab. It was an older model, probably from the nineties, and unfamiliar to him. Maybe she'd driven it here from somewhere else. Like Chicago or New York City. Or Milan.

"I'm Darius, by the way," he said as he passed the driver's-side window.

"Kate." Her tone was much friendlier now, probably because he was doing what she wanted instead of droning on about mud and purposely annoying her. "Be careful near the road, I saw a porcupine right before you showed up. I really appreciate you doing this. Do you want me to get out and help?"

He hid another smile at her obvious reluctance to do any such thing. She'd mentioned her lack of mud boots. He could only imagine the expensive shoes that probably went with that jacket.

"It's all right. One of us needs to be at the wheel. Following my directions," he added.

"Of course. When a knight in white armor appears, it's bad form to argue with him, I suppose."

"Shouldn't that be 'knight in white Armor-All'?" he murmured as he knelt down to insert a block under the front driver's side tire. "Being a truck," he added in case his dumb joke wasn't obvious.

But she wasn't one to miss a joke, clearly. She gave a surprised laugh. "That's not bad."

"Gee, thanks," he said dryly. "Always good to keep your

rescue victims laughing." He stood up and gave the block a kick to make sure it was solidly wedged in place.

"You rescue people often?"

"Yes. It's a full-time job." Literally, it was. Not that she knew that. "Especially in mud season." He passed around the hood of her car to the passenger side. She unrolled the window so they could keep talking.

"See, that's the kind of thing that gets to me. What kind of place has a mud season? Why are people okay with that? Why do people voluntarily choose to live in a place where you have to jump from snow boots, which are unattractive enough, right into mud boots, which are somehow even less appealing?"

He nudged the passenger-side block into place. "You seem awfully worried about shoes."

"Just go ahead and call me shallow. I don't mind."

He stood up and smiled. "So long as you promise not to mace me."

She pulled a funny face at him. "It's bear spray. And no promises."

"Are you always this prickly when someone's trying to help you out?"

She paused, cocking her head as if she had to think about that one. "Well, I can't really say. Generally I don't need help. And if I do, I just pay the person for it. It's a cold, cold world out there, Darius."

"Is it?"

He moved to the rear of the car to install the remaining blocks. He put them behind the tires so the car couldn't roll backwards.

"Sad to say, it is." Her grave tone piqued his curiosity. He got the feeling she was referring to something specific. "I don't want to crush your illusions, Knight in White Armor-All, but most people are crap. Even more to the point, most *men* are crap. So I suppose I haven't perfected my help-receiving manners because it just hasn't come up very often."

He finished his task and stepped to the side. "I'm going to overlook that insult to my gender. At least for now. Want to give it a try? Nice and gentle on the accelerator."

She turned the key in the ignition and fired up the engine. The car rolled forward, the weight of the front end pressing the forward blocks into the mud. He held his breath as the tires fought for purchase on the wood. Should he have put more blocks down? He hefted the extra length of two-by-four that he'd brought over. A little more wood ought to do it.

And that way they could continue their conversation. Maybe he'd even find out why she was so cynical when it came to men in particular, and people in general. Not that he disagreed, entirely. People could be crappy. In his case, that included a couple of women. More specifically, his ex-wives.

The car lurched forward and slid from side to side in the muck. A rooster tail of mud slammed across Darius' pants, even though he tried to jump back in time. The Saab climbed onto the gravel with a squeal. As soon as she'd made it all the way out of the mud, Kate hit the brakes.

"You did it," she called to him. "Thank you so much!"

He shook mud off his right pants leg, like a dog. Damn, now he was going to have to change before he drove out to the Moose. That meant he was probably going to be late for his gig. "No problem," he grumbled.

"I owe you one. Really."

"You don't owe me anything." The very thought irritated him —even if it wasn't his job, people helped each other out around here. It went with living on the edge of the wilderness. "Just be more careful in the mud. If you hit a slick, don't slow down. Just keep going or the mud will suck you in."

She pushed her sunglasses back up her nose. "Now that sounds like life advice I can follow. Don't slow down, just keep going. Got it. Thanks again, Sir Armor-All." With one more salute of thanks, she zoomed off down the road at least fifteen miles over the speed limit.

He shrugged. What the hell, he was a fire chief, not a state trooper. It wasn't his job to make her obey the speed limits. Good thing, too. She didn't seem the type to obey anything except her own wishes.

Even if they left a guy alone with his wood, all covered in mud.

And if that wasn't the story of his life, he didn't know what was.

DARIUS SWUNG BACK into his truck and grabbed his phone. He fired off a quick text to the band manager. *Running late, but I'll be there.*

The bassist for a band from Oregon had gotten food poisoning and their manager had called him in as a last-minute fill-in. He loved getting a chance to play again—it was a great break from his current problem.

Someone was setting nuisance fires around Lost Harbor, and it was starting to piss him off.

He hit the speed dial for Nate Prudhoe, the only other full-time member of the Lost Harbor Volunteer Fire Department.

"Same as the others," he told him. "No real damage, but one pissed-off home owner. I guess that bear cache dated from the 1930s."

"Damn. Any clues?"

"Not a one. Who would have a motive for burning down a bear cache? Other than a bear?"

Nate chuckled. "Ding ding, we have ourselves a suspect. They are coming out of hibernation right about now."

"We need to have a crew meeting about this. We're lucky none of these fires have done much damage."

"Except to our reputation."

Darius swore. "This idiot is going down, whoever it is."

"Right there with you, Chief. I'll set up the meeting."

"Thanks, Nate."

He hung up his phone and noticed that a new email had come in while he'd been sliding around in the mud. It was from the woman who'd been driving him nuts for the past week, Catriona Robinson, Attorney-at-Law.

What kind of person felt the need to attach that information to every single email?

The same kind of person who would try to evict a guy for absolutely no reason, in the middle of gearing up for tourist season. He didn't have time to hunt for a new apartment. Housing was surprisingly difficult to find in this little town, unless you were willing to buy. But he'd only been here for a little over a year, and he still wasn't sure he was going to stay. So he preferred to stick with a rental.

But he disliked apartment hunting so much that he'd actually offered to buy the house from Catriona Robinson, Attorney-at-Law, instead of having to move before he was ready.

She'd rejected that idea right away, and their email correspondence had gone downhill from there.

I have a signed lease. I have no intention of moving until my lease is up. I've already paid next month's rent. You have no right to evict me without notice or cause.

That sounded properly legalistic, but it didn't seem to impress her.

I'm sorry to say that your lease wasn't signed by the actual owner. It was signed by my grandmother. I'm the owner, and I wasn't informed of said lease. I am ready and eager to claim possession of my property.

So this obnoxious lawyer was Emma Gordon's granddaughter? He'd never heard about Emma having a granddaughter—or even a husband or children, for that matter. Obviously this attorney didn't live here or know how things worked in Lost Harbor.

So you're putting the blame on your grandmother? I signed in good faith and so did she. Emma is a friend and a solid member of the community. You should talk to her. She'll straighten this out.

Emma Gordon was a very unique and iconoclastic woman with some wild stories to tell. She'd supplied a dozen orders of peonies to a volunteer fire department fundraiser, but that wasn't the only way Darius knew her.

He and Emma both owned Harleys and had bonded over that fact when he'd picked up his bike from the ferry it had been shipped on. Apparently everyone knew to call Emma the instant a Harley came to town. She'd tracked him down at the firehouse and they'd gabbed for hours about their bikes. He respected the hell out of her, and felt sorry for her that her granddaughter was such a shark.

My grandmother has nothing to do with this. She signed the house over to me in exchange for taking care of her chickens when she dies, the lawyer had written.

He'd laughed out loud at that—typical Emma. One time, Emma had stopped by the firehouse and asked him how much money he would want to dig her a grave on her property.

"That's not happening, Emma," he'd told her. "Is it even legal?"

She'd gone on a long rant about lawyers at that point.

Amen to that. None of his experiences with lawyers had been good. Divorce, liability, fire department lawyers—he'd rather forget all of them. One nice thing about Lost Harbor was that there were only three lawyers in town, and one of them was on the verge of retirement.

He looked at the subject line of her latest email and burst out laughing.

Subject: Your refusal to be reasonable.

Excellent. He was getting under her skin. Maybe she'd give up trying to evict him. His stubborn streak had been activated and he truly believed that he was in the right here. Emma had never told him that she didn't actually own the property. He only had three months left on the lease, anyway. Why couldn't Ms. Attorney-at-Law leave him in peace until then?

He scanned her email and composed his own subject line.

Subject: Chickens

If you can prove that you know the names and varieties of Emma's chickens, I'll consider your suggestion that I move out.

P.s. She has thirty-two chickens, at last count.

P.s.2 They all have names.

P.s.3 You're lucky I'm not asking what their favorite treats are.

Out of the corner of his eye, he spotted the porcupine Kate had warned about. Its quills were settling back into place.

Okay, enough fun tweaking the attorney at law. He had to zip home to his house—while it was still his—grab his bass and find something else to wear tonight.

CHAPTER THREE

Back at Petal to the Metal Peony Farm, Kate changed into her mud boots and unloaded the bags of fertilizer into a wheelbarrow. She trundled them down the path past the *Duchesse de Nemours* plot, where the creamy crown-shaped beauties were cultivated. Right now, all the peonies looked more or less like spears rising from long Typar-covered beds, but soon they'd be leafing out into a glorious symphony of white, deep rose, coral, and blush-pink blooms.

The farm consisted of an enchanting spread of grassy slopes punctuated by outbuildings, peony fields, and plastic-covered greenhouses known as "high tunnels," where Emma grew vegetables and a few other flowers. Perched on a ridge above the town of Lost Harbor, overlooking Misty Bay and the stunning peaks of Lost Souls Wilderness, its thousand-foot elevation and southern exposure were perfect for growing peonies.

Right now, at eight in the evening in mid-April, the fluffy clouds drifting past the bluff held a hint of apricot from the oncoming sunset. The view was enough to make this property spectacular, and when you added in the beauty of the peonies in summer bloom, it could have come straight from a fairy tale.

And then there was Emma Gordon, Kate's mother's mother and the most ornery being on the planet. At eighty-two, she still worked her ass off on the farm, in mud boots and track suit, with a bomber jacket for warmth.

"Did you make that steer manure yourself?" Emma grumbled as Kate brought the wheelbarrow to a halt next to her in the high tunnel. The moist air inside smelled of rich soil and fresh growth.

"I ran into some trouble."

Kate didn't feel like admitting she got stuck in the mud. Alaska had a way of humbling a person, and she'd already been humbled enough by recent events.

"Trouble, trouble. Always in trouble. Reminds me of your teenage years."

Kate took one end of a bag of fertilizer, Emma picked up the other, and together they unloaded it onto the ground.

"With a granny like you, what else would you expect?" Kate gave her a sunny smile. She and Emma had always enjoyed a kind of affectionate bickering relationship.

"I sure wouldn't expect a lawyer. I blame your father for that."

Kate let that jab pass, because it had a big foundation of truth. Her father bore the blame for a lot of things. Her current career implosion was completely due to him.

But when her father—a charming but mostly harmless grifter—somehow ended up with a choice between a dire prison sentence and a vengeful ring of criminals, she couldn't very well abandon him. She'd left her respectable law firm, represented him on her own, gotten him a sweet deal, then hightailed it out of LA to avoid her father's former "associates."

"Can we not go there right now, Emma?" she muttered. "Yell at me about some other stuff, why don't you."

Emma's black eyes snapped at her. "Don't mind if I do. Got a call from Maya. She says you're ignoring her. That's rude, and I raised you better than that."

"Oh my God, I'm not ignoring her, I'm helping out my favorite ancestor."

"I'm not in the ground yet. Though I did pick out a good spot the other day."

"If you're going to talk nonsense like that, you're on your own tonight. I *will* go out clubbing with Maya."

They both chuckled at the word "clubbing." Lost Harbor didn't have "clubs." It had bars and saloons.

"Good, then she'll get off my ass and go solve some crimes."

"What crimes? The biggest crime here is that we have to wear these mud boots everywhere."

"Then go change and get outta here. Have some fun."

"Are you implying that fertilizer isn't fun?"

"Never."

Kate laughed at her grandmother's dry humor.

"Go. Dance a little, drink a little. See Maya. Let off some steam."

Honestly, it sounded like exactly what she needed. The past few months had been unimaginably stressful. "Maybe I will, if you've got this."

Emma waved her away, and Kate dashed back to the old farmhouse to change into some "clubbing" clothes—really, anything that wasn't mud boots and Carhartts would do.

In the tiny cramped guest room filled with unpacked suitcases, a new wave of frustration came over her. She *had* to move into the house on Fairview Court. It wasn't optional. She needed more space, and between the roosters crowing in the morning and the geese honking, she was getting grouchy.

If Project Evict Boone didn't pan out, she'd just move into the upstairs apartment, which was empty. The upstairs space was about half the size of the downstairs because it had a huge front deck. But it would be more livable than this, and it had what she most wanted—some quiet and privacy.

To brighten her mood, she threw on a red halter top and her best pair of skinny jeans, along with her favorite sparkly, strappy dancing shoes.

Her LA life felt incredibly far away right now. But for one night, she could pretend that life wasn't dead and gone, and that angry criminals hadn't threatened to find her and make her pay for the deal she'd gotten her father.

A twinge of pain pulsed across her skull. No. Not a migraine, not now. Not when she was finally about to have a little fun. She took a few deep breaths and it dissipated. Thank God.

Bring on the fun! Maybe there'd even be a man to flirt with. She needed to exercise her flirting muscles. That way, if she ever met Darius the Knight in White Armor-All again, she'd be ready.

AS SOON AS Kate laid eyes on Maya Badger, the urge to down several shots of tequila and tell her the whole sordid story of her father nearly overcame her.

But even though Maya wasn't in uniform—a gold lamé top and black pants was definitely not her uniform—a rural police chief was never really off the job. So Kate stuck with the several shots of tequila and skipped the confession.

Even so, it was hard to fool Maya. At a rickety table crammed into a back corner of the Moose is Loose Saloon, they hugged and shouted greetings over the raucous band.

Which *rocked*, by the way. The second she'd walked in, the deep thump of the upright bass had grabbed her like a dance partner about to swing her off her feet.

After they both sat down, Maya began the grilling. "You never come here in April. Something's up. Are you in trouble?"

"Oh come on, I'm not that rebellious teenager anymore."

"Really? Naughty Kate is history?"

Kate grabbed a cut lime and bit into it so she wouldn't have to say any more. With two Kates in their loose group of teenage friends, one had gotten the "Nice Kate" nickname, while she'd gotten the one that suited her troublemaking style.

"Okay, fine, I see you don't want to talk. That's okay, I have my ways."

Kate waved a hand at her, her mouth puckering from the lime. "You can't use your police superpowers on your best friend. That's not cool."

Maya raised an expressive eyebrow. She wore glittery eye shadow that made her look completely different from her on-the-job persona. "Fine. At least tell me the basics. Are you staying with Emma? Is she okay?"

"Yes, she's okay, and yes, I'm staying there for now. But we're driving each other crazy so I'm going to move into her old house in town."

"The one on Fairview Court?"

"Yup. But there's a very irritating person living in it, so I'm working on evicting him."

Maya laughed and shook her head. "Damn, Kate, look at your badass legal self. Why do you have to evict him?"

"Because it's my house and Emma never should have rented it out, and I like my own space."

"I'll bet you a cocktail that you'll end up letting him stay." Maya gave her a knowing smile. "I know you. At heart, you're softer than a roll of Charmin."

"Did you just compare me to toilet paper?"

"Toilet paper is one of the best inventions in the world. Only the best people deserve to be compared to toilet paper."

Kate rubbed at the spot between her eyebrows where tension always gathered. "Things have been crazy lately. I really just need a place where I can be alone, you know?"

Maya narrowed her perceptive brown eyes at her. "Trouble, just like I thought. Let me guess. It's a man's fault."

Oh, it was definitely a man's fault. "You're absolutely right about that."

"Don't tell me you broke your own no-romance rule."

Kate laughed at the reminder of the old rules she and her friends used to joke about all summer.

"Oh no. I'm still one hundred percent Team Sex."

"And I'm still one hundred percent Team Romance," a soft voice sounded in her ear. She turned to find Jessica Dixon opening her arms for a squeeze. "You're back, Kate! Yay!" They hugged for an extended moment, rocking back and forth with the music.

Damn, that band was good. Especially the bassist. The fast-paced vibrations traveled through her, as if the musician was playing her tendons and nerves instead of an instrument.

"It's so good to see you!" Kate told Jess as she settled into the chair Maya had saved for her. Jessica, with her soft auburn hair and angelic smile, owned the Sweet Harbor Bakery and totally looked the part of the nurturing baker—until you got to know her wild side.

As fun-seeking teenagers on those long summer days, Kate had definitely seen her wild side.

"I fought off three longshoremen and a lumberjack for that chair," Maya said from across the table.

"What are your police powers for if not that?" Jessica lit up with laughter. She had the best belly laugh, always had.

"Good point." Never one to be distracted for long, Maya turned back to Kate. "I was just grilling Kate about the broken heart that brought her back to Lost Harbor in the middle of mud season."

"Oh no." Jessica clasped her hands together. "I'm so sorry."

"I'm fine. No broken heart." Not that kind, anyway. "You guys know me. I'm not the heartbreak type. I've always relied on myself and I always will." With a jaunty smile, Kate tossed her hair over her shoulder.

But Jessica was still eerily perceptive. "Maybe not, but there's something wrong. Isn't there, Maya?"

"Oh yeah. I noticed as soon as she came in and walked right past the hot bouncer." Maya indicated him with a gesture of her head. Then her face sobered. "But seriously, Kate. If there's something wrong, you know you can trust us."

Kate swallowed hard. She wanted to spill all her troubles. It would be a relief to tell the whole story to her friends. But one of these particular friends also happened to be the police chief. And that complicated things.

"You want to know what's wrong?"

"Of course. You can tell us anything." Jessica fiddled with the woven bead bracelet on her wrist. Kate had one of those too, somewhere. So did Maya, but obviously it didn't go with a police uniform. Jessica was the only one who still wore that relic from their teenage summers.

"What's wrong is that this band rocks and I haven't danced or had any fun at all in forever. And we're sitting here talking! That's what's wrong. Who is this band, anyway?"

"They're from out of state—Oregon, I think. But don't change the subject." Jessica shook her head at her, setting a hand on her arm to keep her in her chair. "Maybe what's wrong is that you're avoiding your feelings just like you always have."

"I haven't *always* avoided my feelings. Just when they try to ruin my mood."

Maya laughed at that and tilted her shot glass for a toast. "I hear that."

Kate downed her shot and finally felt a buzz set in. "Sorry, Jess, but you know I'm never going to be Team Talk About Your Feelings, aka Team Romance. We all decided that a long time ago."

Sunbathing on the deck of Jessica's family's fishing boat, they used to discuss things like destiny and soulmates. Jess had been a believer, Kate the cynic, and Maya the neutral observer.

"People change," Jessica insisted. "I know I'll win you over someday. I mean, I won't. A man will. It just has to be the right man."

"The right man?" Kate gestured to the passing waitress for another shot. "The right man is the one who's going to help me forget my crappy life tonight. Like whoever's on that bass. He's already making me forget. Anyone who can play like that can make me forget all kinds of things."

Maya and Jessica exchanged a glance filled with something Kate couldn't quite identify. "The bassist? Do you know who he is?" Maya asked casually.

"Doesn't matter who he is. I don't want to know. I'm Team Sex, remember?"

"What if he's eighty with a beard down to his waist?" Maya teased.

Kate twisted around to peer through the crowd toward the stage. Too many people were in the way, so she stood up. Even though she was on the tall side, all she could see over the sea of bobbing heads was the neck of the bass—a hand working the strings—and a black cowboy hat.

Okay, she could work with a black cowboy hat. And that hand moved so smoothly across the strings. It was a large hand, with long fingers and a wide spread. A man's hand.

And then the crowd shifted just enough so she could see all

of him. He was a big guy, just...big. Wide in the shoulders and long in the legs. Tall and powerful and husky and fit and tall. He played standing up, bent over the upright bass, pouring all of his attention into the strings he was plucking and slapping. Along with the black cowboy hat, he wore a black t-shirt and black jeans.

She couldn't see his face under the cowboy hat, but just then he looked up and—*pow*. He grinned at her—or maybe it was at the crowd in general—the kind of smile that spread across his entire face and made her want to do wild and naughty things to him.

And wait—was that—holy shit! She almost hadn't recognized him.

She dropped back down on her seat. "I do know that guy. I mean, I don't *know* him, but he pulled me out of the mud earlier today."

"It's destiny," Jessica said excitedly. "Clearly there's something going on here. He pulls you out of the mud. Then he pulls you out of your bad mood."

"You should talk to him," Maya agreed.

"Are you guys trying to get me into trouble?"

"At least it's the good kind of trouble." Maya and Jessica laughed and exchanged a high five.

Kate sucked down more tequila. It was kind of odd that her friends weren't warning her away from the bassist. Normally they would because he was a stranger. Except he wasn't totally a stranger, since he'd already rescued her from the mud. But maybe they agreed with her that she needed some fun. Or maybe the tequila was blurring things just enough so she didn't care.

Was he from Oregon, like the rest of the band? If so, what had he been doing on the muddy back roads of Lost Harbor? Visiting friends or family? Sightseeing?

If he was from Oregon, what was the harm? There would be

no chance of running into him at the bank or the grocery store or Gretel's Cafe.

She could follow Maya's suggestion and go ask him.

She hadn't come out tonight for anything other than seeing Maya and Jessica. But life had been very challenging lately, and maybe she really did need a distraction.

Like dancing.

"Come on, you guys. Remember when we used to secretly borrow Jess's dad's car and drive up here to go dancing? Why are we just sitting here! Let's move!"

She jumped to her feet and ditched her jacket.

Maya shoved her chair back and rose to her feet, already moving to the beat. "So long as no one takes any damn selfies."

"Why are you even worried? You don't look anything like your usual self. I didn't even quake in my shoes when I saw you," Kate teased her. "It's amazing how effective that uniform is."

"It's not her uniform," said Jessica, making her way to her feet. "It's her natural authority."

Maya froze her face into a severe frown, then relaxed it again with a laugh after Kate's eyes widened.

"Damn. You really are good."

"Yup. It works on everyone except the guys I happen to like. Makes them disappear."

They all laughed as they carved out a spot on the dance floor. The crowd was a mix of couples and amorphous groups dancing together—like them. The music pulsed right through her system, lighting her up from the inside, like a switch turning on.

Kate threw her head back, letting the beat take her wherever it would. All the mess in LA faded away. It was all so far away now. Her legal career was dead. Her condo sold. Her future unknown.

And right now, none of it mattered.

Next break, she was going to tell Sir Armor-all what a magician he was. Maybe ask him where he lived.

Just then, he looked up and caught her eye. And winked. Obviously he recognized her too.

She must have made a sound, because Maya and Jessica both slowed their dancing and looked in the direction she was staring.

"Wow," Kate breathed. "That man might make me break my biggest rule."

Maya shot her a curious look. "Which is what?"

"Only one stupid thing a night. I already got stuck in the mud, so I've filled my quota. On the other hand, he's possibly from Oregon, so maybe it isn't all that stupid."

She caught another of those odd glances between Jess and Maya.

"What difference does Oregon make?" Jessica asked her.

"The men here aren't really my type."

Maya's eyebrows climbed up her forehead. "Oh really? But that man up there behind that upright, he is your type?"

Kate looked at him again, her mouth literally watering. "I don't know if he's my type, specifically. It's more like he's anyone's type. I mean, look at him. Would you kick him out of bed?"

Maya exchanged another glance with Jessica, this one filled with secret laughter. There was some kind of joke that Kate was missing here.

"I see your point. So what are you going to do about it, Team Sex?" Maya asked.

Jessica nudged her. "Did you know the owner has fishing cabins out back that he rents out?"

"Oh ho, so the Moose is Loose is for lease?"

Kate giggled at her own joke. She was pretty loose herself right about now. Loose was good. Loose was great. She felt loose and relaxed and happy, and it wasn't just the tequila.

It was the juicy thrill of attraction. The glance across a room. The connection sizzling through the notes of that deep bass. They were dancing together, her and Sir Armor-all, even though he was still onstage. She could feel each note he played curl into her bloodstream.

After everything she'd been through lately, couldn't she allow herself one flirtation with a smoking-hot man? Did that even count as a "stupid thing?" He'd already rescued her once. He was very likely from out of town. How risky could it be?

CHAPTER FOUR

Oh man. How was Darius supposed to concentrate on "Light My Fire" when the woman from the stuck Saab was out there dancing in that red top? And those curve-hugging jeans? And those flirtatious hair tosses?

Darius caught a glance from the band's singer as he came close to falling behind the beat. After getting held up by the mud-rescue situation, he'd barely made it up the peninsula in time for a quick rehearsal. Luckily, they were pros, and he was pretty damn good himself, for an amateur. He used to play back in Texas, and still did when he could find someone to jam with.

Oh shit. Now the woman—Kate, he remembered—was tossing back an entire glass of something that looked like tequila. That couldn't be good. The friends she was dancing with would probably take her home, and he wouldn't get to lust after her from his spot behind the bass anymore.

The crowd moved, and he realized with a shock that the woman's friends were none other than Police Chief Maya Badger and Jessica Dixon from the Sweet Harbor Bakery.

Kate was friends with the police chief.

He too was friends with the police chief, more or less. They had their conflicts, as firefighters and police officers often did, but he respected Maya Badger. He definitely respected her enough to stay the hell away from her friend.

Maybe he should stop staring at her and focus on his job. At least for now.

The song ended and he sat down on his stool and took a break while the singer talked to the crowd.

Kate had disappeared, possibly into the bathroom. He caught Maya's eye and beckoned to her. A few minutes later, she appeared next to the stage. Honestly, he barely recognized her in that gold top with her hair all wild.

"Question for you. Your friend Kate. I met her earlier tonight. I don't want to step on—"

"It's all good. Go for it."

He narrowed his eyes at her. Maya could be hard to figure out because she played her cards close to the vest. "That was quick."

She wagged a finger at him. "Just don't tell her who you are, that's my only advice. Also, don't tell her where you live."

"What the hell? Why not?"

"Look, just go with it. She's great. And she thinks you're hot. So far as I know, that's the only thing really wrong with her."

He scowled at her. "Save your insults for the job, why don't you?"

"But why would I, when they're so fun no matter what the circumstances?"

With a growl, he took a sip of the water the waitress had left him. "I only have a couple minutes before the next set. Come on, give me something more or I'll tell everyone I saw you dancing in a gold lamé top and Lost Harbor will never be the same after that."

She smirked and folded her arms across her chest. "You wouldn't."

He raised one eyebrow and held her gaze. But this was Maya Badger he was dealing with, and he quickly caved. "Okay, I probably wouldn't. I'm not that kind of guy."

"Aaaaand, because you know I don't care all that much."

"Good point. Okay, at least give me the lowdown on your friend. Is she single?"

"She's single. She's very cool. Smart, funny, weird taste in men. She's from the Lower Forty-Eight. But she spent summers here growing up."

From out of state. That was a good thing. It could be hard dating in such a small town. A woman who lived somewhere else...yeah, that could work.

"But look, you should get to know her for yourself. Want me to pass a note to her or something?"

He gave her his most intimidating lip curl. "I can take it from here, thanks. I just want to make sure I'm not going to get on your bad side."

"What makes you think you were ever on my good side?"

"Believe me, nothing makes me think that," he said wholeheartedly, making her laugh. "I just don't want to backslide."

"You have my blessing. Just..." she hesitated.

"Just what?"

"Keep me out of it."

"Why?"

"This is girls' night out. We're trying to have fun. I don't want her pestering me about you. The two of you are on your own, okay? Either you click or you don't. I don't want to be involved."

"Fair enough."

She leaned in just a little farther and gave him a quick wink. "Word has it the owner rents the cabins out back."

"I know. They gave me one for the night as payment for filling in. They're pretty nice." At least from what he'd seen; he'd barely had time to drop his bag on the bed before the mini-rehearsal.

A wide grin spread across her rich brown face. "Sounds like destiny to me. But what do I know? I'm just a cop. Have a fun night, Chief."

"You too, Chief."

They added a high-five to that, completing their usual send-off. Maya disappeared back into the crowd.

The singer picked up the mic again, sending a twang of static through the sound system. "All right, who's ready to keep on rocking?"

And it was back to work.

But not without one more glance at Kate. This time, she was looking back. Their gazes caught. And held. And she gave him the naughtiest smile this side of reform school.

He missed his cue. Oops.

Well, it wouldn't be the first time a woman had completely thrown him off track. Judging by the electricity sizzling between him and Kate, it would be worth it.

At least she wasn't from around here, so she couldn't do any permanent damage to his life.

ALL THE STRESS. All the worry. All the annoyance at her father. It all went floating away as Kate threw herself into dancing. Sometimes you just needed to let loose and have fun. Especially when your life had gone to shit. Here she was at the ends of the Earth and the beat was insane and the tequila was kicking in and for the first time in a long time...Kate felt fine.

And Darius in the black cowboy hat looked even more fine.

Their eyes kept meeting...they kept smiling at each other... and every time she looked his way, he got more attractive. She was dancing *for him*. He was playing *for her*. He kept looking at her as if he wanted to jump off the stage and eat her alive.

This was really happening, even though it felt almost surreal, as if she was dreaming the entire thing.

She was very, very out of practice at anything that didn't involve legal filings or growing peonies. Even drinking, for that matter. The Moose is Loose poured generous shots and the waitress was keeping them well-supplied. Was Maya ordering them? Jessica? Did it matter?

The moments blended together in a happy, seamless blur. The taste of lime on her tongue, the thump of the beat, the smell of her own sweat.

At some point Maya went to the restroom. Jessica had gotten into a soulful conversation with a cute guy. Kate was basically dancing alone.

This was it. Time for Naughty Kate to make a move on that mud-rescuing, cowboy-hat-wearing, bass-playing hottie.

On the one hand, she knew perfectly well that she was hellaciously buzzed and probably not making the best decisions. *But that was the entire point.* She wanted to do One Stupid Thing. Well, technically...One More Stupid Thing. This was happening, damn it.

As long as he was definitely from Oregon.

Hauling in a deep breath, she slid through the crowd, dodging elbows and beer bottles.

"Ow, ow, ow," she kept saying; her dodging skills clearly needed some work.

Finally she made it to the stage. Darius hadn't noticed her; he was sitting on a stool next to the standup bass, casually propping it up with one hand as he leaned back to listen to the something the drummer was telling him.

She reached onstage and tugged at his pants leg. He didn't notice because he was too wrapped up in the conversation with the drummer. So she rapped lightly on his shin with her knuckles.

It was hard as a tree, that shin. This man was packed with muscle, every part of him.

When he still didn't turn around, she tried again—harder.

So hard she activated an automatic response and his foot jerked toward her, kicking her on the shoulder.

"Ouch!" It didn't hurt so much as surprise her, but the word popped out anyway.

Darius swung around, an appalled expression on his face. "Good God, did I just kick you? Are you okay?"

As he reached toward her, the speed of his movement knocked the bass out of balance. It slid out of his grip and toward Kate. He lunged to grab it.

"I got it!" she announced.

She stepped forward and caught the rounded lower part of the bass in her arms, dodging the endpin with its rubber cap. The instrument was so large; that thought sounded kind of naughty.

"Kate Robinson to the rescue!" she continued. Sweet lord, was she buzzed. "Coulda shattered all over the floor. Nothing but splinters."

She grinned up at Darius, who still wore a concerned frown. "Don't move," he said sternly. "That thing's too big for you to handle."

"That's what they all say." Did that sound flirty like she'd imagined? Or weird? She blinked at him, replaying it in her head.

Yup, weird. Definitely weird.

"I mean—"

"I'm coming down there," he interrupted. "Hold on."

"You're so bass-y. I mean bossy. Get it?" Was that any better?

The instrument slipped in her grip, so she adjusted the placement of one foot. Suddenly she was sliding on someone's spilled drink and she staggered backwards.

Oh shit. She was going to fall. *She couldn't fall.* That would be so humiliating, not to mention painful. She teetered on the backs of her heels, fighting to stay upright.

Then she blinked to clear her vision, because either she was really really buzzed or she'd never seen another human move so fast. In a blur of black, Darius leaped off the stage and landed at her side with a thump. His cowboy hat went flying off his head and she caught a glimpse of thick dark hair.

Somehow, within moments, he'd settled his arms around her to keep her from falling.

A warm male wall of pure muscle was holding her up. Her entire body relaxed with a sigh. All her troubles melted away and she leaned against him. He felt like heaven, like every fantasy male she'd dreamed about before she'd lost all her illusions about men.

In her distraction, her grip on the bass loosened. It tilted to the side, ready to slide to the floor. The man with his arms around her didn't budge; clearly he was more concerned about her than the bass.

Which was nice, but that bass had given her a lot of pleasure in the hours she'd been dancing here. No way was she going to allow it to crash. She pushed away from Darius' chest so she could reestablish her hold on the instrument. At the same moment, another bar patron—probably trying to help—grabbed the neck of the bass, which had the effect of swinging it up toward Kate right when she was reaching for it.

Bonk.

The edge of the bass struck her on the side of her forehead. Stars gathered at the edge of her vision. This time the pain was real. This was not *at all* the good kind of trouble. *Not* the One More Stupid Thing she'd imagined. She let out a weird sound that she knew she was going to regret. And then she slumped into Darius' arms as everything turned off like a computer booting down.

CHAPTER FIVE

Jesus. With his arms full of unconscious woman and everyone rushing to help, Darius could only watch as the Moose is Loose degenerated into pure chaos.

The other band members jumped down from the stage. A few drunk patrons seized the opportunity to throw punches at each other. A security guy yelled and waved his arms for everyone to be quiet. He had no idea what had happened to his bass. Someone must have saved it because it was nowhere to be seen.

Then a voice from the mic cut through the noise. "Cut it out, everyone."

Maya Badger, in her gold top, glared at the crowd from the stage. "That's enough," she ordered. "Everyone get a grip and calm the F down." She caught Darius' eye and gestured with her head. He interpreted the move as "get Kate out of here."

"We have an injured party, so I need everyone to make way." The crowd had already quieted down, so she didn't even have to raise her voice anymore. Damn, she was good. Even in her party outfit, she knew how to make people do what she said. The Lost Harbor Police Department was in good hands.

He nodded his thanks and scooped Kate into his arms. She was tall and not exactly light, but her weight felt good to him. Jessica appeared at his side. "Is she okay?"

"I'll check her out as soon as I get her out of here."

"Is it okay if I stay with Maya? I know she's got this, but she might need some support."

"Yeah yeah, don't worry, I'll take care of Kate. I'll text Maya after I've assessed her."

He had EMT training, of course. The majority of the calls they got at the Lost Harbor firehouse were medical. He felt very comfortable with his ability to handle her injury. If she needed more than he could offer, he knew exactly where every urgent care, ER, firehouse and police station in the entire Misty Bay peninsula were located.

Everyone gave him space to carry Kate toward the exit. For privacy's sake, he didn't want to examine her in the middle of the Moose is Loose, or even in the kitchen. And he had that cabin, after all. It would double as an exam room.

He kicked open the side exit and turned at an angle to maneuver her out the door. It was actually dark outside, which meant it must be very late. This time of year, the sky stayed light until after ten. Even now, a halo of sunset lingered near the horizon, arching seamlessly into an achingly deep midnight blue scattered with stars.

The pure air felt clean and brisk after the steamy heat of the bar. He drew in deep breaths as sweat gathered on his forehead from the effort of carrying her.

Opening the door of the cabin was another trick. Why had he locked the damn thing? He didn't have anything valuable in it. The only important thing he'd brought was his bass, and who knew where that was at this point.

The cabin was one of those prefab "log cabins" put together from a kit. A simple A-frame with room for a bed, a chair and a nightstand. A minuscule bathroom with only a toilet and sink. Perfect for someone who needed a place to crash after a night partying at the Moose is Loose.

But it was clean and quiet and he had no qualms about setting Kate down on the bed so he could examine her wound.

Gently, he lifted her hair off her face. The thick glossy locks flowed across his fingers in silky waves. With her eyes closed, he missed her vivid presence and bright smile. But she was still a knockout.

So to speak.

A bruise was already developing on her forehead. Ice. He needed ice.

He squatted next to his bag, where he always kept a first-aid kit. He found the quick-freeze ice pack and snapped it to activate the cooling crystals.

After shielding her skin with a washcloth from the bathroom, he positioned the ice pack over the bruise.

The cold of the ice pack woke her up. Her eyebrows drew together and she groaned, then her eyes fluttered open. He hadn't been close enough to really see her eyes before. They were the deep, near-black of a midnight sky. She stared at him for a long moment, a perplexed line forming between her eyebrows.

"The hot bassist."

He gave a snort of laughter. "It's Darius. How's your head feeling?"

Her hand went to her temple. "Hurts."

"Yeah, I'm not surprised. There's a bruise forming. Mind if I do a little test?"

"For what?"

"I want to make sure you don't have a concussion. You got bonked pretty hard."

"Really? I don't remember what happened." The line between her eyebrows deepened. "I remember dancing. I came up to talk to you, didn't I?"

He found a penlight in his bag and held it in front of her face. "Can you follow the light?"

Her eyes tracked it just fine. Her pupils weren't dilated, though her eyes were such a deep color he couldn't be entirely sure.

"Let's try some basic questions. Can you tell me your name?"

"Is that a pickup line? Because you already have me alone on a bed."

He ignored that. She was in no shape for a hookup, though she didn't seem to realize that.

"Do you know what year it is?"

With an irritated expression, she pushed his hand away and tried to sit up. "I'm fine. This is ridiculous. I need to get back to..." She fell quiet with a frown.

"Which brings me to my next question. Where do you live?"

"You're very nosy." A flush rose on her cheeks. "Where do *you* live? Is this your house? Did we go home together?" She glanced around the cabin and a look of horror came over her face. "You *live* here?"

"No, I don't live here. It's a fishing cabin. A rental. Listen, I'm starting to think you might have a bit of concussion. Your memory seems a little sketchy."

"I remember that we were supposed to be flirting, not playing doctor." She shrugged. "I guess that works too."

This woman was TROUBLE with a capital everything.

He handed her the ice pack. "Why don't you hold that against your head. It'll help that bruise."

She sniffed and took the pack from him. "I didn't know that bassists carried ice packs."

He laughed a little, admiring her spunk. She might be a little fuzzy, but she wasn't intimidated by him. Which was interesting, because he knew that many people found his appearance, and especially his size, intimidating. Then again, some women found that to be his best quality.

"I'm not just a bassist. I'm a firefighter too. I'm mostly a firefighter, as a matter of fact. I just play bass on the side."

"Oh. You're really good."

"You should see me put out a fire," he said dryly.

"Kinda hoping I don't get that opportunity," she answered, echoing his tone.

"Right. Good point. So how do you feel other than the bruise? Anything else? It was a little crazy there for a minute."

That blank expression came across her face again. "I just don't remember." He caught the beginnings of panic in her eyes.

"Never mind that. Focus on right now. Any other pain anywhere? Can you do a full-body scan of yourself?"

He waited patiently while she did so. He noticed that she had a few freckles on her nose and that her hands looked strong and capable and had a little dirt under the fingernails.

In the bar she'd said, "Kate Robinson to the rescue!" The name had rung a bell, but he hadn't pursued it. *Robinson.* Wasn't that the name of the crazy lawyer trying to evict him? Weird coincidence.

"What kind of work do you do?" he asked, just in case.

"What?" She blinked a few times, her long, dark lashes fanning up and down. "Why talk about work? Can't we just flirt instead?"

He bit back a smile. "How's that body scan going?"

"That kinda sounds like flirting, but not really."

He adjusted the ice pack on her forehead. "Sorry, but we're going to have to put the flirting on hold, Kate."

She sighed deeply. "Of course we are. Nothing goes my way anymore. There's a good chance I'm cursed."

"Nah. If you were cursed, a firefighter wouldn't have been *right there* when you got hurt."

Her dark eyes scanned him. "Guess I got lucky. Without getting lucky." She pulled the ice pack away from her face. "How does it look?"

"Bruised. But better."

She yawned and turned her head gingerly from side to side. "I should get going."

"You're not going anywhere," he told her firmly. He laid a hand on her shoulder, pressing her back down. She didn't object, probably because she wasn't stupid. "You're staying here for the night and in the morning we'll figure out what happens next."

She nestled her head on the pillow and adjusted the ice pack. "Are you staying here too?"

"Yeah. I don't feel right leaving you here when you can't even say where you live."

"It's not a very easy question, that's all. It's complicated. There's where I used to live, where I live now, and where I want to live." Her eyelids drifted down.

He took out his phone and shot Maya a quick text.

Kate is conscious. No concussion, but a little confused.

Can she stay there for the night?

Of course.

I'll leave her purse and jacket with the owner.

Ten-four.

"Okay, you're all set," he began in a cheerful tone, before he saw that Kate's eyes were closed. He modulated his voice. "I'll be in the chair if you need anything. See you in the morning."

"Thanks, bassist."

"Darius," he reminded her.

"Hot Darius," she murmured.

Okay then. He supposed he could live with that.

He watched as her eyes closed completely and sleep relaxed

her face. Her hand fell away from her head and the ice pack rolled across the pillow.

Gently, he removed it and stowed it back in his bag.

He rose to his feet and stretched his arms over his head. The cabin ceiling was so low that his fingertips brushed against it. His hands were sore from his stint on the bass. He didn't get enough practice these days. It was probably a good thing that this night hadn't ended the way he'd originally hoped it would.

He glanced again at the sleeping woman on the bed. She'd rolled over onto her side and was now lightly snoring.

He settled into the chair, which was designed for someone a foot shorter than him. Ah what the hell. He'd slept in more uncomfortable quarters than this.

He took out his phone and texted Maya one more time.

Make it back to Lost Harbor yet?

Why? My own father doesn't ask me that.

Really? Harris asks me that.

He and Harris Badger jammed together sometimes back in Lost Harbor. When things went late, Harris had a habit of checking in on his drive home.

He probably likes you better because you play. I'm a big-ass disappointment ever since I dropped piano.

Bullshit. I know how he talks about you. He ain't disappointed, Chief.

Whatever. I'm home. Wouldn't be texting if I wasn't.

He chuckled. Maya was a very law-abiding police chief, which apparently was unusual for faraway spots like Lost Harbor, Alaska. Most law enforcement officers had to be pretty flexible in dealing with their independent, quirky populations.

Is Kate a lawyer?

He had to know if Kate was Catriona Robinson, Attorney at Law, before this thing—whatever it was—went any further.

Good night.

Is that a yes?

That's a "keep me out of this."

Great. Was it possible that he'd just rescued the woman trying to evict him—twice? Worse, that he'd developed an insane attraction to her?

Damn his luck. Kate had it all wrong. She wasn't the one who was cursed—he was.

He tossed his phone aside and stretched out his legs, which reached almost to the opposite wall.

Amazingly, in about fifteen seconds, he was asleep.

CHAPTER SIX

There was a man in her room.

Kate almost screamed, but she remembered just in time that alerting the intruder she was awake might be a bad idea.

So she lay still, heart racing. A few terrifying moments from the past couple of months rushed back to her. Hearing someone at her window. Footsteps following her through her parking garage. The sound of a letter dropping through her mail slot.

Where the hell was she? This didn't look like her LA condo. Or her room at Emma's farmhouse. And yet she was tucked into a cozy bed and someone had obviously been taking care of her. A box of tissues lay next to her head.

Cautiously, she lifted her head just a bit. Would the man notice? Would he come after her? He was slouched in the chair, arms folded across his chest, long legs stretched out to infinity. His thick hair was mussed as if he'd been in bed, his face shadowed.

He was a big man, huge in that inadequate chair.

Big man...holy shit, it was the hottie bassist! She searched her mind for his name. Darius. The one who'd rescued her from the mud.

How had she ended up here with Darius, and why weren't they *both* in the bed? Was this the least successful one-night stand ever?

Her head throbbed. Hangover. *Oh, right.* In bits and pieces, it all came back to her. She'd been doing shots with Maya and Jess, and then they'd danced, and then she'd gone up to the stage to flirt with Darius and then...she wasn't entirely sure what had happened after that. She had a vague memory of getting hit on the head, but the details were still foggy.

Darius must have brought her back here and treated her. She remembered concerned gray eyes behind a pen light. Something cold. Trying to flirt and getting shot down.

Ugh. She had to get home. As long as blood wasn't pouring out of a gash, there was no reason she couldn't drive back to Lost Harbor.

Carefully, she pushed the blanket off her, realizing that she still had all her clothes on. That One Stupid Thing she'd been dreaming about—yeah, that obviously hadn't happened.

Just as well, she really couldn't afford to do anything stupid. She'd maxed out on stupid when she'd sacrificed her career for her deadbeat dad.

She swung her legs over the side of the bed and gave herself a minute to adjust. Her head was pounding, the pain centralized around a spot above her temple. She touched it and found the raised surface of a bruise.

Add one more disaster to the heap of crap that was her life.

She tiptoed across the room. He didn't budge. Should she wake him up and thank him? Or at least get his contact info? There wasn't really any point. She'd regressed to Naughty Kate days and completely embarrassed herself. At this point, she was better off heading home and putting this entire mortifying incident in the rearview mirror.

Seeing no sign of her purse or jacket, she gave Darius one last look, committing his hotness to memory, and slid out the door.

Dawn was already turning the wispy clouds a shy pink, like a flock of blushing maidens. The cabin was one of several arrayed behind the Moose is Loose Saloon. She saw her Saab parked where she'd left it, along with a few other vehicles.

The roadhouse had a rough-and-ready look, like an old drunk sleeping off a late night. A nearly life-sized carved moose stood watch by the door, perched on its wooden hind legs. Giving it a wide berth, she pushed open the door. Unlocked, which wasn't surprising around here.

The place was empty and still held the detritus of last night—empty bottles, dirty floor, even a couple of customers passed out on the tables. The stage was empty of everything except Darius' standup bass, which lay flat on its back, as if it too had drunk a little too much.

"Hello?" she called, in case anyone was around.

No one answered, so she lifted the pass-through and stepped behind the bar. Jackpot—her bag and jacket were crammed onto a shelf against the wall, along with a random assortment of other lost objects—including a black cowboy hat.

That brought back a flash of lust. Darius in that black cowboy hat, playing his heart out onstage. Flashing that wild grin at her.

She still didn't know if he lived in Oregon. Fingers crossed, he did and would be back there soon.

Her head throbbed and she decided to skip any more trips down memory lane. She extracted her jacket and put it on, then did a quick search of her bag and found nothing missing. Most importantly, her car keys were still there.

Okay then. Things were looking up.

Outside, the fresh dawn air kissed her face, reviving her even further. She slid into her Saab and let out a deep breath of relief.

Let that be a lesson, she told herself as she turned the key in the ignition. Kate Robinson can't afford any Stupid Things.

No matter how hot they looked in a black cowboy hat.

EMMA WAS ALREADY UP and about, tossing feed to her beloved chickens and her flock of "guard" geese, when Kate crested the sloping drive that delivered workers and occasional visitors to the farm. She wore her purple flannel pajamas and clogs—her usual morning chores outfit.

Emma had lived a wild life. Her past careers included dog musher, crab fisher, city councilperson, and that was just scratching the surface. Occasionally she'd drop a casual comment about cooking at the North Slope or hitching a ride on a cargo ship that would blow Kate's mind.

The first time Kate's parents had sent her to Lost Harbor to stay with Emma, they'd been negotiating their divorce. Kate had been a hurt and angry pre-teen who'd had no idea such a thing as a peony farm existed.

She'd thrown herself into the summer peony harvest because it was something to do, and because she adored her grandma. Emma didn't mind if Kate acted like a brat and dropped curse words. She seemed to understand why she got into so much trouble.

After all, Emma was a hard-core adventurer whose one marriage had lasted only long enough to have a baby girl. She'd decided at the age of sixty-five that she wanted to slow down and smell the flowers. For someone with her degree of energy, that meant buying a piece of land and creating a peony farm.

The name Petal to the Metal pretty much described her

entire attitude toward life. It also paid tribute to her lifelong love of Harleys.

Emma knew that something bad had happened in LA, and she knew that it involved Kate's dad, Frank Robinson. She even knew that Kate had come back to Lost Harbor because she was afraid. Kate had tried to spare her the details, but much of the story had slipped out.

The day after Kate had arrived, Emma had shown off her collection of firearms. "I won't ask any questions, but just in case," she'd said, hefting a hunting rifle in one hand. "I want you to know I'm ready."

"Ready for what? A peony uprising?"

Even though they'd both laughed, Kate was grateful for the thought.

However, the last thing she wanted was for Emma to get into a shootout with anyone from her father's orbit.

One more reason to move into the house on Fairview Court.

As Kate stepped out of the Saab, Emma waved her over.

Kate zipped up her jacket and picked her way across the grass in her high-heeled boots. A wandering goose honked at her as she passed.

"Juicy night?" Emma asked with a wink.

Apparently the "no questions" policy didn't apply to the ol' walk of shame.

"Not even close," Kate told her. "Well, it might have been close. I did wake up in a strange bed. But the man in question was across the room asleep in a chair, so that doesn't really add up to juicy."

"Eh." Emma cocked her head and made a clucking sound at one of her hens. "First late night since you got back, and no story to tell. Sure is different from your teenage years."

Kate laughed. "Maybe I'm waiting until I'm in my own place with no nosy old lady waiting for a report."

"Don't talk nonsense." Emma scattered a handful of feed to her favorite Rhode Island Red hen. "You can't move into town. I rented the house out."

"Yeah, I noticed. I'm working on that, but until then, I'll just move into the upstairs."

"The upstairs? It needs to be redone. That's why I haven't rented it out. The floors need to be stripped, the—"

"Emma. I can handle all that. I'm not a princess, despite all this glamour." She gestured wryly at her bedhead hair and wrinkled clothes. "It's better for both of us if we're not on top of each other. I'll still be helping out through the harvest."

"Such a stubborn thing you are. Don't know where you get it from."

"Yeah, it's a real mystery," Kate said wryly.

Emma turned to the hen. "You featherbrained piece of fluff, what are you waiting for? That's an avocado peel. You love those and they cost five bucks apiece. You might as well be a tea cozy for all the brains you have."

Kate smothered a laugh at the way her affectionate tone contrasted with her berating words. The hen didn't seem one bit bothered, though it did deign to peck at the avocado peel.

"I'm going to change my clothes and shower off." Her hand involuntarily went to her head, which drew Emma's attention.

"You're hurt?" A frown gathered on her forehead.

"Oh, just your everyday ordinary bar brawl. Flying bottles, crashing basses, that sort of thing."

An image from last night swam to mind. Darius leaning over her with an ice pack. The impact of all that thick dark hair and those gleaming silvery eyes, that sexy jaw stubble and heady masculine scent. He sure packed a powerful punch of pheromones.

Too bad she'd never see the man again.

"Are you okay?" Emma was asking.

"Oh yeah. Fine. I just need some coffee. I'll do some work on the new plantings, then later I'm going to drive down to Fairview Court and check things out, maybe move a couple of boxes down. Mind if I borrow a truck?"

"It's pointless to argue with you, I suppose."

"It is. My mind's made up."

"Then I'll just argue with these chickens instead. They're more reasonable."

Emma turned back to her flock. Kate headed for the farmhouse, which had been built in the early days of Lost Harbor's existence. Everywhere she looked, there was a piece of antique equipment—an old-fashioned clothes wringer or an ironwork boot scraper. It was part of the charm of the place, and about as far from Kate's LA condo as could be.

Her little guest room had an enamel bowl and water pitcher, along with an aluminum lidded chamber pot.

Cute, but she drew the line at chamber pots.

After a lengthy shower, she filled an insulated thermos with coffee and wandered down to the peony fields. Emma had organized the plots according to their harvest time and the color of the cultivars, from the gorgeous deep pink of the *Edulis Superba* to the much-in-demand coral of the *Coral Sunset.*

The Alaska peony industry existed only because it was one of the few places in the world where peonies bloomed from July to as late as September. Since Alaska thawed so much later than anywhere else with appropriate growing conditions, Alaska peonies bloomed after everyone else's had already gone by.

So if you were a summer bride who wanted fresh peonies for your wedding, your only option in the entire world was one of the peony farms in Alaska.

Kate knew that most people thought of salmon or king crab or goldmining when they thought about Alaskan industries. But peony farms did pretty well too. Emma spent most of the year protecting, weeding, and irrigating the bushes, then went through an insanely busy few weeks of harvest in the summer. Petal to the Metal had several huge walk-in coolers where they stored the stems before they were shipped out.

Right now, in late April, the big task was scouting for botrytis, a gray mold that caused cankers to form on the peony stems. Every canker had to be cut out with a knife—which made it the perfect job for Emma's afterschool worker, a teenage girl named S.G., who'd arrived in Lost Harbor with a hunting knife and clothes made from animal hides.

Even in a town full of eccentrics, the girl stood out because of her mysterious origins. S.G. stood for Spruce Grouse, a name she'd chosen herself because she didn't know her real name. She'd been raised in Lost Souls Wilderness by a trapper who refused to say where he'd found her.

Kate spotted her working a row of *Edulis Superba*. She wore a "botrytis bag" around her neck to stash the scraps of mold in. With her lower lip between her teeth, she was carefully carving a canker from a stem.

"Morning, Kiddo," Kate greeted the girl. "Getting in a couple hours before school?"

S.G. shrugged. "School's boring today. I don't want to go."

"Oh no. You're not skipping school for this job. That's one of the terms and conditions of your employment, remember?"

She winced at her own legalese. Sometimes she forgot to phrase things like a regular person.

"But Kate, it's really seriously very boring today. There's a job fair. And I already have a job." She popped the piece of diseased stem in her bag, then used a bottle of alcohol to disinfect her blade. It was very important not to spread the botrytis through the crop.

Kate squatted next to her. In her overalls and mud boots, her pale hair in two braids, S.G. looked like any other Lost Harbor kid, but she'd been through so much. After running away from the trapper, she'd hidden out in the local firehouse for weeks. She'd used their shower, filched food from their refrigerator, and spied on the firefighters.

Firefighters...that reminded her of Darius. That man had a pesky way of popping into her thoughts at random moments. She wondered where he was now. Probably on his way back to Oregon with the band.

"Kate?" She started. S.G. was frowning at her, and she realized she'd completely zoned out thinking about Darius.

"Sorry. Job fair. It's a good thing. You might want to learn about other jobs. Fishing boats, barista like Gretel, police officer like Maya."

"Doctor like Bethany?"

"Absolutely. Or a lawyer like me."

S.G. shrugged and wrinkled her nose, making Kate laugh.

"I saw that face. I'll remember that if you ever need a lawyer."

She rose to her feet and took a deep breath of the pure air, which was saturated with the rich scent of spring soil and a tinge of isopropyl alcohol.

"Hey, kid, since you're already skipping school, would you like another job for the day?"

"What job?"

"I could use a hand moving my stuff into my new house."

S.G. frowned in confusion. "You don't have hands?"

"It's a phrase. It means to help someone."

Since S.G. had been raised in the wilderness, her vocabulary and understanding of the world could be very sketchy. She knew everything about hunting and nothing about math, for instance. The trapper, who'd turned out to be a criminal on the run, hadn't bothered to give her an education, so now she was making up for lost time. She was being fostered by Denaina, who owned the property next door, which was how Emma first came to know her.

Kate had clicked with S.G. right away; she'd always connected to teenagers and their troubles. She'd even spent some time helping her with her schoolwork. S.G. was learning fast, but every once in a while a gap in her education would surface—and it could be something completely unexpected. Like the phrase "give me a hand."

"You want my help moving? Why are you moving?"

"So Emma and I don't kill each other before the peony harvest. That's a bad joke, by the way." S.G. didn't always get sarcasm. "I'll pay you the same as you're getting here and I'll even throw in lunch."

"Okay." S.G. shrugged and stood up, wiping her hands on her overalls. "Cheeseburgers?"

"Cheeseburgers. Sure."

"Do you want to go now?"

"I still have some packing to do. I should be ready by lunchtime. Thanks, kid."

On her way back to the farmhouse, she stopped to admire Emma's newest plot. She'd planted it three autumns ago, and this would be its first year to produce sellable blooms. Even though Kate had seen photos of their enormous brilliant pink blossoms, she couldn't wait to see one—and smell their intoxicating rose-like fragrance—for herself.

With a laugh at her own excitement—what self-respecting cynical lawyer would get so carried away over a *Mon Jules Elie*—she hurried back to the farmhouse.

CHAPTER SEVEN

Emma had thrown open the door to the barnlike structure next to the house. It was more of a warehouse than a barn, since she didn't keep farm animals.

"I got all the furniture you could ever want in here," she called to Kate. "Things I've been collecting here and there. You can take what you need."

"Seriously?" Kate joined her and gazed into the crammed space. "That's amazing. You could probably furnish ten houses with all that. Is there a brand-new mattress in there, by chance?"

"Couple of them."

That was just one of the reasons Kate loved her grandmother. She knew how to offer the right kind of support at the exact moment it was needed.

Kate slung an arm over her grandmother's shoulder and pulled her in for a hug. "You're the best, Emma." She dropped a kiss on her gray-streaked black hair. "Where would I be without you?"

"Women's Correctional Institute?"

"Very likely. I'll go through this stuff later. I'm going to keep it simple for this first trip. Boxes and suitcases."

After she'd loaded Emma's pickup, she called out to S.G.. The girl came dashing up the slope from the peony field, shooing away geese as she ran. Kate tried to imagine another teenage girl who would work nonstop from morning to lunch without a single break or complaint, and failed. One more bit of proof that S.G. was no ordinary girl.

"Can I try driving?" she asked as soon as she'd hopped in the passenger seat.

Okay, maybe she had some normal teenage tendencies.

"Some other time. My load's a little too precarious."

As she pulled out of the turnaround, she sent nervous glances in the rearview mirror toward the pile of boxes in the bed of the truck. She'd run a strap over the load, but something told her she hadn't done it right. The boxes were already shifting around and they hadn't even hit the muddy part yet.

"Should have let me do it," said S.G. matter-of-factly. "I'm good with loads."

"That doesn't surprise me," Kate murmured. "You're a true Alaska chick."

"I'm a chicken?"

"It means girl. Sorry. Actually, forget I said that. You don't need to know *all* the words."

They reached the road that led into town. The snow had melted enough to reveal patches of green, which grew more frequent the closer they came to town. Spring took its sweet time coming to Lost Harbor, but it was worth the wait. The wistful call of a varied thrush floating through the morning air could make a grown woman cry.

"I found a boy," S.G. said as they took one of the hairpin curves in the road.

"Uh oh. That sounds like trouble."

"He might be in trouble. I don't know."

Kate frowned, her attention divided between S.G. and a box that was now threatening to tumble off the truck. "What's his name?"

"He doesn't want to tell me."

"That's not a good sign."

"I think he's afraid."

Kate could well imagine that S.G., with her unusual history, could be intimidating to the boys around here. To any boys, really.

"Because he knows how good you are with knives?"

"No. I mean, he doesn't know that. I don't carry my knife anymore, the school won't let me."

"Seems like a reasonable policy."

S.G. shrugged. She was very attached to her hunting knife and unnervingly skilled with it.

"So this boy...do you know him from school?"

S.G. didn't answer that question, instead posing one of her own. "Can he work at the farm too? He needs a job."

"Maybe. We'd need to know his name, though. Bring him by and we'll talk to him. Okay, this is the street. Fairview Court. Pretty, isn't it?" The street took a slow, lazy curve just above town. Between homes she got peeks of the sparkling blue waters of Misty Bay. Birch trees and spruce offered some privacy, but this was a much more populated neighborhood than the ridge where the farm was located.

"So many houses." S.G. gave a little shudder.

"Yeah, well, I grew up in the suburbs, so this is normal to me. You might not know what a suburb is, but this neighborhood is as close as Lost Harbor gets. There, that's the one!" She pointed to a fairly new split-level house with oyster-pink siding. A staircase painted blue marched along the outer wall to the upstairs. It was going to be a pain in the ass to move her stuff in. On the upside, the upstairs had a huge front deck and sliding glass doors with a view of the ocean.

The downstairs, on the other hand, had all the other good stuff—a deluxe master bedroom and a fully modernized kitchen. More importantly, it had a security system. That alone made it worth fighting for.

She pulled into the driveway next to a motorcycle that was already parked in front of the garage.

Great, the tenant was here. Perfect timing. She could give him his thirty days' notice. She even had the paperwork ready. Noticing that her bag had slid off her lap onto the floorboards, she bent down to grab it.

"Hey, there's Darius!" exclaimed S.G..

Kate jumped, and her head hit the steering wheel. "Crap," she muttered. Of all the random names, why did S.G. have to say that one?

Carefully, she maneuvered her head from under the steering wheel, bag in hand. "You scared me, S.G.."

"Darius isn't as scary as he looks," the girl said cheerfully. She waved at someone Kate couldn't quite see. "He's actually nice. He taught me how to play darts at the firehouse."

Uh oh. A sinking feeling settled into Kate's stomach. The firehouse? Darius had said he was a firefighter. He couldn't possibly be...

She craned her neck to see who S.G. was waving at.

And there he came, striding down the sidewalk with a dog bouncing at his heels. Looking just as big and mouthwatering and lust-inspiring as he'd looked last night. The black t-shirt was gone, and in its place he wore a faded t-shirt with a band she couldn't make out. His workout sweats were ripped off at the knees, revealing unbelievably muscular calves.

Apparently he'd been running, because his hair was thickened with sweat and a triangle of dampness darkened his t-shirt.

He lifted the bottom edge to wipe sweat off his face. The sight of his muscular abdomen and the dark covering of curls sent heat lancing through her.

This was just bad on every possible level.

"You know Darius?"

"He's the fire chief."

"Of Lost Harbor?"

"Of course. Where else?"

"No," Kate moaned out loud.

"Yes. He was pretty mad at me at first when he found out I was hiding there. But then he got over it and he's my friend now. I'm going to say hi." S.G. hopped out and scampered down the sidewalk to greet him.

Kate felt as if she was watching a movie unfold in slow motion. Darius dropped his t-shirt and gave S.G. a wide grin. The dog, who looked to be some kind of husky mix, sat on his haunches and watched alertly as they conversed.

Slowly her breathing returned to normal. So Darius lived in Lost Harbor—was the fire chief of Lost Harbor—and he was jogging through the neighborhood. So what? It was just a weird coincidence, or one of those things that happened when you lived in a small town. That didn't mean they'd be running into each other all the time.

Luckily, they hadn't actually done anything last night.

Taking in a deep breath for strength, she got out of the truck and tucked her hands in her pockets. Strolling down the sidewalk toward them, she decided it was her turn to give someone else a shock.

"Hello there, Darius."

He turned to greet her, but he didn't seem surprised. "Hi Kate."

Managing a friendly smile, she walked down the driveway toward him. And toward S.G., of course, except that somehow the girl was little more than a blur at this point. All she could see was Darius' wide shoulders and tousled hair. In the daylight, he was even more attractive, which didn't happen very often, in her experience. The firm lines of his face, the set of his jaw, the sensual curl of his lips, all were details that she hadn't noticed the night before.

"How are you feeling—" He paused, glancing down at S.G.

Which was a very thoughtful touch that she appreciated. S.G. didn't need to know their business.

"So you're the Lost Harbor fire chief," she said quickly, changing the subject. "Fancy that."

"Yeah. And you..." His gaze shifted to her truck and her load of boxes. He raised an eyebrow. "You're delivering something?"

"Oh, just myself and my possessions," she said cheerfully. "I'm moving into this house. I had no idea the first neighbor I met would be the fire chief. Do you live around here?"

"Pretty close."

She glanced at S.G., who was now crouched down next to the dog, cooing and petting him. Oblivious to anyone else. ""Listen, about...last night. I...uh..."

"I was worried about you when I woke up this morning." He deepened his voice to an intimate level that sent shivers through her. "Didn't think you should be driving."

"Well, it was fine. And...thank you, for helping me. I...uh..." His physicality was so distracting, she was having trouble forming a complete sentence. "I thought you were from Oregon. If I'd known you were from Lost Harbor, things never would have gone so far."

"A little too close to home, huh? Okay, I guess I see the logic." She watched one corner of his mouth lift into a slow curve. There was a sexy draw to those lips. A fullness, a promise of reckless naughtiness.

Was she swaying toward him? Good God.

She took a determined step backwards. "Awkwardly enough, apparently we're neighbors. My first order of business is dealing with the tenant who lives downstairs." A bright idea struck her. "Maybe you can help me with that."

"Sure. Happy to. What are you thinking...rent reduction? Maybe some renovating?"

She blinked at him in confusion. A slight wisp of an ache drifted behind her eyes, like a flashback of a headache. "Why would I do that?"

"Don't tell me you're about to do something nasty and kick him out. That could definitely get you off on the wrong foot in this neighborhood."

"Why do you say that?"

"Because people tend to be protective of their local fire chief."

All the pieces settled into place—and she couldn't believe she hadn't realized it right away. She also couldn't believe her bad luck. Maybe she really was cursed.

"You're D. Boone," she groaned.

"Fraid so. Darius Boone." He smirked at her as he stuck out his hand. "Guess you're my new landlady. Nice to meet you. You're a lot different in person. In your emails, you came across kind of...antagonistic."

Without returning his handshake, she wheeled around and headed for her truck. The pulse behind her eyes was blooming into a full-fledged ache. She probably *should* still be in bed. He was probably right about that. And she hated that he was right about that, because he was a jerk.

Okay, a jerk who had taken care of her last night.

And a jerk who was nice to S.G..

And a jerk who had rescued her from the mud.

She stalked past the bed of the truck, brushing against one of the boxes that had shifted during her drive down the hill.

"Watch it!" he called after her. She flung her arm up in an "I got this" gesture—and hit the box.

Which tumbled off the pile and headed for the ground. She lunged for it, hoping to stop it in midair, before it spilled her possessions all over the lawn. But she was a second too late, and instead it landed smack on her right foot.

She held back the swear words that wanted to fly from her mouth. Cursed was beginning to seem like too mild a word for this string of bad luck.

Wincing from the pain in her foot, she crouched down and picked up the box.

Darius stepped to her side and frowned at the pile of boxes in the bed of her truck. "Could have secured that load a little better."

As she gritted her teeth, the box slipped from her grasp and landed on *his* foot.

Obviously, their tenant/landlady relationship was off to a fantastic start.

CHAPTER EIGHT

Darius ignored the pain in his toe. First of all, the box was pretty light. Second, it was nothing compared to the confirmation that the woman he kept running into—the woman he was definitely hot for—really was the same woman who wanted to evict him. He could barely believe the warm, laughing woman from last night was the all-business shark behind those emails.

He had to get this situation sorted out.

"Listen, why don't I help you unload these boxes and then you guys can come in for some coffee. I'm due at the firehouse soon but I have a little time."

"I promised I'd take S.G. out for cheeseburgers." After a moment of tension, her face relaxed. "But maybe we can talk later. I'll...email you."

"Right. Looking forward to that."

She laughed reluctantly, and just like that, the woman from last night was back. No red halter top this time. She was wearing a cambric work shirt and her dark hair was caught back in a ponytail. The sparkly high heels had been replaced with mud boots.

And yet she was still sexy to him. Tall and curvy and outrageously attractive.

The palms of his hands twitched, and he curled them into fists, then stretched out his fingers.

"Your email address...dboone@lhfd.org. All this time I assumed your name was Daniel Boone."

He tilted his head back and laughed. "Family legend says we're related, but who knows? You always signed your emails Catriona. I didn't make the connection to Kate."

"I go by Catriona at work. Or I used to, anyway. Now I'm a peony farmer named Kate." A wry smile quivered in the corner of her mouth.

His pager buzzed. He checked it and swore out loud. Message from Nate.

Dispatcher called. Nuisance fire number gazillion out on the mudflats on the boardwalk. No address, just meet me at the firehouse in two minutes.

"Gotta go. We'll be in touch." He turned to S.G., who was still cooing to the neighbor's dog. "Hey, S.G., can you take Thor across the street before you leave?"

Since it was the quickest option for the short trip to the firehouse, he hopped onto his Harley.

Kate planted her hands on her hips as he maneuvered the bike down the driveway. "A Harley. Let me guess. That's why Emma rented this place to you."

He grinned at her and hit the kickstarter. "You got it. Guess Harleys are thicker than blood."

He zoomed off, leaving her shaking her head in rueful defeat.

DARIUS CHANGED into his gear in record time and hopped into the already moving Engine 1 as it left the apparatus bay.

Nate drove the rig, setting the flashers to clear the way through town.

Not that there was much to clear, ever, except in tourist season. But visitors didn't generally start heading to Alaska until later in May. Only a few of the boardwalk businesses were even open yet. They encountered no obstacles during their race to the long finger of land that extended into the bay like a claw.

Darius watched the snowcapped mountains across the bay draw closer while the crew—Nate, Rick Puente and Betty Riley—speculated about the fire.

"Punk kids," announced Rick. "They're ready for school to be out. I know my kid is."

"Could be the hippie dude who lives in an old bus on that property. Maybe he wants all the mud to himself," said Betty.

"If it's the hippie guy, then it could be a one-off." Nate frowned at the road ahead. "But it sure seems like it's connected to the others. It's a pile of soaking-wet lumber on a mudflat. How does something like that even burn?"

Rick adjusted his gloves. "It's got to be connected. This time of year we're usually fighting mud, not fires."

Even though Darius was relatively new to Lost Harbor, he knew the pattern. The most intense time for firefighting was the summer, when massive brushfires could develop in the wilderness. Sometimes they encroached on the settled areas, in which case it was all hands onboard to set fire lines and backfires.

Here in town, structure fires just didn't happen all that often —because there weren't many structures. Emergency medical calls took up the bulk of their time.

But this was the eighth time in the last couple weeks that a random fire had broken out. A shed behind the feed store had caught fire. A burn barrel at an empty homestead had been knocked over and sparked a small brushfire. And now an abandoned houseboat was burning.

Darius glanced over at Nate, who'd grown up here and knew the territory inside and out. "What do you think, Nate?"

"You know what they say. Strange things happen around Lost Souls Wilderness."

All the others said the last words along with Nate, while Darius rolled his eyes. He'd only heard that saying about a hundred times since moving here. It seemed to be a point of pride with the locals, but he preferred a more reality-based approach.

"How about we see what's going on with this fire before we speculate," he ordered the crew.

And that put an end to that.

The fire had broken out at one of those quirky Lost Harbor locations that didn't fit a conventional location marker. On the long, narrow arm of land that led to the harbor, there was a stretch of marshy mud flats where a series of old boats had been abandoned over the years. Ancient fishing boats and dinghies rotted away into the mud. Some of them still belonged to people, some didn't. One old fishing vessel occasionally flew a pirate flag.

They found the houseboat fully engulfed in flames, spewing thick black smoke into the air. A haphazard pile of old rowboats and skiffs and ropes and other gear extended from the houseboat all the way to an RV park. Someone should have cleaned up that mess years ago.

At the other end of the trail of junk was the office building that serviced the RV park. Restrooms, a gas pump, a small convenience store. The houseboat was a goner, but they had to protect those structures.

Darius issued swift orders to hose down the debris closest to the houseboat and clear the area adjacent to the RV park. He helped Nate haul the three-inch hose to the jumbled junk pile of marine detritus. He held the hose in place while Nate went to turn on the flow.

Unlike every previous place he'd worked, the tiny town of

Lost Harbor didn't have many fire hydrants. Engine 1 was equipped with a seven-hundred-and-fifty pound water tank. If that wasn't enough, sometimes they had to find other sources of suppressant—ocean water would work in this instance. Just one of the ways in which firefighting in a remote location was new and different.

As he saturated the weathered old dinghies and buoys and broken crab traps, he kept an eye on the blazing bonfire that had been a houseboat. The wind was blowing the smoke toward the bay, creating a trail of dark swirls that wafted into the sky.

Why would anyone want to torch that old thing? *Had* someone set this fire? At first glance, he saw no other reason why it would have caught fire. Nothing electrical, nothing chemical, nothing weather-related.

It probably wasn't insurance-related. There was no way an insurance company would cover this old hulk. None of it made any sense, but then again, at this point, he just needed to make sure the damn fire didn't spread. After that, he and Nate would come in and look for signs of an accelerant or anything else that would indicate arson.

Along the road out to the boardwalk, cars slowed to watch them work, and a few people took photos out their windows. The fire made a spectacular sight against the backdrop of silver mudflats and snowcapped peaks.

This was a piece of Lost Harbor going up in flames; it had once been someone's home. Maybe a newlywed couple or a retired couple looking for peace and adventure.

Sad, when he thought of it that way. Romantic dreams gone up in smoke; he knew how that went.

"Who owns this thing?" he asked Nate as they watched the sparks swirl across the mud.

"The houseboat? The story goes that a smuggler bought it as a way to launder his ill-gotten funds. Then he hooked up with a local baker, who wanted to turn it into a bed-and-breakfast. They fought so much that one of them—not clear who—shot a hole through the hull and it foundered. Instead of trying to salvage it, they towed it here and beached it. They never spoke a word to each other again."

Darius stared at him, noting the usual laughter in his gray eyes. Nate was an easygoing guy who loved a good laugh, so there was a good chance he'd made up that entire story. "You're serious?"

"I know it sounds far-fetched, but yeah. If you don't believe me, ask Jessica at Sweet Harbor Bakery. That baker was her mother. After the boat sank, the Dixons opened up the bakery and never looked back."

Darius shook his head with a laugh. "Seems like there's a moral in there."

"Don't launder money?"

"I was thinking more like a metaphor. All the stages of a relationship are right there. You start with the naive dream. You progress to the fighting, which ends up with a bullet hole in your planks. Then you drag the rotting remains to a mudhole and try to forget about it."

Nate waved away an ember riding past on an air current. "Such a romantic."

"Hey. I was. That was the problem."

Though why he was getting onto that topic, he had no idea. He didn't really care for digging around in the past.

Nate took over the hose. "If you're trying to get me to disinvite you to the wedding, not gonna happen. You're coming, romantic or not."

"Of course I'm coming." Nate and Bethany were planning a summer wedding, and it was already marked on his calendar. Hard for a fire chief to ignore his crew's big life events. "I'm not against marriage. Fuck, I did it twice. I'm against marriage *for me.*

You and Bethany, different story. I think you two might have a chance."

Nate gave a hearty laugh. "The optimism, it burns."

"Sorry. Translate that into happy-fluffy language and you know what I mean."

"You think I'm happy-fluffy? Seriously, man, I was the last person who thought I'd be getting married this summer. I used to be as cynical as they come."

Darius didn't buy it. Nate was the kind of guy who would do anything for anyone. A solid, loyal, down-to-earth man loved by all. Also, he hadn't been married and divorced twice, the way Darius had.

They shifted to stamping out hotspots, bringing the heavy stream of water closer to the houseboat to hem it in. The fire was losing its fuel, dying back, like a dragon collapsing into itself.

It occurred to Darius that he might be able to quiz Nate about his new landlady.

"Do you know someone named Kate? Friend of Maya and Jessica Dixon?"

Nate squinted off at the ocean. "Couple of Kates in town. Does she run that Thai place with her husband?"

"No, no. Not Kate Saelim. Kate Robinson."

Nate kicked at a smoldering plank, which split open and disgorged a pile of sparks onto the mud. "Oh, you mean Naughty Kate."

Darius gave a double take, nearly losing his footing on the smoldering debris. "Naughty Kate?"

"It was a nickname she had for a while, to distinguish her from Nice Kate. She was kind of a wild child when she used to come here. Her grandmother runs that peony farm up on the ridge."

"Right. Emma Gordon."

Nate gave him a speculative glance but went on without any

ribbing, which Darius appreciated. "Emma's daughter ran away and got pregnant. Married a dude who turned out to be a small-time grifter type. Then they got divorced and sent Kate to Lost Harbor every summer just to get her out of the way. Kate did a lot of acting out, I guess you could say. Shoplifting, underage drinking, minor stuff like that. But then she got her life together and became a lawyer. I haven't seen her in years." Nate jerked the hose to unkink it. "Is she back?"

"She's back. I pulled her out of the mud the other day."

"Now that's interesting. She and Maya used to be best friends. Why don't you ask Maya more about her?"

Darius shrugged. "It's not that important, that's why."

"Bullshit, boss. This is the first time you've asked me about a specific woman since you've been here. There's gotta be some kind of reason."

"Yeah. There is."

"I knew it!" Nate jogged back to the engine to turn off the stream of water. Darius shook off the remaining droplets and began the process of coiling the hose for stowage. Still talking, Nate jogged back to help him. "My romantic Spidey sense never lets me down."

"She's my new landlady," Darius said with a smirk. "That's all. I want to know what I'm in for."

Nate crowed with laughter. "So Kate Robinson is your new landlady. Wait—*Kate's* the one who's been threatening to evict you?"

"Yup. That was before she met me, though."

"And now?"

"There's a good chance she'll bring a shotgun with her when she kicks me out," he admitted. "She's a fiery one."

For some reason, Nate couldn't stop laughing. "Man, this should be fun. I'm gonna be needing weekly reports, Chief."

"And you're gonna need your ass kicked." They reached the

fire engine and together hefted the hose back onto its reel. Darius closed the hatch and latched it with a sharp click.

"Speaking of which, we're down to our last few games before summer hiatus. You playing this weekend?"

"Probably." They both played on the local hockey team, the Lost Harbor Puffins—or Lost Harbor Losers, according to their competitors. "Unless I'm looking for new lodgings."

"Eh, you'll be fine. Who would evict a fire chief? Not even Naughty Kate is that crazy."

CHAPTER NINE

"Apparently I can't evict a fire chief," Kate told him, sounding none too happy about it. They met in the driveway a few nights later—"night" being an odd word to use, since it was still light out. A chill had fallen even though darkness still hadn't. Kate had rattled up the driveway with a full load of furniture. He noticed dark shadows under her eyes and a hint of purple at her temple. She must be exhausted, but that didn't affect her spunk level.

"Did you check the city code or something?"

"No. I asked my grandmother. Let me just say that I got an earful."

Darius refrained from pointing out that she could have done that from the beginning. "Technically, that's not true. You have every right to evict me."

She pointed at him in triumph, her work glove aimed at his chest. "Exactly. Didn't I say that a few times in my emails?"

"You did. More than a few. It was annoying. Want a hand with your furniture? The outside stairs are a bear."

Reluctantly, she nodded. "I lost my helper. So sure, that'd be great. I can handle most of it, but the couch—"

"I'm happy to help," he cut her off. "Don't worry about it."

They moved toward the bed of the truck. The sight of the load made him cringe. Did she know nothing about loading trucks? "Where are you from?"

"You mean, where am I moving from? Petal to the Metal, my grandmother's farm. Let's start with this rug."

"No, I mean where'd you come to Lost Harbor from?" He moved aside a chair that had made the trip balanced between a coatrack and the rolled-up rug.

"Why are you asking?"

"Why not? For instance, I moved here from Texas."

She narrowed her eyes at him as she grabbed onto the end of the carpet roll. "Okay."

"In Texas, we learn that it's important to use ratchet straps and bungee cords to secure your load, otherwise something could fly off and hit someone. That's one of the reasons why I'm curious about where *you're* from."

"I'm from the Kingdom of Cities," she said grandly. "Home to an amazing invention known as a moving company."

He chuckled as he helped her slide the rug off the tailgate. "I've heard those legends, but I paid them no mind. Surely such tales can't be true."

"Many wonders can be found in the Kingdom of Cities. Imagine food brought right to your door. It's called 'delivery.'" Together, they carried the rug toward the blue staircase.

"Impossible. Next you'll be telling me the WiFi always works."

She giggled, looking behind her to make sure she wasn't missing the bottom step. Her ponytail swung over her shoulder, drawing his attention to the tanned skin of her neck. Farmer's tan, the kind you could get even in the chilly temperatures of April because the sun stayed so long in the sky.

He found it sexy as hell—that, and the way her twisted position emphasized the deep curves of her chest and waist...

He fixed his gaze on the carpet and as a result, stumbled a bit as his foot hit the bottom step.

She swung her head back to check on him. "You okay?"

"Yup. Keep going." He adjusted his grip on the roll. "Do you have a body wrapped up in here or something?"

A laugh floated across the carpet. "Knowing Emma, anything's possible."

"I believe it. She heard about my Harley and tracked me down to talk shop."

"She's a badass. Best grandma ever. Even though she doesn't want me to move out, she's helping me furnish this place. She insisted I take this rug because the floors need finishing."

They reached the landing of the upstairs apartment. Kate fumbled for the doorknob as she propped the rug on one knee. When it turned, she pushed it open with her foot. He followed her through a short hallway to the front room with its breathtaking view of the town and the bay beyond it.

The floors were unfinished plywood and the pink fluff of insulation showed through a few gaps in the walls, but other than that it was a lovely space. Much smaller than his apartment, but that view made up for it.

"Here." She stopped in the middle of the front room and set her end of the carpet roll down. He followed suit.

"Let's roll it out," he suggested. "See how it looks."

Her face brightened eagerly. "You don't mind?"

"Sure, why not? We carted it all the way up here, why not get some satisfaction?"

"Let's do it. I've never actually seen what the rug looks like. She told me it's an antique from India." She crouched down and grabbed one end, holding it in place while he unrolled the bulk of it while backing across the room.

A bit of dust rose into the air, along with a faint sweet smell, like old rose petals.

"You might need a vacuum. Not to mention some weights to keep the corners down."

"We can use boxes for now. Stay there." She hopped to her feet and dragged a box his way, then used another one to anchor her end. "There!" She gazed at the unfurled carpet, and slowly her expression turned puzzled. She tilted her head, then walked around to the other side of the carpet.

He rose to his feet and stepped to her side. Then blinked.

Was he really seeing what he thought he was seeing?

"Is that..." He pointed to what looked like a...a penis. About to touch the mouth of a smiling woman. Who was being held by a naked man fondling her breasts. Who was....Where did it end?

"Oh my God." Her face turned red as she took in the decadent backdrop of the carpet. "Emma gave me a Kama Sutra carpet."

They both stared down at the panorama of naked figures in naughty and astonishingly flexible positions. Then they both burst into gales of laughter.

Darius' whole body shook with the force of his amusement, so much so that he had to bend over and rest his hands on his knees, gasping for breath.

"I didn't...even know...such a thing...existed."

As soon as she could stop laughing, Kate blew out a breath, sending strands of her hair wafting away from her face.

His hands twitched again. He wished he could touch her.

"Oh, Emma. You win." Kate planted her hands on her hips and gazed down at the carpet. A light flush still colored her cheeks. "No wonder she wanted me to have this. She's probably laughing her ass off right about now. I need to get her back somehow."

"What's your move?"

"I don't know." Thoughtfully, she tapped a finger against her chin. "I'm kind of tempted to pretend there's nothing unusual about the rug. I bet that would drive her crazy. Oh!" She clapped her hands together. "I can tell her that the floors are just fine without a rug, and that I'm going to donate it to her church—in her name." Her cackle of glee made him smile.

"You could probably sell it on eBay for a ton of money. It's such a find."

"That's true." With a thoughtful expression, she traced the border with her toe. "I think it might be hard to part with, though."

He lifted his eyebrows. *Hard* to part with? Was that an intentional double entendre?

Her eyes went wide, and she clapped a hand over her mouth. "Sorry, that just slipped out."

She clapped her other hand over her mouth, realizing she'd done it again.

He burst into laughter all over again. "Blame it on the rug. Bad influence."

Above her hand, her eyes flashed with naughty laughter. Lust tugged at him, hot and fierce.

He cleared his throat and stuffed his hands in his pockets, hoping that would hide the beginnings of his erection. "So you've decided that you can't evict me. That's good news."

Her entire manner shifted back to all-business and she dropped her hands from her face. "The correct way to phrase that is that I *can* evict you. I have the right to, according to the lease. But I'm not going to."

Uh oh. He saw a loophole there he didn't like. "Then we should both sign a new lease that says you can't evict me. I don't want you changing your mind on me."

She lifted one eyebrow. "Trusting, aren't you?"

"I'm a trust-but-verify kind of guy. And I'd like a real lease. It can be short-term if you like."

"Are you considering moving out?"

"Depends on how much noise my upstairs neighbor makes. The rug should help. On the other hand, that particular rug could lead to a lot more noise."

She pulled a face and jammed her hands into her back pockets. "No need to worry about that. The other night's close call was enough to teach me my lesson."

He folded his arms across his chest. "Are you talking about us?"

"There was no 'us,'" she said firmly. "That's the other thing we should talk about. Let's agree the other night didn't happen."

"What didn't happen? Are you referring to the part that didn't happen or the part that did happen?"

She blinked at him, bringing his attention to the brilliant dark fire of her eyes. "That doesn't make any sense."

When he started to explain, she lifted her hand to stop him. "It's okay. We don't need to relive it. None of it happened."

He eyed her curiously. "What are you so worried about? Even if we had slept together, it's no one's business. We're both single." It occurred to him that he didn't know that for sure. "At least, I am."

"That's not the issue," she said, irritated. "Of course I'm single. I'm as single as can be."

"I didn't know there were degrees of single."

"Well, there are." She ticked off a list on her fingers. "There's single but looking for a mate. There's technically single but committed to one person. There's happily single. Miserably single. Single but still having lots of sex." She gestured at the rug as she mentioned that one. "Single but may never have sex again. Think of it as a spectrum."

"Hmm." Tired of standing, he crouched down next to the rug

and rested one forearm on his thigh. "Interesting breakdown. Where do you land on that spectrum?"

She followed his lead and sat crosslegged on the carpet. "Maybe you should answer that question first."

He shrugged. "Is there a spot on that spectrum for a twice-divorced, never-again kind of guy?"

Her eyes widened. "Two divorces? Okay, you might have me beat."

"You've been divorced too?"

"No. Never been married. But I haven't had sex in two years, so there's that."

He whistled slowly. Apparently they were letting everything out in this conversation.

"Any particular reason why?"

"Many reasons why, and many reasons not to tell you why. For instance, we just met. And I'm now your landlady. That's why I'm talking about all this, because I want to make sure we understand each other perfectly. Even though we're both single, nothing like that night is going to happen again."

Was it his imagination, or was she going out of her way to insist on that? He hadn't initiated anything last night. She had. Maybe she should give this little lecture to herself.

"So the other night..."

"Was the closest I've come in two years." She smiled ruefully. "And I came away with a bruise on my head, a massive hangover, and a fuzzy memory. I'm taking it as a sign that I shouldn't try that again."

He had to admit, he found her decision disappointing. They had some pretty great chemistry, and he enjoyed talking to her. She had a funny way of stating things and a fast-paced style that kept him on his toes. She was also gorgeous to watch, the way expressions flitted across her face and an occasional dimple appeared an inch below her mouth, to the right, almost on her chin.

Sometimes he almost lost track of what she was saying because he found the play of her expressions so absorbing.

Maybe this wasn't her final decision. There might be a way to change her mind. He could be patient.

Assuming he wanted anything to do with his new landlady, who seemed like big trouble. He didn't need to get burned again. The last remnants of his formerly romantic heart couldn't take it.

"When you say fuzzy memory..."

"Well." Her right eye twitched. He wondered if that was a tell. "I know I was coming onto you. Flirting with you. Just so you know, I didn't really mean it. I was pretty buzzed and uh... confusing things with a book I'd just read."

Under his skeptical gaze, she maintained an expression of perfect innocence—which he didn't believe for a second. "What book?" he finally asked.

"Excuse me?"

"I'm just curious what the book was. I've been looking for something good to read."

Not true in the slightest. He didn't have much time for reading, other than fire science journals and reports from the forest service. But he would *like* to read. That much was true.

"Oh, it was nothing you'd be interested in. It was a romance novel."

"A steamy one? I'm interested now."

"No, not at all. It's...uh...Amish."

"An Amish romance novel?" That didn't seem at all plausible to him. "Is that really a thing?"

"It really is. You can look it up." With a look of triumph—as if she'd won that round—she pushed herself to her feet. "So now that we're on the same page, I'll draw up that lease and leave it in your mailbox."

"Great." He too maneuvered himself back upright, noting the ache in his legs. It had been a long day.

He caught her quick glance at his thighs as he gained his feet. Her throat moved as she swallowed.

Good. He'd go along with her little fiction about the flirting not being real. But he didn't believe it for a second. She was just as attracted to him as he was to her. Patience. That was the key.

He headed for the door. "Should we get that couch next? Or do you plan to hang out on the Kama Sutra carpet reading Amish romance novels all night?"

CHAPTER TEN

"You knew, didn't you?" Kate confronted Maya the next time she ran into her, which was at Gretel's Cafe a few days later. Gretel's was within walking distance of Fairview Court, so she'd gotten into the habit of stopping in for a hazelnut latte.

"I generally know everything, so the answer's probably yes. But what, exactly?"

"You knew who Darius was."

"Darius?" Gretel smiled brightly as she handed over their coffees. She was new in town, a magenta-haired, fun-loving free spirit who Kate had liked immediately. "Everyone knows Darius. You don't know Darius, Kate? I can introduce you. He plays hockey with Zander. And he runs the fire department. He also plays on Open Mic Night sometimes. You should come!"

Oh no, she wasn't going to take a chance on watching him play bass again.

"I'm good. Thanks, Gretel."

Kate tugged Maya to the sunny table by the window and plopped her down. "You knew Darius wasn't from Oregon. You even knew he was renting the Fairview Court house."

"Guilty." Serenely, Maya sipped at her coffee. "Your point?"

"Not only did you not warn me, you pushed me toward him!"

"You didn't need any pushing."

"Fair point. So why didn't you tell me who he was?"

"Because." Maya tore open a packet of sugar and stirred it into her coffee. "You would have shut it down. I like Darius. I think you'd be good together."

Kate's mouth fell open. As teenagers, Maya had never approved of the boys she went for. "You were playing matchmaker?"

"Sort of. Believe me, if I didn't know Darius was such a standup guy, I would have warned you. Really, I should have warned him about *you*."

Kate rolled her eyes at that. "You know my Naughty Kate days are behind me."

"So you say. And yet you still won't tell me what's going on with you." Maya's expression turned strict, more in tune with the police chief uniform she was wearing.

"I will. I promise."

Maya waited a beat, but Kate wasn't about to spill everything in the middle of the breakfast rush at Gretel's. "So how's the house-sharing working out?" Maya asked.

"Good," Kate admitted. "He's an excellent tenant."

"Not surprised. Told you he's a good guy. I gotta get to work." She gathered up her things, and they both headed out to the sidewalk, where they waved goodbye and went their separate ways.

Kate headed for Fairview Court, enjoying the radiant sunshine pouring from the cloudless sky.

Good to know that Darius had the Maya Badger seal of approval.

Not that it mattered. She barely saw the man. Not only did he work a lot, but he had a busy life beyond the firehouse. Hockey practice, jam sessions, city council meetings at which he delivered reports. He was rarely home, and when he was, he took care not to disturb her.

Then there was her worry about the lack of a security system. She added an extra deadbolt and slept with her can of bear spray nearby, but it turned out that living above a big strong fire chief made her feel much safer than living alone.

She slept like a baby knowing he was downstairs—that was, when she wasn't thinking naughty thoughts about him.

Darius also had a habit of doing thoughtful things that took her by surprise. He trimmed the unruly hedges that Emma had planted. He shoveled moose poop off the lawn. When they started running out of hot water in the mornings, he let her get first crack at a shower.

And then there was the railing of the blue staircase, which had broken during her move-in. Fixing it was obviously her responsibility.

But there he was, on this beautiful sunny morning, hard at work on it.

Tool belt and everything.

She practically had a hot flash when she caught sight of him. It took several moments for her to catch her breath as she came down the sidewalk.

He stopped in the midst of hammering the last nail into the new length of wood he'd installed.

"I was going to fix that," she told him. "That's what landladies are for."

"I had a few minutes, and it's an easy fix. I had the wood in my stash already."

"Your stash?"

"Leftovers from other repairs around here."

"Well, I'm happy to take it off your rent."

He laughed and tucked the hammer back into his tool belt.

"Not necessary. I had to get a box of threepenny nails, you can reimburse me for that if you want."

"Sure, how much was that?" She reached into her back pocket, where she still had change left from a fertilizer purchase.

"A dollar and seventy-six cents," he said dryly. "Or a return favor, if you prefer."

"What kind of favor?" she asked warily. Chances were, it would be harder to deliver than a dollar and seventy-six cents.

"Ever heard of the Lost Harbor Puffins?"

"Your hockey team?"

"Yeah. We have a game tonight, and I promised S.G. I'd bring her. But it turns out I have to get out to the rink early to help set up. She knows you, so I thought maybe you could bring her."

She pretended to think about it, tapping her finger on her chin. "Can I just drop her off or do I have to watch the game too?"

His smiled dipped. "Up to you. I can take her home, no problem."

"I'm just joking." She gave him a light tap on the arm and got yet another reminder of how damn hard his muscles were. "There's nothing I'd rather do than watch sweaty men fight over an inanimate object while skating across the ice."

He narrowed his eyes at her. "You know it's not just men, right? We have two women on the team. So I'll thank you to keep your sexist remarks to yourself." He followed that up with a grin.

She actually did feel a bit embarrassed by her assumption. "Point taken. Thanks for enlightening me."

He lifted his eyebrows in surprise.

"I can admit when I'm wrong," she said with all the dignity she could manage—even though she hated being wrong.

Still smiling, he began unbuckling his tool belt.

"What are you doing?" she asked nervously. It was such a sexy move, whether intentionally or not.

"Gotta get out to the rink. The railing's fixed, though it could use a coat of paint. The game starts at seven, and S.G. won't want to miss a thing. I'll leave you both tickets and I'm happy to spring for popcorn or peanuts or—"

She stopped him with a gesture. "That's okay, I'll take care of it. See you there at seven. Knock em dead. Or knock their teeth out, whatever it is that hockey players say for good luck."

He laughed as he headed for his own door on the other side of the garage. She turned as he passed her. Yup, the rear view was just as mouthwatering as the front one. "We generally just say 'have a good one,' or 'loser buys the first round.' But thanks for the visual."

She could definitely say the same as she watched him disappear around the corner.

THAT VISUAL WAS JUST A TEASE, as it turned out. An even better visual awaited her at the hockey rink. She'd never been inside the building that contained the rink, but she'd passed it many times on her way to the harbor boardwalk. To her, it seemed strange that a place with so many frozen lakes and ponds would have an ice rink.

But once she saw the way the game was played, she understood. They needed those boards along the side for the players to crash against. What fun would it be if you couldn't body slam a piece of plexiglass while skating fifty miles per hour?

She actually had no idea how fast they were going, but she could barely keep track of who was who as the players sped back and forth across the ice.

Except for Darius, of course, who was the tallest person on the Lost Harbor team. The other team, from Kodiak, had an extremely tall Russian player, but they wore dark blue jerseys instead of white, so it was easy to keep track of Darius.

For a big man, he was pretty agile out there on that ice. He used his size to intimidate the opposing players, or to sneak his stick between two people and whip the puck over to someone on his team. She recognized Zander Ross, Gretel's boyfriend/fiancé/ex-husband, but no one else on the team.

"How do they even keep track of that little thing?" she marveled to S.G. as they shared a bag of corn chips.

"It's black and the ice is white." S.G. sat on the edge of her seat, completely wrapped up in every move the players made. "Did you know they're not supposed to punch each other?"

"I did not. How unfair," she said dryly.

S.G. waved at someone on the other side of the rink. Kate followed her gaze and saw a boy sitting alone on the far bleachers. He wore a thick gray fleece hoodie against the chill of the rink, so she couldn't make out his face. He was watching the players very closely.

"Friend of yours?"

"It's no one," said S.G..

Interesting. S.G. was generally one of the most truthful people Kate knew. She usually only lied by omission, as in neglecting to mention that she had homework to do. In answer to a direct question, she always told the truth.

But obviously the boy wasn't "no one." In fact, the two of them seemed to be conducting a kind of silent communication by way of tilts of the head and shoulder movements.

"Why don't you just go and talk to him?" Kate finally said, exasperated by all the twitching going on next to her.

"What do you mean?"

Fine, so she still wanted to play dumb. Have it her way.

"Goal!" the girl shouted and jumped to her feet, thrusting her arms into the air. "Darius just scored! Go, Darius!!"

Damn, she'd missed his big moment. She applauded and whistled along with the rest of the crowd. Darius circled the ice, waving his hockey stick in the air to acknowledge the applause, and she could have sworn he aimed a grin her direction.

Shortly after that, the first period ended. Darius pulled off his helmet and glided toward the area where Kate and S.G. were sitting.

"Come on, let's go say hi," said S.G., jumping to her feet. They made their way down the bleacher steps until they reached the protective boards placed around the rink.

"Nice goal," S.G. told him. "I thought you were passing to the forward."

"That was the plan, but I saw an opening." He shoved a sweat-soaked chunk of hair off his face. "You guys having fun?"

"Actually, yeah," Kate told him. "Other than freezing my ass off, I've had a great time."

He blinked sweat out of his eyes, looking a little self-conscious. "Did you catch that last goal?"

His expression was just too cute for words. She hated to break it to him that she'd missed it.

"Sorry, I was distracted." She pulled an apologetic face. "Next time, I'll make sure to watch."

"*Next* time? You think that happens often? It'll probably be next year by the time I make another goal." He laughed as he tugged his sweaty jersey away from his chest.

"How was I supposed to know that? I'm more of a basketball fan. People sink baskets all time."

"Guess I'll have to switch sports, then." He skated backwards a few strokes, then forward again. Probably trying to stay loose. "Anything to impress my landlady."

Oh, she was impressed. That wasn't the problem. The problem was pretending she wasn't.

She glanced at the spot next to her, only to realize that the girl had skipped away somewhere. Scanning the bleachers, she spotted S.G. huddled on the bench next to the boy in the hoodie. They were deep in a conversation.

"Hey, do you know that kid?" she asked Darius. "I think he's a new friend of S.G.'s, and she's being very weird about him."

He turned to look for himself, then shook his head. "Doesn't look familiar, but I can't really see his face."

A horn blared, which was apparently the sign for the players to resume their spots on the ice.

"Watch closely," Darius warned as he plopped his helmet back on his head and fastened it. "I'd hate for you to miss another big goal."

"Does it even count if no one saw it?"

He fastened his chinstrap with a flourish. "Read the scoreboard, baby. Read it and weep." He dug the blade of one skate into the ice and turned with a swish, ice particles flying through the air. With swift, lethal strokes, he rejoined his teammates.

His use of the word "baby" sent the weirdest thrill through her. She imagined him saying it in bed, right before he stretched his big body over her. *What do you feel like, baby? You want it fast or slow? Hard or soft?*

Oh for fuck's sake. She was totally losing it. Maybe she should have slept with Darius at the Moose is Loose after all. Then she wouldn't still be fantasizing about it.

Flawed logic, obviously. She might still be fantasizing about it, except she'd have more concrete details to fill in the blanks.

CHAPTER ELEVEN

Over the next few weeks, five more fires got called in to the station. None of them caused any damage to a residence or a person. An empty woodshed out on MacKenzie Ridge burned down. A junk car got torched near the campgrounds. Two of the fires involved stacks of pallets. Other than the fact that they were minor fires, Darius could detect no pattern.

Even residents outside the volunteer fire department noticed the unusual fire activity. People started coming up to him on the street and asking him what was going on.

It was frustrating as hell.

Even more frustrating than living below Kate, listening to her move about upstairs, wondering what she was doing or wearing or saying.

Even though they kept a careful distance from each other, he'd noticed a few new things about her. For one, she was extremely cautious. She'd installed extra locks on the door. In a town like Lost Harbor, where some people didn't even have locks, that was surprising.

When she hopped out of her Saab, she always held her keys

so they could serve as a weapon. Who was she defending herself against? Stray porcupines?

He asked Maya about it one night at the city council meeting. The two of them were working on a bond issue to construct separate buildings for the fire and police departments. Right now they were located in the same compound and things could get a little tight.

As they waited to deliver their report to the city council, he leaned over and whispered, "Kate Robinson. My new landlady. Is everything okay with her?"

"What are you talking about?" Maya was in full uniform, with her hair slicked back and pinned tightly to her head. He wouldn't be surprised if she gave him a ticket for talking.

"She seems a little extra vigilant."

She folded her lips together, looking thoughtful. "Honestly? I don't know. But trouble has a way of following Kate around. Always has."

"But she's a lawyer."

"And? She's still Kate. Also, her family is..." She trailed off, shaking her head. "Will you keep me informed if there's anything I need to know?"

"As her friend or as the police chief?"

"Both, I guess."

The mayor called her up to the stage at that point, while he chewed that over.

Was Kate in some kind of danger?

If she were, would she tell him about it?

And was she ever going to relax her "no-flirting" policy?

He could be patient. Patience was one of his strengths. He'd worked on it over the years, as he'd risen in the ranks of the fire service. Patience when dealing with young rookies, patience with city councils, patience when dealing with lonely elders who called the fire department for trivial things.

Sometimes he wondered how his two marriages would have gone if he'd had more patience back then. But since he'd only been nineteen the first time around, he'd barely even known the word "patient."

The second marriage might have gone differently, but he doubted it. Amelie hadn't been looking for patience from him. She'd wanted "rough" Darius, the rougher, the better. He'd given her what she wanted, until he didn't want to be that person anymore. At which point, she'd dumped him.

But everything was different now. He was older, wiser, more jaded, more realistic, and more patient.

If the right time came, and he and Kate were both still feeling the vibe, maybe things would go his way. If not, he wasn't going to cry about it. He was all grown up now and he knew that life was no fairy tale—or even an Amish romance.

That didn't stop his pulse from kicking up when someone knocked on his door one morning. He had a rare weekday off from the firehouse and had slept in.

He was still shirtless and barefoot, having just come out of the shower. He reached for a t-shirt, then decided that Kate wouldn't mind a look at his bare chest. He'd seen the way she snuck glances at him. Besides, he had to seize every opportunity to remind her of what had almost happened between them. And what could happen, if they chose it.

But when he opened the door, he found himself facing a man instead of a feisty brunette. The stranger was almost as tall as he was, with alert eyes that sounded an alarm for Darius. Despite his friendly smile, this man had an agenda. A law-enforcement-related agenda. Even though he wore jeans and a hunter's jacket, he clearly wasn't a local. Something about his hair and clean-shaven look signaled "not from around here."

"Sorry to bother you so early. My name is Ethan James." The man pulled out a plastic ID case and flipped it open. "I'm a private investigator from California. Nothing alarming, I promise."

Doing his due diligence, Darius took the ID and studied it. The James Agency, based in Los Angeles, California. No reason to doubt it.

No reason to start off on a bad foot, either. As the fire chief, he too was part of the law enforcement system.

"Darius Boone." He offered his hand and they shared a firm handshake. "Give me a second, I'll be right with you." He stepped aside and pulled on his t-shirt. "Want some coffee?"

"Nope, I just grabbed some at Gretel's Cafe. Didn't it used to be called something else?" Ethan stayed at the threshold of the door, which Darius appreciated.

"You can come on in," he offered. Ethan took a few steps inside, revealing a slight limp as he did so.

With a mug of coffee in hand, Darius sat on the arm of his sofa and scrutinized his unexpected guest. "You've been to Lost Harbor before?"

"Yeah, I played bodyguard to a friend for a few days. Fell in love with this little town."

"Let me guess. Padric Jeffers?"

Padric was the only real celebrity from Lost Harbor who might conceivably need a bodyguard. He was a globally famous rock star who had grown up here and recently returned, at least part time.

Ethan just smiled slightly, which was another point in his favor in Darius' book. He wasn't here to discuss his clients, obviously.

"So how can I help you?" Darius asked after a sip of his coffee, black and scorching the way he liked it.

"I'm looking for someone. A woman."

Darius tried to keep his expression neutral, but he must have shown some kind of reaction, because Ethan quickly continued.

"She's not in any kind of trouble or danger. I was hired by a law firm to find her because her testimony could be useful for a case they're building."

"Must be really useful, to send someone all the way to Lost Harbor."

Ethan smiled. "I'm not privy to the details. I'm just doing my part."

"What's her name?"

"Her birth name is Catriona Robinson. But she's also known as Catriona Fletcher."

Darius kept his expression completely neutral. Kate had more than one name? That was a bit of a shocker, and he didn't like it one bit. He wanted to find out more before he gave away any information to this investigator.

"Never heard of a Catriona Fletcher. But I'm relatively new in town. You might have better luck talking to Maya Badger, the police chief. She knows everyone. That's not an exaggeration."

Ethan nodded amiably. "Always an option. But my information led me to this location."

"Well, sorry. Give me your card, I'll call you if anything comes to mind." He got to his feet, ready to be done with this conversation.

Ethan pulled out his phone and clicked on a photo. "I have a picture of her. She might be using a different name." He aimed the phone in Darius' direction.

A woman's face filled the screen. It was the kind of photo taken for work ID purposes—no smile, straight to camera. She wore a black blazer over a light gray silk top—it looked expensive. In the unflattering lighting, it was hard to see the color of her eyes.

But it was definitely Kate. A professional career woman version of Kate.

"This photo is a few years old," Ethan said as Darius stared at it. "Keep that in mind."

It might be plausible that he didn't put "Catriona Fletcher" and "Kate Robinson" together. But to say he didn't recognize the woman in the photo would be a lie.

Still, Ethan James was just a P.I., not an actual officer. He wasn't breaking any kind of law by not telling him everything.

Darius made a split-second decision. He lifted his gaze to Ethan's and shook his head. "Sorry."

After a long moment of scrutiny, Ethan accepted his answer. He handed Darius a business card. "I'll be here for a few more days if anything comes to mind. Just call that number."

Darius accepted the card. "Enjoy your time in Lost Harbor."

"I always do. Thank you for your help." With a civil nod, he headed for the door, that same hitch in his stride.

"Wait," Darius called after him. "Could you email me that photo?"

"Sure."

Darius gave him his personal email address. Best to keep this whole situation away from his official duties.

As soon as Ethan James left, Darius closed the door behind him. He watched through the front window until he'd driven away in a vehicle that he recognized as one of Lost Harbor's five rental cars.

He pulled out his phone and searched through his email inbox. When he found the photo, he saved it to his phone and stared at it for a good long while.

What was going on with Catriona/Kate/Robinson/Fletcher?

A footfall sounded from upstairs. Kate was awake and moving around. Even though the soundproofing was generally pretty good, occasionally he heard a thump or a crash. He figured she was moving furniture around on her own, refusing to ask for his help. Independent as ever.

Pocketing his phone, with the photo cued up, he downed the rest of his coffee and pulled a sweater over his head. He'd done Kate a huge favor by buying her some time. The least she could do would be to answer some very reasonable questions.

Then again, so far he'd never had any luck predicting what Kate would do.

CHAPTER TWELVE

Kate wasn't quite prepared for the high-octane impact of Darius at her door first thing in the morning. In a heathery-brown hand-knit sweater, with his sweatpants molding to the hard muscles of his thighs, he was just...a lot. A lot of man. A lot of gleaming silver-blue eyes and husky shoulders and thick, mussed hair.

Given her two years without sex, shouldn't she be renting to someone a little lighter on the testosterone?

She sighed and tamped down her automatic reaction to him. "Good morning. You're up early."

"It's not really that early. I'm surprised you aren't at the farm already."

"I was up late." No need to tell him that her sleeplessness was partly his fault. "What's up? Urgent landlady business?"

"Not exactly. I had a visitor this morning."

"There's a lot of that going around, apparently. What's wrong with people?"

A good smell wafted from him. Coffee was somewhere in the mix, along with freshly showered skin. He must have shaved, because for once she saw no dark stubble on his jaw. Morning

Darius—clear-eyed and clean-shaven—was just as attractive as all the other Dariuses she'd encountered.

He didn't respond to her jab the way he usually did, with light humor. His firm lips didn't curve into that smile she'd come to anticipate. "This visitor was from out of town. California, in fact."

Fear stabbed through her, hot and fast. She reared backwards, away from Darius.

Shut the door. Get him out.

She nearly slammed the door in his face, but he stopped it with one hand. Before she could get a word out, he stepped inside and closed the door behind him.

"Kate, it's okay."

"Did he threaten you?"

"What? No." He frowned in confusion. "Why would he threaten me? He was quite friendly and professional."

Professional. A professional assassin maybe? She shook herself back to reality. Her father's crew might be criminals, but they weren't killers.

"Who was he?" she asked. Might as well get this over with. "Did he give a name?"

"He's a private investigator named Ethan James, from Los Angeles."

A private investigator! Her eyes went wide. She'd been careful not to give anyone any forwarding information, just in case it got into the wrong hands. Apparently it had taken an investigator to track her down.

"He was looking for you," Darius went on. "Two different names came up."

"What did you tell him?" she asked nervously, biting on a fingernail. She had no clue what an investigator wanted with her, but it was clear what Darius wanted. Answers.

"Nothing. I got rid of him. I figured I'd let you tell me what was going on."

Oh God, this was bad. Darius probably thought she was on the run from the law, using a fake name, or some other nefarious thing.

His eyes held hers. She read concern in them, but also some suspicion.

She couldn't blame him for that.

She wrestled back the impulse to tell him to butt out and mind his business. He'd done her a favor just now. If any man was trustworthy, it might be Darius Boone. It was worth a shot, anyway.

She hauled in a long breath. "Better come in." She led the way to the living room, which she'd just finished furnishing a few days ago. The infamous carpet was now covered with a coffee table, along with a few strategically placed throw rugs.

Morning light poured through the window and danced across the hardwood floor in honey-colored beams. Her mug of coffee sat steaming on the coffee table, next to her laptop. She'd been peacefully answering emails, sipping her hazelnut French roast, before Darius had shattered her calm.

Darius went to the sliding glass door that let onto the deck and scanned the street out front. "Just making sure he's gone."

"Did he say what he was after?"

"Like I said, he was looking for Catriona Fletcher or Catriona Robinson. He showed me a picture." Darius came toward her and showed her his phone. Her old work photo from the law firm. Wonderful.

"Crappy photo, huh?" she said lightly. "Why are work photos always so unflattering?"

He didn't smile. "It's from your old job? When you were a lawyer?"

"Yes. From the law firm of Bustos, Bagwell and Gonzalez. I

was a lowly second-year associate when I left. And yes, they knew me as Catriona Fletcher. I used that name for…" she made a face. "Reasons."

"Reasons," he repeated flatly.

She tried a winning smile, but it made no impression on him.

"You're going to give me more than that, right? Because I have his number right here on this card and all it will take is a phone—"

"Extortion? Really? You'd stoop so low?"

"Legal terms? Really? *You'd* stoop that low?"

She pressed her lips together and turned away from his gaze, which seemed to see right through her. "It's…it's embarrassing. The kind of sordid story you'd read about in a tabloid. But if you really want to hear it…"

He plopped himself down on the couch, his thighs spread like twin oak trees. "I really want to hear it." That voice left no room for doubt.

She sighed and sank down on the couch cushion farthest from him. "I don't even know where to start," she groaned.

"How about this? I'll ask questions. I'll start with why you looked so scared when you heard about Ethan James."

"No, no, that's a terrible place to start. That's practically the end."

He rolled his eyes at her. "Good God, you're stubborn. Start wherever you want. How about your name. Why the two names?"

But that didn't feel like a good place either. "Just…" She waved him away. "Let me tell it. I'll start with the day I was emancipated. I was seventeen years old and I got tired of being yanked around between my father the grifter and my mother the gypsy. So I emancipated myself and I chose my own last name just to make the point extra clear."

She snuck a glance at his impassive face.

"I used Catriona Fletcher all through college and law school and at work. I didn't want my professional reputation associated with my father. He's slightly notorious in Southern California. I didn't want people connecting me with a small-time criminal. I mean, I had my own issues, you may have heard."

"Naughty Kate."

She cringed. "Exactly. But that was kid stuff, and I wanted to put it behind me. Kate Robinson was a pile of trouble. Catriona Fletcher, on the other hand, had her shit together."

He cocked his head, waiting for more.

Oh God, this was hard. Her habit of secrecy was so ingrained. "Hey, you want some coffee?"

He laughed, the deep sound rolling through her. It was oddly reassuring to hear that laugh, in a "not everything has been destroyed" kind of way. "You don't have to be so squirrely, Kate. I'm not the enemy, I promise."

"I know you're not." For a moment she wished she could lean against his broad, solid chest and forget about all this. "Though we did start out that way."

"Only until we met." His silvery eyes gleamed at her. She sighed and tucked a lock of hair behind her ears. She hadn't even showered yet this morning, let alone brushed her hair. She probably still had sleep in her eyes. She'd barely remembered to grab her old UCLA hoodie before opening the door.

It just showed you how quickly life could change.

"Hang on," she told him. "I'll be right back."

"You aren't going to disappear out the back door, are you? If so, can I have dibs on the rug?"

She laughed despite herself. "No, I just want to put on a bra. You caught me by surprise. You can't expect a girl to bare her secrets without some support."

His lightning-fast glance at her chest gave her some satisfaction.

Once she'd put on a bra and brushed her hair into a more orderly ponytail, she felt more ready to deal with this situation. She poured another mug of coffee and brought it to Darius, who was standing at the sliding door again.

"Just so you know, that investigator won't give up easily," he told her. "I'm keeping an eye out for you."

She nodded and handed him the coffee mug. Propping her butt on the arm of the couch, she picked up her own mug and took a long bracing gulp. "Where were we?"

He leaned against the wall and cupped the mug in both hands. She wished they were still next to each other, but knew it would be easier this way.

"Working at a law firm, following the straight and narrow?"

"Yes, exactly. It was everything I'd imagined. Everything I'd worked for. I was completely independent. I had a mortgage on a condo in Westwood. I had a red Miata that I drove to the office. I worked all the time. *All* the time. When I wasn't working, I'd go to brunch or dancing with my girlfriends. I dated now and then but it was never my priority. I rarely heard from my parents. It was a completely selfish existence, exactly what I used to dream about. I was one of those kids who basically raised themselves because their parents had no clue and also didn't care to learn. Emma was my only real 'parent' growing up. And I only saw her in the summers. Anyway—" She took a break for a sip of coffee. "Is this boring you?" she asked hopefully.

"Absolutely not," came Darius' firm answer.

She sighed. Of course not. Darius looked like he'd been permanently planted there next to her view of Misty Bay.

"So then one day my father surfaced. He was in trouble with a group of lowlife scammers who ran a fake supplement ring, among other things. They also sold fake timeshares and forged yacht titles and I don't even know what all. He had a kind of salesman role with them—that's his forte, he can talk anyone into anything." She flashed a wry smile. "I may have inherited my ability to argue a case from him. He's not all bad."

Darius lifted an eyebrow, looking unconvinced about that. "Let me guess. He needed legal help."

"Yeppers. The DA had started an investigation, and the others were trying to set him up as the ringleader. He was almost out of money and couldn't get a lawyer to help him. So." She hauled in a long breath. It still hurt to think about this part. "My law firm wanted nothing to do with it, so I left the firm and represented him myself. I got him a deal that allowed him to testify against the others in exchange for house arrest. Pretty fricking great deal. Apparently the DA found him 'charming.'"

She put that last word in air quotes because she herself no longer found Frank Robinson at all charming.

"Do you have any idea how much I wish there was whisky in this coffee?" she quipped.

Darius gave her the most sympathetic smile she'd seen from him yet. "You're doing great. But I have a feeling the worst is yet to come."

"It is." She hauled in another long breath. "After my father gave his testimony, scary things started happening. Death threats on my phone. Graffiti on the door of my condo. Tires slashed. I looked into hiring a bodyguard."

"Didn't the DA help?"

She shook her head impatiently. "It had nothing to do with them. I like to handle my own problems."

"At least some things haven't changed," he said dryly.

Point taken.

"I knew it was the scammers. I kept hoping they'd forget about me. But then it escalated. Someone broke into my condo one night. I had already put a deadbolt on my bedroom door and mapped out an exit just in case. So I got out of there before they came in. But it was terrifying. They broke the door and ripped up my favorite pillow. Goose feathers everywhere."

Weeks later, she could sort of make a joke out of it. But not really, especially with Darius looking like a thundercloud leaning against the wall. "Jesus. Where was the bodyguard?"

"He was just a part-timer, it was all I could afford. Anyway, at that point I decided that I needed to leave town. My career was in shambles anyway. I didn't feel safe anywhere I went in LA. I wanted to get as far away as possible, and Lost Harbor, Alaska, fits that description. I sold my condo and bought a plane ticket here, where no one has ever heard of Catriona Fletcher. Until now. Now, I'm screwed."

Darius came over to her and put a hand on her shoulder, reassurance radiating through its weight and warmth. "Are you worried that Ethan James is working for those criminals? I don't think so."

"You don't know that. Criminals hire lawyers too. If I wanted to represent bad guys, I could make a fortune."

He absorbed that with a flicker of his eyelids. "He seemed like a decent guy. He said something about wanting you to testify in a case. He left me his card. How about if I act as a go-between so I can find out more from him? If I get any hint of anything suspicious, I'll drop it."

She chewed at the inside of her mouth. If the scammers from LA were involved, would they really give her a head's up by sending a polite man with a business card?

"I want to find out who he's working for. That will tell me a lot."

He scanned her face closely. "You're thinking of meeting with him?"

"I can't exactly ignore him. It's a small town, and if he's any good, he'll keep on popping up. Unless I want to flee into Lost Souls Wilderness, I should probably just face him. And believe me, I'm not the roughing-it-in-the-wilderness type. Jess and Maya can confirm."

"Let's do some research on Ethan James and his agency first."

He pulled out his phone, but she reached out a hand to stop him. "You don't have to do that. This is my problem. You have a whole firehouse to worry about."

His blue-gray gaze clashed with hers. "Oh hell no. You're not pushing me away on this. I'm in the middle of it and I'm not going anywhere."

A sneaky thrill of pleasure shot through her at his words. Not just his words, but his manner, like some kind of Highland warrior ready to take up arms to defend her.

"Fine," she conceded. "You can look up Ethan James while I make a few calls."

He did more than that. While she curled up on her couch and talked to her contact at the DA's office, he wandered into her kitchen and came back with breakfast.

A plate of blueberry pancakes, to be exact. Which he must have made from scratch, because she didn't have any pancake mix on hand.

Impressive.

The pancakes were the perfect balance between hearty and fluffy. She gorged herself as she listened to the ADA talk about a class-action suit filed against the doctor who had vouched for the fake supplements.

"These are amazing," she told Darius when she'd finally completed the call. "How'd you learn to make such good pancakes?"

"I always make pancakes when I work an overnight shift, so long as I'm not out on a call. My crews expect it now. I've spoiled them. We don't work a lot of overnight shifts here, just in the summer. But the tradition continues. So what'd you learn?"

"Sounds like they're busy with other things. My contact

thinks the chances that they've sent someone to Alaska are zero. Anything on this Ethan James?"

"Clean as a bottle of detergent. Excellent reputation. Stellar record. I forgot to mention that he's friends with Padric Jeffers. You could also contact him for a reference."

"Oh sure, just call up Padric Jeffers out of the blue." She was familiar with the rock star, but only through Zoe Bellini, his fiancée. "That's okay, I'm willing to take a chance and meet him for myself."

"Good." He tugged a business card from the pocket of his sweats. "Want me to call him or do you want to call him yourself?"

"I'll call him myself, of course." She plucked the card from his hand and looked at the name and contact information printed on it. *The James Agency. Los Angeles, California.* The words gave her a sudden chill. They brought back those fearful moments during her last days in LA.

And she realized...she didn't want to do this alone.

"But I...would be grateful...I mean, if you have the time..."

It shouldn't feel so awkward to ask for his help. But she was so used to relying only on herself.

"Want me to come with you? You got it." He grinned at her widely, his teeth gleaming like a pirate's. "I was afraid you'd never ask."

"Weird thing to get excited about." She nudged his thigh with her foot—for no other reason than to remind herself of those hard muscles. "It's not like it's a hot date."

"We'll see."

CHAPTER THIRTEEN

Darius had left out one important detail about Ethan James—the guy was a hottie. They met him in the lobby of the Eagle's Nest Resort and Hotel, by far the most expensive hotel in Lost Harbor, and one of the few that stayed open all winter. With his easy smile and penetrating eyes, Ethan James was instantly appealing.

But not quite as appealing as the big guy at her side.

"Call me Kate," she said immediately upon shaking Ethan's hand.

"Ethan. Thanks for meeting with me."

They claimed a quiet nook with a stunning view of the restless gray ocean and the icy peaks on the other side. Misty Bay was living up to its name today, with long fingers of fog drifting past like smoke.

They had the lobby to themselves. The reception clerk was watching TikTok videos on his phone, and the only other noise was the quiet bubbling of a fish tank.

"I have lots of questions, Ethan." she told him, after making sure the clerk had his headphones in.

"Of course you do. I would too. Let me start with who sent

me up here. My client is the law firm of Cotton and Bryant."

Her eyes widened. That name was famous in California legal circles. It was one of the most respected law firms in the country. "That's reassuring."

"Good. I can't say that I know the ins and outs of your situation, but I do know that they're not trying to put you in danger. They want your testimony in a case."

"What's the case?"

"Class-action suit against Dr. Robert Kramer."

So the ADA had been right on about that. "The supplement fraudster."

"That's the one. Your...ahem..." He cleared his throat delicately, glancing at Darius.

Kate gritted her teeth. "You don't have to dance around it. My father was working with him. Darius knows all the dirt at this point."

"Good. Then I can speak freely?" Kate nodded, and he continued. "Thirty victims of the supplement scam are filing a five hundred million dollar class-action lawsuit against Kramer's company. Cotton and Bryant's team thinks your testimony can be useful."

"I'm not going to testify against my father," she said flatly. "First of all, I was his lawyer. Also, he's my father, and even though he wasn't much of a parental figure, I couldn't do that to him."

Ethan shook his head with a frown. "No no, not that. We've gathered evidence that Kramer ordered his operatives to harass you and intimidate you. That's the testimony we're after. All you have to do is recount everything that happened before you left LA, and the steps you took to protect yourself. Just tell the truth. That's all. The law firm will pay all your expenses to fly to LA and you can tape your deposition."

Her heart skipped a few beats. *Fly to LA.* Sunshine. Freeways. Maybe a brunch with a few friends. A taste of her old life.

"With your testimony, you could help bring the victims' families some closure."

Her eyebrows lifted. "I'm sorry, don't you mean cash?"

"That too." He smiled slightly. "Before I came up here, I did a little research on you. I found it interesting that you became a lawyer when your father spent so much time dodging them. You could have chosen his kind of life, but you didn't."

She threw up a hand. "I don't need a psych profile, Ethan James. I've spent a lot of time trying *not* to be my father. I know that. I'm sympathetic to the class-action suit. I know what it's like to be scammed. I've seen it many times and it's a terrible feeling. But I left LA because I was being threatened and—"

"All security costs will be covered. Sorry, I should have mentioned that right away."

She stole a glance at Darius, but his expression told her nothing. He had his intimidating poker face on lock.

"When would they want me? For how long?"

"It should only take a couple of days. One day to meet with the team and prep, one day for the depo. Maybe more if the opposing counsel gets frisky."

Two days. That sounded safe, but it didn't leave much time for extras. Brunch with friends was probably out.

And come to think of it, she wouldn't want to expose anyone else to any bad guys catching wind of her return.

"I'd like to choose my own security."

Ethan relaxed back in his chair. Obviously he knew a victory when he witnessed one. "That sounds like a reasonable request."

"I'd call it more of a condition."

He laughed. "I see you haven't lost a step. Condition. Got it. I can almost guarantee they'll agree to that very reasonable condition."

She smiled, finding him charming.

Darius leaned forward; he didn't seem to find Ethan quite as appealing as she did. "There's something else. Maybe you should tell Kate how you found her and how you can guarantee that no one followed you."

She shot Darius a grateful glance for remembering that point. Bringing him along had been a good move.

Ethan hesitated, clearly reluctant to reveal his own trade secrets. "Is it enough if I just tell you that you're still safe here?"

"Not even close," Darius answered for her in a low growl.

It felt really good to have a guard dog by her side. More of a guard bear, taking into account his size.

"Like I said, I did some research and stumbled across the Lost Harbor connection. I figured it was worth checking out. As for guaranteeing Kate's safety, I told my client that I was pursuing a lead but didn't give any details. I turned my phone off before I left the city, took three different flights in case someone was following me, and I've been using a burner phone since I got here."

That sounded thorough to her.

But Darius still didn't look convinced. "We called the number that was on your business card."

"I got that card printed in Anchorage."

"Got a receipt for that?"

As they lobbed arguments back and forth, Kate looked from one to the other. What the heck were they fighting about? Why was Darius being so hostile to Ethan, after saying he was a decent guy?

"Darius, can I talk to you in private for a second?" She tugged him to his feet and led him around the corner to a little nook, where a door led to an enclosed terrace that contained an outdoor hot tub. He pushed open the door and they stepped outside. Immediately, a rough wind jostled them, like sharp elbows on a crowded bus.

Darius positioned himself so his big body shielded her from the worst of it. With his legs braced apart on the deck and his hair tossed by the wind, he looked like a pirate.

"I thought you vouched for Ethan. Why are you so suspicious?"

"Due diligence, isn't that what you lawyers call it?"

"Are you sure we don't call it being territorial?"

His expression shuttered. "You want me to back off."

"No. You're thinking of things I should have thought of. I'm just wondering if you think there's something suspicious going on with Ethan."

He shoved his hands in his pockets and hunched his big shoulders. "No," he admitted. "I think he's being straight. I just —" He made a sound like a growl. "Wish he wasn't such a charmer."

Secret joy sparked inside her. Darius *was* a little jealous. And that was kind of adorable. She kept her face neutral. "Can I ask you something?"

He jerked his head with a nod.

"Big guy like you, have you ever worked private security?"

Surprise lit up his face. "You want me to come with you to LA?"

"I do. I want someone who's not connected to the law firm. Not that I don't trust them, but..." She shrugged. "I'd feel more comfortable with someone I know, someone smart *and* strong. Could you get time off from the station?"

"I have backlogs of vacation time. Nate can take over for a few days. It's not a problem."

"So, Sir Armor-All. Would you like to play personal bodyguard for a couple of days? You and me and a hotel room in LA?"

Heat flared behind his eyes. Her pulse picked up and energy sizzled between them. A gust of wind swirled around them, making her sway toward him. Her nipples pebbled into hard peaks. *This man, between her thighs...*

She took a step back. This wasn't a hookup, for heaven's sake. It was a risky trip into her recent past.

Finally he nodded. "Yeah. I'll be your bodyguard." The roughness of his voice told her he was feeling the same lust that she was.

"Are you sure?" she asked innocently. "I mean, Ethan's an LA local, and I'm sure he's perfectly capable—"

At the fierce look in his eyes, she dropped the act.

"Good," she said simply. "I was hoping you'd want to come with me. I already feel safer."

One corner of his mouth quirked up. "You were teasing me about Ethan?"

"Maybe a little." She shot him her naughtiest grin. "Call it revenge."

"For what?"

"I'll think of something."

He tilted his head back and burst into laughter. She watched the strong tendons of his neck flex and had the impulse to lick his skin, just there.

"Has anyone ever told you you're a pain in the ass?" he asked her when he was done laughing.

"I'm pretty sure you told me that in one of your first emails."

"Well, it's still true." He stepped to the side, breaking their intense connection, and opened the door for her. "But don't worry. I take my bodyguard duties seriously. I won't let anything happen to that ass."

On her way through the door, with her back to him, she gave her ass a naughty twitch.

She didn't have to see Darius' face to sense his reaction to that. She could feel his gaze burning up and down her backside.

This was going to be a very interesting trip.

CHAPTER FOURTEEN

The law firm of Cotton and Bryant booked them adjoining suites in an upscale boutique hotel in Century City, a neighborhood that seemed to consist entirely of high-rises. Even though Darius was a ranch boy by birth, he'd lived in both Houston and El Paso —different cities for different marriages. He enjoyed cities, when he wasn't scanning every passing face for some sign of a threat.

It was a relief to step into Kate's suite and drop out of watchdog mode.

Kate set her suitcase on the floor and surveyed the impeccable room with a happy sigh. Stargazer lilies and a tropical fruit basket sat on the glass coffee table.

"You know, I think it's worth putting my life at risk just so I can have a fifteen-dollar kiwi paid for by a fancy law firm." She plucked a fuzzy brown fruit from the basket and peeled it with her thumbnail. Juice wetted her fingers, and he decided that watching her eat it—her lips on that green flesh—might be too much for him.

"I'm going to do a quick check of the room." He went from window to window, making sure everything was locked from the inside and inaccessible from the outside. He did the same thing in his own suite.

"Do you want this open or closed?" he asked her from the door that separated their suites.

"What's safer?" She paused with the kiwi inches from her lips. Damn. He knew that would be trouble. He lost his train of thought.

"Safer in terms of..."

Her eyebrows lifted. "In terms of not getting surprised in the middle of the night."

What kind of surprise did she have in mind?

He shook off his inappropriate thoughts and got back to business. "Probably open, so I can hear if something happens."

"Okay. Open. But no peeking." She winked at him and bit into the fruit in her hand. Juice ran down her forearm, and she darted out her tongue to catch it.

He wheeled around and pulled the door half-closed behind him. "Taking a shower," he told her in a choked voice.

"Me too," she called after him. Great. Simultaneous showers. He'd have to make his a cold one. "Want to get dinner after that? I'd say it's on me, but the law firm's paying for everything so it's on them."

"Sounds good."

Instead of a cold shower, he turned the heat up and filled the stall with fragrant steam. Then he soaped up his hand and wrapped it around his cock. With the other hand braced against the tiles, water cascading onto his head and back, he stroked himself. Kate's face and lips danced behind his closed eyes. The way she'd licked that juice off her arm...that should have been her tongue on his erection. And it was, in his imagination.

What was she doing right now? Was she too in the shower? Soaping her breasts, covering herself with lather? Maybe her hand was between her legs right this very moment. Maybe she was rubbing herself, touching her own nipples. *Oh God.*

It took only a few strokes for him to come in his hand. Pressure relieved. At least for the moment.

He spent some more time catching his breath, cleaning himself thoroughly, and delivering himself a lecture about proper bodyguard behavior.

When he'd gotten himself dressed in a new set of clothes, he knocked on the adjoining door.

"Come in," Kate called. She spun around as he stepped through the door, and all that hard work he'd done in the shower went right down the drain.

It was just a black dress, but the way it cupped her breasts and pushed them together was a goddamn threat to a man's sanity. The fabric clung to the curves of her waist and hips, then stopped short just above her knees. Not only that, but she wore heels so high she came up to his chin rather than his chest.

"I brought my stilettos with me," she told him cheerfully. "It's not often I can wear them around a man without towering over him."

He grunted, since that was the only sound he was capable of making right then.

"Also, in a pinch, I can use them as a weapon." She bent to slide off one of her shoes, giving him an even better view of the bare upper curve of her breasts. His mouth went dry.

He cleared his throat. "That's okay, you don't have to demonstrate. I feel safer already."

She tugged the shoe strap back into place and stood up. "How's your appetite?"

Wrong question. He lifted one eyebrow and didn't answer. She flushed and ran her tongue over her lips. "There's a great steakhouse around the corner."

"Works for me."

Good God, he had to get a grip. He was here to watch her back, not slobber all over her.

She pulled on a red sweater—forevermore, he'd associate the color red with her—and they headed out the door.

The electric atmosphere between them followed them into the elevator and through the foyer. It must have made Kate nervous too, because she launched into a breathless explanation of how much she'd been looking forward to dipping into her Los Angeles wardrobe again. And then something about makeup and hair stylists and brunch.

When they hit the sidewalk, she wobbled a little on her stilettos, and he grabbed her arm to steady her. She leaned on it for extra support as they walked. Finally he saw the advantage of those shoes, aside from the fact that they made her legs look about as long as a high-rise.

"Look at us, all civilized and going out to dinner in LA. We've come a long way from that muddy road in Lost Harbor," she said lightly.

"And from the Moose is Loose, passed out in that cabin."

"Knocked out," she corrected. "Passed out sounds more degenerate. I didn't have enough fun to qualify for passed out."

"Really?" He gave her a wicked sidelong look. "I did. It was a great night, until I woke up all alone with a goddamn crick in my neck."

She pulled a mock-apologetic face and slid her hand to the back of his neck. "Poor baby. I can make up for it now if you like."

She massaged him lightly, and he groaned. "Now? In the middle of a city sidewalk when I'm supposed to be watching for bad guys? We really need to talk about your timing."

With a smile, she dropped her hand, letting it linger on his back before settling at his elbow. The muscles along his spine tingled, missing her touch already.

"Don't worry, I won't interfere with bad guy patrol. If you

weren't here, I'd be barricading myself in the hotel room and ordering room service."

"Maybe we should—"

"No. It's such a short walk, and there's all this warmth and smog to enjoy. "

He laughed. "Forget what it's like after all that clean Lost Harbor air?"

"I did." She inhaled a long breath. "It's strange being here. I feel like I'm drunk but I'm definitely not."

"I don't even have that excuse," he murmured, half to himself. But he knew exactly what she meant. It was a giddy feeling to be here with her in this enormous, sprawling city in which no one knew their business. No curious volunteer firemen or hockey teammates to be seen. They could do whatever they wanted and no one ever had to know about it.

They could throw every rulebook in existence out the window.

Except for the one that would keep her safe, of course.

To that end, he made sure they were seated in a corner booth, from which he could see everyone who came in and out of Ruby's Steakhouse.

"You seem like you know what you're doing, bodyguard-wise," she commented after the hostess had left them alone with their drink menus.

"I've watched enough Jason Statham movies to get the general idea."

She smiled at that. He loved making her smile. That little divot that appeared near her chin just did him in. Every time.

"Have you always been a fireman?" she asked.

"Mostly, but I started life as a cowboy."

Her eyes lit up. "That hat. I loved that hat. I haven't seen you wear it since that night."

If he'd known she'd be looking for it, he would have done

something about it. "I lost it at the Moose Is Loose. They're hanging onto it for me, but I haven't been up there since that night. Didn't know it meant anything to you. I've had it since I was a teenager riding herd."

"I guess I'll just have to use my imagination," she murmured wickedly.

"I've been using mine overtime, so join the club."

The tip of her tongue slid between her lips. She'd put something in her hair to make it look wild and tousled, and it didn't take much imagination to picture it spread across his pillow.

"I'm trying to ask you serious questions and you keep distracting me." With a stern frown, she tapped on the table between them. "When did you switch from cowboy to fireman?"

"Halfway through college. I was a biology major. Thought I might go on to med school but decided to change to fire sciences. I couldn't stomach any more school. Turns out a good half of our calls are medical anyway. So I get to use those muscles too."

Under her curious gaze, he found himself wanting to keep talking, which was unusual for him.

"When did you become a fire chief?"

"When I moved to Lost Harbor. That's generally how it happens, you have to switch locations to get promoted. I've had a lot of experience with volunteer fire departments because that's how I started, as a volunteer for the county where our ranch was located in Texas."

"Texas to Alaska. That's a long way."

"Yeah." He saw no need to elaborate on that, but she kept waiting so he felt rude not answering. "I had reasons for wanting a change of scene."

"Like what?"

Oh lordy, she really did want to get into it. "Divorce," he said simply.

Her expression shifted from interested to cautious. Not that he could blame her.

"I needed a new start, and it wasn't ever going to happen within a hundred miles of my ex."

"Lost Harbor is a lot more than a hundred miles away from Texas."

"And about six state lines away. Part of its charm." He leaned forward, propping his elbows on the table. "Listen. I don't bad-mouth my ex. Either of them. Those relationships were what they were, and I learned my lessons."

"Which were?"

"Why make things complicated when you can just fuck and have fun?" He said it lightly, but he heard the hollowness of his own words. It had taken a lot of hurt for him to get to the point where he believed that.

He still wasn't completely sure that he did.

"Sounds like you had a rough time." Her sympathetic gaze drew more confessions from him.

He shrugged. "I'm not complaining. I married the first girl I really loved. Gillian. We got married at the end of high school. Then I got busy with college and she got bored. Met someone else and took off. I didn't blame her, but it was a kick in the guts. I was still a naive kid, basically. It blew me away that she could even think about another man. I was so in love, or at least I thought I was."

He could hear the hurt seeping into his voice, and cleared his throat. "Like I said, it was a good lesson."

She touched his hand, making him realize he'd been clenching it. "I'm sorry. That must have been a real heartbreak."

"Oh, yeah. I thought we'd cracked the whole love-and-marriage thing. I was going to get my degree, become a doctor, start a family. Turns out we never made it past my freshman year. Poor dumb kid." He shook his head at his own past self. "I proposed to her on horseback during a roundup. Man, when I look back, I can't believe what a dolt I was."

A funny smile flitted across her lips. "It's very sweet, honestly. From the outside, I never would have pegged you as a sap."

"And you'd be right about that. My sappy days are dead and gone. After Gillian left, my brothers kept telling me to 'buck up, be a man.' I shut the fuck up after that. Got into firefighting and moved on."

What he left unsaid was that if his marriage to Gillian hadn't killed off his romantic side, his nightmare with Amelie would have done it.

"Here's the thing. I was a naive, clueless, horny kid. I thought women were...angels. I idolized Gillian. When she left me, it was like a bomb hitting. I had to rethink everything. I went through a really dark time. Honestly, I went a little over the edge."

"Over the edge? How do you mean?"

He stopped himself before he went any further. "I don't know you well enough yet. Sorry."

Her eyes went wide with indignation. "Now that's a tease and a half. Unfair."

"How is that unfair when I don't know the first thing about your life? Except the two-year dry spell. Can't forget about that. Ever been close to getting married?"

"Nope. Before I came to Lost Harbor, I was one hundred percent focused on my career. Except when I was focused on having fun." She sparkled a smile at him. "I've always kept my relationships...undemanding."

"What were you afraid of?"

His question seemed to startle her. "Afraid? What makes you think I was afraid?"

"Just an impression."

She tilted her head, mulling that over. A basket of breadsticks appeared, dropped off by the hostess, and she cracked one in half and dipped it in olive oil. "Maybe I was afraid. I didn't want to get sidetracked. I didn't want to get sucked back into the muck. I always figured I was one bad decision away from becoming Naughty Kate all over again. So yeah...I guess I was afraid."

"Hm."

She made a face at him. "Hm? What does that mean? Hm."

"I think you're brave. You grabbed your life and decided for yourself what you wanted. And hey, you came to Alaska. Farming in Alaska is no cakewalk."

"That's true. The other day I literally fell through the snow crust while I was carrying a bag of fertilizer to a shed. I fell on my ass and got showered with chicken manure. I even had some in my eyelashes. I think I still might have a few bits of it here and there. Oh, hello!"

The waitress had arrived and, judging by her look of revulsion, had caught that last part. "Sorry, I'm a peony farmer from Alaska," said Kate. "I have stories."

"A peony farmer? That's a thing?"

"It was a surprise to me too. But yes."

The waitress, a gorgeous twenty-something, turned to Darius. "Are you a peony farmer too?"

"No. I'm a—"

"He's my personal bodyguard," Kate interrupted.

He raised an eyebrow at her, but she just blinked at him innocently and picked up her menu. They placed their orders—both of them going for the steak specials, with all the extras.

When the waitress was gone, he allowed a smug smile to curve across his face. "Your personal bodyguard, eh?"

She shrugged one bare shoulder. "If you'd told her you were a firefighter, she'd be flirting with you nonstop. I rescued you."

He decided it would be fun to tease her a little. "You keep telling yourself that."

"What do you mean?"

"You were obviously telling her to back off. You were guarding your territory."

"My *territory*? What are you, the back forty?"

He leaned closer to her. "You called me 'your personal bodyguard.' Not just your bodyguard. But your *personal* one. She got the message pretty quick too."

"Maybe I don't want you getting distracted when you're supposed to be protecting me."

"Maybe you know there's something going on here," he waved his hand between them, "and you don't want anyone messing with it."

"Oh really, that's your interpretation? Isn't that a little bit arrogant?" The quiver in one corner of her mouth took the sting out of her insult.

"It's not arrogance if it's true." He held her gaze, feeling that wild connection flare between them again. It was always there, like background static, and all it took was a little oxygen to make it burst to life.

The muscles of her throat moved as she swallowed. His cock twitched in response. Fuck, why was it that every move she made got a rise out of him?

Their stare down ended when she capitulated. "Okay, say that it is true. Obviously there's something between us. But it's probably just...a physical anomaly. It doesn't mean anything. We're not compatible, obviously. If we were we wouldn't argue so much."

Earlier in his life, that might have wounded him. But he'd grown a thick shield around his heart since his Gillian days.

"Besides," she added, "I decided to not do anything stupid. My close call, remember?"

"I remember. Never was clear on the reasons, though."

Well," she began warily. "If those guys find me, I might have to go somewhere else. I don't want to put anyone else at risk."

"What if that 'anyone else' decides he's okay with that risk? I came down here, didn't I? If I was afraid of risk, I'd be back in Lost Harbor fighting fires and ice storms. Oh wait. That's risky too. Looks like I'm not afraid of risk."

She laughed unwillingly.

"The question is, are you?" He drilled his gaze into her, giving her a preview of what things would be like in bed with his strength and her fire. *Good God.*

She tugged her lower lip between her teeth. "I don't know... lately my most intimate relationships have been with flowers. Peonies, not penises. Then you come along like some kind of testosterone bomb. I'm not sure I know how to handle you." She blinked at him, all innocence.

He threw his head back and roared with laughter. When he was done, he planted his forearms on the table and took her hands between his. "I'm not sure of a lot, but I'm one hundred percent sure that if anyone can handle me, it's you. Of course, there's only one way to find out."

"That sounds like a challenge."

"Oh, it is, babe. It one hundred percent is."

CHAPTER FIFTEEN

Kate was quivering from head to toe by the time they got back to the hotel. Darius had make it perfectly clear where he stood and what he wanted. It was what she wanted too, with every fiber of her being.

But when she reached the room, she found a message on the hotel phone. Cotton and Bryant had been trying to reach her; apparently her cell phone had been off the entire time they'd been at dinner. She'd been so wrapped up in their conversation that she hadn't even noticed the lack of texts or calls.

The phone call with the associate who'd be handling the deposition took over an hour. At some point, Darius disappeared into his room, and when she was done, she tiptoed to the door and peered in.

He lay sprawled on the bed in a twisted tangle of bed sheets and long limbs. A pillow lay across his chest, with an arm holding it in place. His other arm was flung to one side, palm up. A gentle snore floated across the room.

She found it endearing the way he was clinging to that pillow as if it was a Teddy bear. It made her think of what he'd said about his first marriage and how he'd been so crushed, but was told to "buck up." Was that what happened to a guy who had a tender heart but happened to be born into a big rugged body?

Was anything left of that tender heart?

Even though he talked a cynical game, she had a feeling there was quite a bit left. There was a reason Lost Harbor had taken Chief Boone into their hearts. There was a reason he'd chosen the protective career of firefighter. There was a reason a hyper-wary kid like S.G. trusted him so much.

She tiptoed away from the door between their suites and headed for her own bed. With depo prep looming in the morning, she had no business fantasizing about a "challenge."

HER PREP TOOK up all of the next day. The associate offered to come to her hotel suite for the session so she wouldn't have to take any unnecessary risks. Since Darius wouldn't be needed until dinnertime, he took off to check out Century City.

Kate found the prep excruciating. She wasn't used to being on this end of the equation. She was used to asking the questions, not trying her best to answer them. After a couple of hours, a familiar pulse behind her eyes began to throb. She hadn't had a migraine since she'd left LA; she'd nearly forgotten what they felt like.

After running through the kinds of questions they planned to ask her, the associate switched to playing opposing counsel and doing his utmost to trip her up. It was exhausting and when they finally called it a day, she could have cried with relief.

As soon as the associate was gone, she changed into her comfy clothes and guzzled a bottle of water as she looked out the sixteenth-floor window at the endless expanse of streets and buildings and freeways. She'd been one of those busy little bees buzzing around town. Fun times—stressful, but fun.

But something had shifted, and she wasn't as excited to be back as she'd anticipated.

Pain behind her eyes sent her to the couch, where she draped a cool washcloth over her face. That was where she was when Darius returned. She lifted the cloth to peer at him and his overflowing load of shopping bags.

"I see you found the mall."

"I went shop-ping. O.M.G." His imitation of a tween girl made her laugh.

"Find any cowboy hats?"

"Hell no. You have to go to Texas for those. Got something for everyone on the crew, though. Couple things for my hockey team. A knife-holder for S.G.."

"You found a knife holder in the Century City mall?"

"Go figure." He showed off the hot-pink leather holster. "She's going to hate it. I had to do it."

With a groan, she dropped the facecloth back into place. "You're a weirdo."

"How'd it go today?" He lowered himself next to her, as she braced for the effects of jostling on her head. But he was surprisingly gentle as he settled his big body beside her. "Tough day?"

"I'm trying to fend off a migraine. It's the last thing I need right now." She closed her eyes to bring back the darkness.

"What helps with that?"

She shrugged. "Darkness. Quiet. Sometimes the muscles in the back of my neck get so tight..."

"Say no more." A big, warm hand settled on the back of her neck. His thumb pressed along the tendons. An instant long groan spilled from her mouth.

"That feels—"

"Shhh," he murmured. "You need quiet, remember? I bet you've been talking all day."

"Mmmm, hmmmm." After that she followed his directions and held her tongue, losing herself in the soothing magic of his strokes. His fingers were so damn strong. The tightness in her tendons was no match for his gentle power, and slowly the tension eased.

From her experience, if she could head off a migraine before it really took hold, she might be able to sleep it away and not miss the next two days in a fog of agony. Deliberately she relaxed her jaw and her eyelids and any other muscle she had any control over. Calm, even breaths. Coolness. Darkness.

Think of peonies, not depos.

No, not even that. No thoughts. Thoughts hurt. They made her tense up and that made everything worse. Let all the thoughts evaporate like a cloud of mosquitoes. Let peace and calm spread from the back of her neck, from those commanding fingers, through her skull and along her face.

She drifted into a half-conscious state. The feeling of being swept down a river roused her sometime later. But she wasn't on a river; she was in Darius' arms, and he was carrying her to bed.

Second time he's done this, she thought sluggishly. *Next time I want to be conscious.*

Or maybe she'd said it out loud, because a low chuckle vibrated through her from his broad chest.

"Count on it," he murmured as he nestled her into softness. "I'll wake you up in the morning in plenty of time."

He stepped to the window to draw the blinds against the city lights. So light here, all the time. In Lost Harbor, it really got *dark* at night. No streetlights, just moonlight and starlight. Maybe that was why she didn't get migraines there.

Time passed, and slowly the iron band of pain around her skull eased. She snuggled into the covers and slept, and it really felt as if she could still feel Darius' gentle hands on her head, smoothing out every bit of tension and stress. Even though he was gone, it felt as if he was with her, his heated skin against hers, his arms holding her tight against everything out there that wanted to hurt her.

"Kate?" His voice came softly through a white veil of dreams. "Sweetheart? Can you open your eyes?"

At first she wasn't sure if she could. But she wanted to see if it was really Darius calling her "sweetheart," or just one of the nighttime fantasies she'd been having lately. She dragged her heavy eyes open, realizing as she did so that it didn't hurt.

"You called me sweetheart." Her voice didn't make her wince the way it usually did when she spoke during a migraine episode.

"I knew that would get your attention." Sitting on the edge of her bed, he stroked a damp strand of hair away from her face. "How's your head?"

She blinked hard—another test. A faint trace of pain remained, like a shadow of a memory of pain. "Seems okay."

Cautiously, she pushed herself into a sitting position. She still wore the loose clothing she'd changed into last night when she'd felt the first threat of a migraine. "What time is it?"

"Still early. It's only six-thirty. I thought you might want some time to ease into the day."

She nodded carefully. "Good thinking. Thanks, Darius. I think I might be fine." Gingerly, she moved her head from side to side. "You've got the touch. I wish I'd known you when I was cramming for the bar exam. It might not have taken me two tries."

"You get migraines a lot?"

"It happens." He offered her a hand, and for once she accepted without protest, though she wasn't yet ready to try standing up. She had a feeling she'd never reject help from Darius again. He'd proven himself a gem with those expert hands of his. "I need to be at the Cotton and Bryant offices by nine."

"Yup. I already made coffee, and I got you a room service menu. If you want to shower, I'll order breakfast."

Tears came to her eyes. "You're being so nice to me," she moaned, wiping a tear away with the back of her hand.

He looked alarmed. "Want me to stop? Does it make it worse?"

"No, it's just..." More tears came and she let them flow, because recovering from a migraine was a delicate process and couldn't be interfered with. "I get emotional after a migraine. The relief from the pain makes me want to kiss someone's feet."

If anything, he looked even more alarmed. "I wouldn't recommend that. My feet are in steel-toed boots much of the time. They're ugly as hell."

She couldn't help laughing, even though a laugh had a big potential for bringing more pain. But no pangs of electric tension shot through her skull. Amazingly, she really had made it through this episode in almost record time.

"The thing is, when I get a migraine I'm like a wounded bear. I just want to crawl into my den and hide there until it's safe to come out. I don't want any people in my space, I don't want voices or food or anything except maybe a sip of water. Even when I was a kid I just wanted to be left alone."

"Sorry, Kate. I didn't know any of that. I would have—"

She stopped him by planting a spontaneous and entirely shocking kiss on the lips. At least *she* was shocked; he didn't miss a beat. He responded with gentle pressure of his own, a promise of more, much more, maybe later, maybe tomorrow, when they had more time. It wasn't a deep kiss, but it wasn't just a peck either. There was full, tingling, breathtaking contact between her lips and his. His mouth was just as firm and sexy to touch as she'd dreamed.

It came to a natural, easy end and they drew apart. Kate felt as if they'd calmly stepped over some invisible boundary and were safely on the other side.

She touched her lips briefly. "What I mean to say is, don't apologize for that amazing neck rub last night. I don't know why you're not a masseur with these hands."

She lifted his hand off the bedcovers and spread it open, palm up. She traced the calluses that marched across the pads below his fingers. The lines on his palm were strongly etched, and some of them seemed to be nicks and scars.

It was a hand that had been through some shit. And a hand she could trust.

It was also a hand that she wanted to feel all over her body.

"And the way you carried me to bed and tucked me in. Closed the blinds. That was so sweet of you."

His eyes darkened as she continued to stroke his hand. "Do you remember what you said? You said you want to be conscious the next time I put you into a bed." The thick growl of his voice made her nipples peak.

He noticed, too. It was probably hard to miss, since she was wearing a thin tank top with nothing underneath. Her breath came fast as his gaze dropped to her chest. He lifted his other hand, the one she wasn't petting. It came toward her and, for a moment, she knew he was going to touch her breasts, and she wanted that more than anything in the goddamn world.

But then he shifted and settled his hand on the curve of her neck. He pulled her toward him so he rested his forehead against hers.

"You're a sorceress, woman. But you need to get yourself ready for this deposition and I'm not going to be responsible if you miss it."

"But it's hours away," she pointed out.

"Not enough hours for all the things I want to do with you." Firmly, he ripped the covers off her and gripped her by the elbow.

"Come on. Get yourself into that shower and tell me what you want for breakfast."

Sexual frustration fought with her common sense. Of course he was right. Coming out of a migraine, it would be insane to do anything that would raise her heart rate. She needed to be careful.

It was a good thing one of them was thinking straight.

She carefully swung her legs over the side of the bed and stood up. Hardly any wavering at all. She rolled her neck and found barely a hint of pain. Truly, Darius had worked a miracle.

And now she was ravenous. "I don't need a menu. I know what I want. I'll have my traditional pretrial breakfast, please. French toast and hash browns and bacon. Coffee with lots of cream. And if they have any orange juice throw that in too."

With a grin, he unfolded his big body from the bed. "Sounds like you're feeling better. Good to see."

She decided to give him something even better to see, and stripped off her tank top on her way into the bathroom.

Until they could get between the sheets, she'd have to be satisfied with that sexy groan of his.

CHAPTER SIXTEEN

Darius stayed close to her side all the way through the deposition. The lawyers allowed him into the conference room where it took place, although they asked him to sit off to the side.

Even there, she noticed, he made his presence felt. Someone so big, with so much tamped-down power, was hard to ignore.

"Catriona Robinson Fletcher," she said to the camera as she was sworn in. "Home address under file."

Her one request had been that she not be required to reveal her new location. She didn't trust any of these people, on either side of the case, to protect that information. In fact, the only person in the room she truly trusted was Darius Boone.

His quiet presence gave her more strength than he probably realized. Every time she got rattled by a question from the opposition, she drew on his silent support.

They started with questions about how she got involved in the case.

"I was the attorney on record representing Frank Robinson, who is my father. He was peripherally involved with Dr.

Kramer's supplement scheme. He offered testimony against various co-conspirators in exchange for a lighter sentence."

"And you brokered this deal?"

"Correct."

"Did you expect that it would anger the other members of this criminal enterprise?"

She and the associate had agreed on this line of questioning as a way of getting out ahead of a touchy issue.

"I anticipated some hostility, of course. But most of the other suspects had experience with the justice system. They know the drill. And I imagined they'd be more upset with my father than with me. That part took me by surprise."

The opposing lawyer, Tim Chun, who wore a sharp suit and plenty of hair product, started off with a doozy. "Do you consider yourself a naive person?"

"Not at all."

"Stupid? Dumb? Clueless?"

"I'm sure I have my moments. Don't we all?"

She caught Darius' smirk out of the corner of her eye.

"Isn't it true that you *chose* to represent your father? That you went so far as to quit your lucrative position at a respectable law firm in order to do so?"

"Yes. And yes."

"Is that because they refused to touch the case due to your father's sordid criminal past?"

This was suddenly getting a lot less fun. "You'd have to ask them why they didn't want the case."

"Why did you take the case?"

"To help my father."

"Your father, the criminal."

Since that wasn't a question, she didn't answer.

"Isn't it true that associating with criminals brings unintended consequences?"

She glanced at the Cotton and Bryant associate, who should have objected to such a vague question. He was jotting down a note, so she objected herself. "Overly vague."

"Never mind. Do you know who was behind the threatening letters and other incidents you've described?"

"No. But I've been told there's evidence that—"

The lawyer cut her off. "Answer the question only, please."

"No."

"But you assumed it had to do with your father's criminal cohorts?"

"I didn't assume anything. I just left."

That threw the lawyer off stride. "You...just left, you say. You just left behind your career, your entire life? Because you were afraid?"

"Yes."

"And yet you're here today."

She waited a beat. "Sorry, is that a question?"

Chun shuffled some papers. "The question is, if you were so terrorized, why did you have a romantic dinner at Ruby's Steakhouse two nights ago?" He held up a photo of her and Darius laughing intimately together.

Ah. Now she saw where he was going with this.

"Objection," said the lawyer from Cotton. "Relevance?"

"Goes to her state of mind and characterization of—"

Kate held up a hand, shooting a quick look at the Cotton associate. "I'll answer."

Chun looked a little nervous now, but it was too late.

"I had dinner with my bodyguard. I hired him because I'm still afraid."

Poor lawyer, he thought he'd trapped her. He must have gotten thrown off by the fact that Darius was a fire chief and not a professional bodyguard. Best move ever, hiring him.

"And yet, as you noticed so perceptively, I am in fact here. It's a challenge to face your fears. And there's nothing I enjoy more than accepting a challenge."

Out of the corner of her eye, she caught Darius' grin.

Challenge accepted.

"THAT WAS one of the best movies I've ever seen," Darius joked as they left the law firm's offices. "The dialogue was fantastic. The plot was compelling. And that actress who played the lawyer, holy shit she was hot."

And boy, was she, in her tailored cream suit and kitten heels, with her long hair in a twist at the back of her neck.

She gave him a tired smile. He could see her fatigue in the shadows under her eyes and the lines around her mouth. It made him feel protective of her, especially after what he'd witnessed last night. How she'd gone from a blinding headache to kicking legal ass, he had no idea.

But he admired the hell out of her. Just from that short demonstration, she must have been a fantastic lawyer.

"Do you miss your job here?" He scanned the sidewalk out front as they pushed through the revolving door in the law firm's foyer. He kept his arm protectively around her, just in case. If either a bad guy or a migraine hit, he'd be there.

She screwed up her face. "Ask me when I didn't just get shish-kebabbed under oath."

"You did great. You had that guy spinning his wheels."

"Oh, you know me, I like arguing my points. Sometimes I argue with the peonies. I definitely argue with Emma. I've kept my skills honed with a few emails here and there."

She gave him a sly smile that made him laugh. "Do you miss your law firm?"

"I miss the people I worked with. I miss the sense of accomplishment. But surprisingly, I don't really miss my life here. One migraine later, and I'm ready to go back."

She didn't seem to mind the fact that his arm was still around her shoulder, so he left it there as they strolled down the sidewalk. "Why don't you practice law in Alaska? Lost Harbor only has three lawyers, and one's about to retire."

"I know. Emma's told me a few times. But I'd have to take the Alaska bar, and then there's the issue of my name. I'd worry that somehow it would put me back on the radar."

"You happen to be best friends with the police chief. The fire chief's on your side too. You have backup, you know."

She glanced up at him; the seriousness in her eyes took him by surprise. "I would never want anyone in Lost Harbor to have to deal with those lowlifes. Never. I would leave first."

He wanted to argue, but the fire in her eyes told him there'd be no point.

"Listen, I have one more favor to ask you," she told him as they neared the hotel.

"Sure. You hungry? Thirsty? How's your head?"

Another faint smile. "I could use a rest, not going to lie. But right now, all I need is for you to go back to the hotel. I'll be back in a few hours."

He stopped dead in his tracks. "Are you nuts? The hell with that. You can forget it. Wherever you're going, I'm going with you. Period. End of story. Nonnegotiable," he added when she still didn't look convinced.

She folded her arms across her chest and glared at him. "Why do you have to be such a stubborn bastard?"

"Born that way, babe. That's why you hired me." Someone jostled him on their way down the sidewalk, and he moved closer to Kate, shielding her. "Come on. It's not safe to stand out here in the open. Let's go."

Her gaze clung to his, probing his determination. Apparently finding that it was rock solid, she released a sigh. "Okay. Let's go. But before we do, you have to understand that this is private. It's not for anyone else to know about. Not Emma. Not Maya. Not anyone in Lost Harbor. Promise?"

He raised his palm, as if putting himself under oath the way she just had. "You have my word as a stubborn bastard."

CHAPTER SEVENTEEN

Their fourth Lyft driver dropped them off at her father's Brentwood address. His location was protected; she only knew it because she was his lawyer. Ironically, it was probably the least risky place in LA, as long as no one followed them. To that end, they switched Lyfts three times on their way and made sure to get lost in the always dependably congested traffic.

Even receiving her father's message—*Need to see you*—had triggered a migraine, and she hadn't given any thought to it since last night. The depo came first. But now that it was over, it was time to face the music.

"Katiebird!" Her father swung the door open, his face beaming with welcome. She couldn't help a quick check of his ankle. There it was, the electronic bracelet that kept him confined to within fifty yards of this property. *Nice imprisonment if you can get it.*

She'd sacrificed her entire career so he could get it.

"Hi Dad. You look good."

Frank Robinson always looked good. He had to, because his existence depended on it. At all times, his hair was perfectly moussed, his eyes clear and sparkling blue, his skin smooth as a baby's. He could have been a motivational speaker or a wrinkle cream spokesperson. He probably had been both of those things in his checkered career; Kate couldn't keep track of all his occupations.

Around the age of thirteen, she'd finally understood her father's lax attitude toward things like laws and morals. At the age of seventeen, she'd legally emancipated herself. But she still loved him. Not only was he her father, but he was extremely lovable; it was part of his tool kit.

"And you look absolutely marvelous, Katiebird. A bit dirty under the fingernails, but I blame that on your grandmother."

Kate tucked her fingers into her palms, so her nails were out of sight. Trust her father to notice that detail. His observational skills were another ability that contributed to his shady career.

"You sound vaguely British," she told him as she and Darius stepped inside the foyer. High ceilings, terra-cotta tiles; nothing but the best for Frank Robinson, even in home confinement.

"Yes, I'm trying to use my time productively."

"By learning a British accent?"

"Not just British, dahling," he said airily. "I've mastered ten different accents so far. New Zealand, Australian, Irish—"

She cut him off. "Why don't you learn some actual languages? That would be more productive than accents."

"I throw a few words into the mix, Katiebird. But you know me. Why do something difficult when you can take things easy? Who's this tall drink of water?" He eyed Darius with trepidation. "He looks as if he could toss me over his shoulder and lock me in a trunk. Can you tell him I'm already serving time, there's no need to pile on?"

"His name is Darius, and he can speak for himself. Darius Boone, Frank Robinson. My father."

Darius stuck out his hand. Her father grabbed it and pumped

it enthusiastically. "Any friend of my daughter's...*are* you friends? What are you to each other? I sense simmering sexual tension, or perhaps it's simply tension. Ooh, those are the best relationships, when there's friction and drama and conflict, so delicious, reminds me of your mother—"

"Dad!" Kate cut him off before he could completely mortify her. "Darius is my security for this trip. Those goons of Kramer's might still be after me."

"Yes, I understand. Very grateful, very. You're a good daughter. I don't deserve it, I know. At least I've done one thing right in my wayward life." He plucked a silver bell from a knickknack table and rang it. "Lemonade for my guests, please!"

An answering shout came from deeper inside the house.

"You have servants here with you?" Kate asked incredulously.

"One servant. How else am I supposed to live?"

Kate exchanged an outraged glance with Darius, only to find that he looked more amused than anything else. Well, it wasn't his father, so he didn't have to be embarrassed, or angry, or any of the other emotions pouring through her right now.

"We can't stay for lemonade," she said firmly. "It's been a long day and we're leaving first thing tomorrow."

His perceptive blue eyes scanned her face. "Migraine, honey?"

She gave the tiniest of nods. Sometimes her father could be incredibly compassionate, like a Teddy bear come to life. And sometimes he could be crueler than a playground bully. She never knew which Frank would appear, despite a childhood of trying to guess.

"It's hardly a surprise, after the stress I've caused you." Ah, so it was the Teddy bear. "My poor sweet baby, those awful headaches. They began when she was just a tween," he explained to Darius. "Puberty, no doubt. I used to drape blankets over the windows to block out every speck of light. I'd bring her cool washcloths and speak in the softest whisper, like the ghost of Florence Nightingale."

"That's perfect, Frank. Just perfect. You're using my migraines to talk about yourself and your parenting."

He blinked at her as a tough-looking man in a bellhop uniform, with actual epaulets and gold braids, appeared with a tray of glasses. "Lemonade? Hydration sometimes helped."

"No. Thank you," she added to the servant, who left immediately. "Why do you make him wear that uniform?"

"It was all they had left at the costume shop," he said in a reasonable tone—as if that explanation made any sense.

"Why is he wearing *any* uniform? You know what, never mind. It doesn't matter. Why did you want to see me?"

"Sweetcakes, as if I need a reason beyond saying thank you? Yet again?" He turned to Darius. He always had a knack for including everyone in a conversation. "I'd be in prison now if not for my brilliant daughter."

"Well, you're welcome, Frank," she told her father to draw his attention back to her. "I'm glad to see that you're looking so well."

He beamed at her.

"If that's it, we should probably get—"

"There is a tiny matter that has come up." He held up two fingers indicating how extremely small it was. "A dispute that could use your talents."

"No," she said flatly. "I'm not a lawyer anymore."

"Of course you are. You didn't do all that hard work just to walk away. That's not my Katiebird."

Her head throbbed with a flashback of migraine pain. "I'm no longer practicing, Frank. I'm a peony farmer. And a landlady. *Not* a lawyer. Even if I was, I told you at the beginning it was a one-time thing."

"Do you see how ice cold she is to her dear old dad?" So

breezy and witty, her father. So uncaring about any needs but his own. "Can't you talk to her, big fellow? Such iciness from one's own flesh and blood. It's practically inhuman. But then, she's always been so hardhearted—and hardheaded. You must know that by now."

Kate felt heat slowly rise in her face. Just when she thought she was safe, her father twisted the knife right where he knew it would hurt. Hardhearted...did that word really describe her? Was that why she'd never let herself fall in love with anyone?

"I'm not—" she began, but Darius stopped her with one motion of his hand.

"I think he asked me a question."

Her father beamed at him as if they were already best friends. "That I did. Perhaps you're a father yourself, and you understand the pain of—"

"I'm not a father. Haven't been that lucky. But if I were, I'd be pretty freaking proud if she was anything like Kate. Kate's not icy, she's not hardhearted. She didn't have to come here, and if she takes my advice, she won't do it again until you get your head out of your ass. But since she is a little hard*headed*, she'll do what she chooses. And I'm behind her a hundred percent."

Kate felt his hand under her elbow and realized he was nudging her toward the door. Her father's jaw was agape; she'd never seen him stunned into silence before.

That was the thing about Darius. He didn't talk a lot, but when he did, people paid attention. Even Frank Robinson.

"Bye Frank," she told her father. "I'll be in touch."

Her father dragged his fascinated gaze away from Darius long enough to blow her a kiss. "I like him," he called after them. "You have my approval. Always thought you needed a man who could stand up to you. Don't let this one slip away like the others."

One last jab for the road, apparently.

Kate slammed the door behind her on the way out. Her face still felt hot and her fists kept clenching the way they used to do when she had tantrums as a kid. Familiar fury coursed through her system in a hot river of emotion. Frank *always* did this to her. He always turned her into a blubbery mess. No emancipation, no law degree, nothing had changed that. She should never have come here. She should know better by now.

"I'll call a Lyft," Darius said.

"No. I need to walk for a minute."

Right now, she didn't care if a bad guy spotted her. She stalked down the curving drive toward the upscale street with its sycamore trees and bougainvillea hedges. Darius caught up to her with one long stride.

"I'm sorry you had to see all that," she told him stiffly. "I warned you not to come."

"Hey, it's no skin off my nose. Are you okay?"

"I will be. I just need a minute." After a few more steps, her frustration erupted. "Can you believe how stupid I am?" she cried. "I actually thought he'd start acting like a real father if I saved him from prison. I thought he'd appreciate me. I mean, he tried, I suppose. He said 'thank you.' But then he just had to insult me and manipulate me and...I *know* not to trust him. I *know* it. And yet I fall for it every time."

"And you know why?"

"Why?" she asked automatically, even though she doubted that he could possibly know anything about it.

"Because your father's dead wrong. You're not hardhearted. If you were, why would you have torpedoed your legal career for him?"

She spun around to face him. "You know what's a hard-hearted thing to do? Evict a fire chief. I tried to do that before I even met you."

"And a little bit after you met me," he pointed out.

"Exactly. He's right. That was cold."

"Yeah, well." He shrugged his massive shoulders. "You didn't evict me, did you?"

"But...that's..." Maybe it was time to confess something. "Because I didn't want to," she admitted.

He laughed. "Right, because you're not the shark you pretend to be." His silvery eyes gleamed down at her. "And because you wanted me around."

On the verge of telling him exactly that, she snapped her mouth shut. "Because you were so good with things like shoveling the path."

"And giving you hockey tickets."

"And fixing the handrail. You're really a very useful tenant."

He dropped his voice into the register where the hot growls lived. "You have no idea how useful I can be."

Her lower belly clenched with a stab of excitement. Her frustration with her father evaporated as she threw herself into flirting with Darius. "Like with the migraine? That kind of useful?"

"Sure, anything physical like that, it's kind of my specialty."

"I thought fires were your specialty."

"Absolutely. All kinds of fires." His deep voice reached right into her bloodstream and started a fire all on its own. It spread through her veins like warm honey.

"I'll call a Lyft." Her voice, on the other hand, had gone all tight and breathy. She fumbled with her phone as she went through the steps. "But before Dmitri in the red Honda gets here, I want to say something."

He cocked his head, waiting, his eyes steady on hers. Steady as a rock, that was Darius. And damn, it was everything she wanted. Everything she needed.

"No one has ever stood up for me like that," she said softly. "Most people find my father amusing and don't understand why I get upset with him. I love him, he's my father, but I've never felt safe with him. I've always known I had to watch my own back around him. And I had to do it alone. I mean, it was good training for being a lawyer. But—"

A red Honda pulled up next to them. Their driver had arrived, just in the nick of time to keep her from getting carried away.

"Thank you," she finished quickly. "It meant a lot."

He nodded simply. "You got it. Give me a second to check out the driver."

That was Darius, always saying so much with just a few words. Better yet, his words were on point and none of them were trying to deceive. Especially after that encounter with Frank, it was a little dose of bliss.

Actually, a tall and broad-shouldered dose of bliss.

CHAPTER EIGHTEEN

Darius lectured himself all the way back to the hotel about hopes, and not getting them up for nothing. But it was useless. The fact was, he'd been lusting after Kate for so long that he couldn't ignore it anymore.

He wanted her so badly his scalp prickled.

Meeting her father didn't change things at all. The opposite, actually. That dose of father-daughter dysfunction had made him understand so much more about Kate. Her independent spirit, her fire, even her prickliness—it all made sense now that he'd seen her with "dear old Dad."

"Did you grow up mostly with your father?" he asked her as they sped toward the hotel in their third Lyft—taking the same precautions as before.

"Mostly, yeah. He and my mom split up when I was eight. I went back and forth between them until I was thirteen or so. Then she got together with a music producer who lives in Japan. I could have gone to live with them, but I didn't want to leave my friends and I've always been bad at learning other languages. Maybe I should just learn accents like my dad."

He slid his hand onto her thigh. "Just so you know, I have a thing for an Italian accent."

"Hmm...espresso!" She made an Italian-ish gesture with her fingers. "Pasta, linguini! Bellini! Minestrone!"

"Now you're just making me hungry." He tightened his hand on her thigh, the firm curve of her flesh filling his hand. "So you stayed in California with your father?"

"Until I could emancipate myself. Had to wait until I was seventeen. But every summer I'd go to Lost Harbor and help Emma with the peony harvest. In a lot of ways, she's the one who raised me. Things like morals and ethics and integrity and little things like that, they all came from her. Both my parents are a little sketchy in that realm."

He scanned her profile and the clean lines of her face, like an artist's quick and confident brushstrokes. "What's your mother's story?"

"My mom is a pleasure-seeking wanderlust type. Always falls for the shiny object. I always had to vet her boyfriends but she never listened. Her husband is decent, though. I don't worry about her anymore. She had some kind of fallout with Emma, so they're on the outs. I'm sure Emma must have been a difficult parent. But she's an awesome grandparent." She gave a sudden yawn. "Wow, seeing your sociopathic imprisoned father really takes it out of you." She stretched her neck from side to side. "I feel like I could sleep for a week."

His heart sank, and he gave himself another little mini-lecture. *She's had a nightmare couple of days. Take it easy, big guy. Just because this is our last night at the hotel. Just because we've been dancing around this thing the entire trip. Doesn't mean a damn thing unless she wants it to.*

Their Lyft pulled up outside their hotel. Kate took care of the payment while Darius stepped out and wrestled back his low-grade arousal. He could be patient. He *was* patient. He'd just have to make that patience last a while longer.

In the meantime, there was always the shower.

As soon as he'd made sure that Kate was safely in her suite, door locked, he disappeared into his own suite. He stripped off his clothes on his way to the bathroom and headed straight for the shower.

With the scalding water streaming over him, he touched himself briefly, but went no further. It wasn't enough, not anymore. He wanted Kate in the flesh, not just Kate in his imagination. He'd hold out for that. Maybe when they got back to Lost Harbor, he'd launch a full-on "get Kate into bed" campaign. Romantic dates across the bay, flirty emails, flowers, whatever it took.

Maybe not flowers, since she got enough of those at Petal to the Metal.

He'd figure something out. Maybe something involving his bass and his cowboy hat—possibly his bare chest as well. He knew she liked all of those things.

Chuckling, he stepped out of the shower and grabbed a towel. He was still drying his hair when he stepped into the bedroom and stopped in his tracks.

Kate posed on his bed in the kind of seductive posture that belonged in a lingerie ad. She lay on her side, with her head resting on her hand, propped up by her elbow. One knee was bent, the other leg stretched out, emphasizing the long slope of her hip.

She wasn't wearing her cream suit anymore, or at least not all of it. The skirt was gone, as was her blazer. The charcoal blouse was half unbuttoned, revealing a silky black bra and a creamy curve of cleavage. He couldn't see if she wore any underwear, since the blouse was covering just enough of her hips—such a tease. And her legs—my God, they went forever, a long, languorous line of firm smooth flesh.

He realized that he was dripping water on the carpet as he gawked at the vision on his bed.

Oh, and he was stark naked as well.

Which she didn't seem to mind, since she was doing the same thing he was. Staring like a sex-starved teenager.

"Hi," she said softly. He could hear the tentative question in her voice. *Is this okay? Do you want this?*

"Hi back."

Her face relaxed as she got his message: *Fuck yeah, I want this.*

"Mind if I check something?" He stepped next to the bed and put his left hand on her thigh, just above her bent knee. He spread his fingers across her warm skin, his thumb reaching almost to the edge of the blouse, and his little finger touching her kneecap. She shivered under his touch. "Just wanted to make sure you're real, and not a fantasy I brought with me from the shower."

A spark of humor lit up her dark eyes. "That's funny. I was thinking about you in the shower just yesterday."

"Is that right?" He smoothed his hand down her leg. Over the knee, circling lightly around her kneecap, then along the side of her calf. Her skin was pure satin. "What were you thinking?"

"It wasn't so much thinking as imagining." A wicked smile went along with that comment. "I have a very good imagination, but it turns out that reality is even better." With her free hand, she touched his naked thigh, close enough to his cock to make it stir. "I mean, Darius. Jesus."

He wasn't entirely sure what she was referring to, but it didn't much matter. As long as she had that look in her eyes, he'd take it. Desire spread through him in a slow fever.

"I was imagining some interesting things in the shower as well."

"Care to share?"

"Well, you were definitely in there with me. But you didn't have all these clothes on."

"All these clothes?" she laughed at him. "I'm practically naked."

He came to the end of the bed and put one knee on the mattress. She rolled onto her back so she could watch him, and bent one arm behind her head, supporting it. That position tugged her blouse higher up her body, so he could see her panties. Hip huggers in a sexy fire-engine red.

Of course she'd be wearing red. Just the bright cherry on the cake of this sensual scenario.

"*I'm* naked. You're still dressed. And you're in my bed. This is a naked bed, just so you know. Anyone who comes in here is required to be naked."

"Oh really? Who enforces those rules?" Teasingly, she rested her bare foot on his thigh. He wrapped his hand around her ankle and tugged her closer. The blouse rode up even higher, revealing the firm mound of her belly. All that tender skin under there. And more clothes. Damn, that bra needed to go.

"Security," he said gruffly. "It's a tough job, but I volunteered and I can handle it."

Her eyes widened as he took hold of one of her feet. Cradling it between his hands, he pressed his thumb into the instep, the spot where nerve endings gathered and carried messages to the rest of the body.

At least that was how the reflexologist he'd dated had explained it.

She gasped and arched her back as he massaged the sole of her foot. He watched her responses closely, enjoying the way her body moved with his strokes. Each time she twisted and moaned, her blouse revealed more of her bra and the lush curves under it.

He feasted his eyes on her as he worked her other foot. When he was done, he set her leg back on the bed and watched it fall open to the side. Damn, what a sexy sight that was.

Braceleting her ankles with both hands, he spread her legs even farther apart and kept her still, just like that, so he could look at her.

The flash of red panties over her plump mound made his cock jump. The sound of her panting breath made his throat close up, and the scent of her intimate flesh sent him over the edge.

"Undo the rest of your blouse," he told her in a rough voice. "I want to see you."

Her eyes flared as she caught the undercurrent of command in his voice. He could give her a lot more than that, if she wanted. But not yet. They were still figuring each other out.

"Kind of bossy," she grumbled as she slid a button through its hole.

"I'm a fire chief. Comes with the territory."

"Good to know." A sensual smile curved her lips. The blouse fell open even farther. Her bra had patches of lace through which he could see glimpses of flesh and a hint of dark nipples. "Right now I feel too good to complain about anything. That thing you did with my feet...Oh my God. Dreamy." Her fingers paused mid-button, so close to her nipples he could cry. "What's it called, what you were doing?"

"Hmm?" He was so riveted by the slow reveal of her bra that he'd lost track of what she was talking about. "Sorry, what?"

"What's the matter, big guy?" With a teasing smile, she skimmed her fingers across her bra cups. "Nothing more to say? No more bossy orders?"

He wrestled himself back under control. His cock was rock

hard now, rearing between his thighs. "You want orders?" He took hold of his aching cock with one hand. "Show me your tits. Let me see those nipples."

Was his language too rough for her? She was a fancy lawyer, after all. She probably didn't like words like "tits." Only one way to find out.

Her chest rose and fell and a flush came into her cheeks. Smoky desire hazed her eyes and she cupped her breasts. "You mean these tits?"

Oh yeah. The game was on.

"You're teasing me now?" He put a dangerous edge into his voice. "That's not very nice. Do you know how many times I've imagined your breasts?"

"Uh oh. What if they don't live up to your imagination?"

"Ain't possible. Get that bra off before I rip it off with my teeth."

Her lips parted and her breath sped up even faster. "Promises promises. I'm thinking you should come and get it." She trailed a finger along the soft curves above her bra.

Sounded like an invitation to him.

In a swift move, he pounced on top of her and stretched his body over hers, his hands planted on either side of her head. Maybe four inches separated them, and that space sizzled with heat.

She gave a squeal of surprise and laughed up at him. "That was fast."

"Let's hope that's the last time you say that." He lowered his head to her bra and took the upper edge of one cup between his teeth. Her hands fluttered to his shoulders. She traced the muscles she found there with a lingering touch.

He hoped she liked what she felt. Because everything about her pleased him on a primal level of "Woman—good. Want. Touch. Taste. Good."

Details swam through his senses. The warmth of her skin against his tongue. The scent rising from the dip between her breasts, that heady feminine dampness. The firm rise of flesh above the naughty peekaboo lace. The push of her nipples against the fabric.

With his teeth, he dragged the cloth down to expose her breast, inch by slow inch. He took his time so as not to miss a moment of the glorious show. One nipple revealed—a pop of Chianti red against her pale skin. He slid his tongue across her flesh and watched the skin around her nipple pucker in response.

She whimpered, and he felt her legs move beneath him with the same restless need that was driving him. He circled the aureola with his tongue, near enough to the nipple to feel it harden even more.

"Jesus, Darius. You're such a tease," she gasped.

"You asked for it." His hot breath surrounded her nipple, giving it another shot of arousal. "You could have just showed me your boobs like a good girl. Instead you had to be naughty."

Unable to wait another second, he took her nipple into his mouth and claimed it with a deep suckle.

She arched wildly and tightened her grip on his shoulders. "Holy fuck, Darius."

Now that was what he liked to hear. Unbridled yelling and cursing. With his mouth and tongue and even a touch of teeth, he ravaged her nipple until it felt like rock candy against his lips.

Then he shifted to the other nipple, because balance was important. She groaned as he lavished attention on that one as well. "Hang on," she gasped. "There's too much...wait a second... this damn thing..."

He had to admit, he loved seeing her at a loss for words. It hardly ever happened.

She struggled to reach behind her for her bra clasp.

"I got it," he told her. He rolled off of her, and she twisted her torso to give him easier access. Fuck if that wasn't just as hot as everything else about her. Strong, sleek muscles lining her spine, along with a little tattoo at the base of her neck.

He couldn't tell exactly what it was. Vaguely round, kind of ruffly, like a weird mushroom.

He unfastened her bra and traced the tattoo with his finger. "What's your tattoo?"

She gave a laughing groan. "You really can't tell?"

"Not at all. Hedgehog? Porcupine?"

"No! It's a peony. I let my friend practice on me when she was learning to do tattoos. I thought a flower would be easy, but apparently not." She twisted to look over her shoulder. "I tend to forget about it because I don't see it. Is it ridiculous?"

"No." He smoothed his thumb across it. The fact that she had a peony tattoo made him wonder if she was more attached to Lost Harbor than she let on. "It's sweet. Does Emma know you have a peony tattoo?"

"Nah. I don't want to get her hopes up. She's always thinking I'll move to Lost Harbor and take over the farm."

Aaaaand, let that be a lesson. Kate was not planning to stay in Lost Harbor.

"Then why'd you choose a peony?"

She sighed and shifted position so she could work the bra straps off her body. "Interesting timing, big guy. You're the man of few words and now you want to talk tattoos?"

She slipped off the bra and tossed it aside. He didn't answer, because his attention had now shifted back to the front of her body, and the part of him that responded primitively to the sight of bare breasts had taken full charge.

Like a red cape at a bull fight.

He reached for those beautiful soft mounds and filled his hands with them. "Sorry, did you say something?" He brushed his thumbs against the tips of her nipples. Her head fell back and her hair went tumbling against the headboard.

"You wanted to hear about my tattoo."

"Tattoo?" he said blankly. Those nipples. So proud and erect and deep, dark red. The tempting color of the first sip of a freshly poured glass of burgundy.

He flicked his thumbs against both nipples and felt them harden just a bit more. She tugged her bottom lip between her teeth with a moan. He felt her legs move and knew exactly what she needed.

Keeping his mouth busy with her nipples, he slid his hand down her belly, savoring the tautness of her muscles under her smooth skin. He lingered on the soft rise of flesh below her navel. And then came a nest of silky hair and damp flesh. Delicately, he searched the tender folds for the nugget lurking inside. That sweet, juicy, swollen nub of flesh that surged against his fingers when he found it.

Kate lifted her hips to meet his hand. Her urgent movement sent a bolt of heat to his cock. Then a hot hand surrounded him and held him lightly. *Kate's hand.* Fuck. Her hand was on his cock and he didn't know if he could handle that.

His erection swelled to bursting. He gritted his teeth and mentally reached for something that would take down his hard-on. Flat tires. Popping balloons. Burnt toast.

That worked enough so he could continue exploring the soft wetness between her legs. Her head was still tilted back, her eyes half-closed and hazy. As he scanned her features, watching every reaction to his fondling, their eyes met and an incredible sensation swept through him. It was a feeling he'd never experienced before, not in all the times he'd taken a woman to bed.

It was the sense of seeing someone perfectly. No illusions, no deceptions, no lies. And being seen in exactly the same way. No need to pretend or hide. Kate could handle him, every part of him.

And he intended to prove he could handle her. Anything she threw at him, from emails to fake names, he could handle.

Except maybe not the way she was lightly stroking his cock.

"Ah God, that feels good," he groaned. "Too fucking good."

"No such thing," she whispered. She circled the top of his penis with soft fingers. "You're shaking."

"Trying to hold back," he gritted through clenched teeth. "No condom."

"You came all the way to a fancy hotel in California without any condoms?"

"No, I have some. But not on my dick. Got a box in my bag."

"An entire box? So optimistic." Then she did something that very nearly made him lose his mind. She touched her own pussy, nudging his hand aside to gather moisture. Then she brought it back to his erection and wrapped her newly slick hand back where it had been—except it felt even better now with her juices sliding across his hot skin.

Back to the teeth clenching and flat tire imagining.

Except this time he pictured tires stuck in the mud and a sassy brunette behind the wheel. The breasts he'd wondered about *at the time* were now bare naked before him, and he had to lick those nipples again, had to lash them with the flat of his tongue. And what about her clit? It pulsed against his fingers, wanting pressure and hot stroking, and so he gave it to her because he'd give her anything she wanted, especially when his cock was in her hand and his balls were going tight and heavy, and she needed a finger inside her, or two, down to his knuckle, so the heel of his hand could grind against her hot little clit and *fuck* ...

No flat tire in the world could stop that explosion. He erupted with a growl like a wounded bear. At nearly the same time, she arched against his hand and let out a long, low cry that rose and fell with the waves of her orgasm. His brain nearly split in two from the effort to keep the pressure on her clit while his climax ripped through his body. *She* was what mattered, not him.

But damn, every second of that release felt so fucking good, and it was such a long time coming.

Or so it felt. Maybe it had only been a few weeks, but in lust-years, it felt like forever. Didn't matter how long, this woman had taken over his thoughts completely.

When they'd both completed the downhill slide of their orgasms, he gently drew his hand from her pulsing sex and lifted his body away from hers. Damn, he'd spilled all over her. Her belly was damp with his semen. "Let me take care of this," he said gruffly.

"Hey." She caught his shoulders to keep him where he was. He met her eyes, their dark brilliance drawing him in deep, so deep. "That was...really something."

He waited, thinking she was going to say more. She appeared to be fumbling for words. When she didn't continue, he pulled away again.

Again, she held him in place. "Wait. I'm trying to say something and it's not working."

His eyebrows lifted. "Kate Robinson at a loss for words? Mark it down."

She laughed, and that seemed to return some of her usual focus and fire. "I'm good at some kinds of talking and I suck at other kinds. Like this."

He wasn't sure what kind she was referring to—post-sex? Emotion? Cleaning his goop off her tummy? "No rush, sweetheart. I'm not going anywhere except to get a washcloth. I came all over you and I didn't intend for—"

She shook her head, smiling slightly. "I was going to shower anyway. I nearly got into yours with you, but you're so big I figured you'd hog all the water. Kind of like you do back home."

He laughed down at her. "I never had a problem until my new landlady showed up."

"Oh I know, she's such a nightmare." She rolled under his arm and stood up. She still wore her red panties, and they were just as much of a turn-on as ever. He rolled over onto his back and relaxed, arms spread wide, soaking in the afterglow. Now that he didn't have to get up, he was happy to stretch out like a lump on a log.

She lifted one naughty eyebrow at him. "I'll be right back, big guy. Don't go anywhere."

"Couldn't if I wanted to," he murmured.

Halfway across the room, she spun back around and faced him. "The thing I wanted to say was, you're very different from the men I've known. And I—I appreciate you coming here with me." Her expression of discomfort was adorable. She obviously didn't like talking about things like this. Honestly, it was endearing to see this vulnerable side of her. He had a feeling that not many people got to see it.

"You're welcome," he said simply.

She gave him a bright smile, the kind he was more used to from her. "Also, what we did just now was even better than what I've been picturing in my head."

He smiled a lazy grin. "I'd like to know more about what goes on in that head of yours. I bet there's some naughty stuff in there."

Her eyes flashed wickedly as she turned toward the adjoining door. Her ass twitched back and forth in those little red panties and he groaned loudly.

"You're killing me, Kate in the red panties."

With one last provocative hip check, she disappeared through the door to her suite.

CHAPTER NINETEEN

Kate's heart was still hammering when she stepped into her shower. She and Darius hadn't even had sex and still that experience ranked in the top five sexual experiences of her entire life.

And the other four involved her vibrator.

Why was fooling around with Darius so different from the other times she'd had sex? She'd always enjoyed sex. It was a great release. That was why she appreciated her vibrator. All the release but none of the drama. You didn't have to talk to someone afterwards, or worry about their feelings for you—or lack of feelings. It didn't lead to hurt for herself or a partner.

Obviously a vibrator didn't offer the full sensory experience of sex with a man, which was why she still made room in her life for dating and even the occasional friends-with-benefits situation. She'd always gone for short-term relationships because her life didn't have room for anything else.

At least that was what she'd always told herself.

But maybe the fact was that no one had really intrigued her enough to try. And no one had taken the time to get past all her layers of wariness and mistrust.

Until a big, gruff, stubborn bastard of a fire chief had come along. Slowly but surely, she'd come to trust him.

Also, he could do things with his hands that she hadn't known a man could do. How were his hands so big and yet so sensitive? He knew exactly how to touch her, and how hard, and how long.

She lost herself in the blissful recollection of the last half hour or so of her life. By the time her shower ended, her system was back to the low hum of arousal that she'd been experiencing ever since...well, probably ever since that first glimpse of his hard stomach when he'd wiped sweat off his face after his jog.

Or no—when she'd seen him onstage at the Moose is Loose.

Or even when he'd stopped to help her. It was very possible that his good deed combined with his powerful physique and kind silver-gray eyes had delivered the first blow to her defenses.

The question was, what did he want now that he was behind the castle door?

What did *she* want?

She shook the question away as she dried her hair with a bath towel. None of that mattered yet. They had one more night in this hotel—really just a matter of hours at this point—and the only thing she really wanted was to make the most of it.

She barely heard the knock on the front door of her suite, but she did hear Darius' deep voice ring out with a firm, "Be right there."

It could be someone from the law firm, or maybe from the hotel itself. She was hurrying to finish drying off when she heard Darius call, "Stay where you are until I say the word, Kate!"

Holy hell. In a flash, the terror from those last few weeks in LA came rushing back. She hadn't been careful enough—she'd gone to see her father—she'd eaten dinner at a restaurant—she'd gotten lax. Her worst fear had come true—one of Kramer's goons had found her. Maybe his lawyers had tipped them off. Now they were threatening Darius and he was trying to protect her, probably risking his own life in the process.

Her heart jumped into her throat and adrenaline flooded through her. She couldn't let Darius get hurt. Not on her account. She had to help him. *Phone. Call for help.* No, she'd left her phone in the room.

Bear spray. She had the canister Emma had given her. It was in her rolling suitcase, which she'd dragged into the bathroom with her rather than sorting through it for clothes. Yes! She pounced on it and rummaged through to the bottom, where she'd stashed the can. She'd declared it at the airport, and hadn't pulled it out since. It was really just a crutch at this point.

Her hands were shaking so much it was hard to get a grip on it. She checked the button to make sure she was orienting it in the right direction. More fears multiplied like bunnies.

What if she missed and sprayed Darius instead? What if she blinded someone? She didn't want to hurt anyone. She just wanted them to leave her alone!

I don't even have to use it, she decided. *This is about bluffing. And I learned bluffing from the master.*

She straightened her shoulders, getting into character—badass with a weapon. At which point she realized that she wearing a fluffy white bath towel and nothing else. No time to change now. She cinched the knot tighter. She'd just have to hope it stayed on.

Gathering all her nerve, she swung the bathroom door open. As she leaped into the room, the towel snagged on the doorknob and fell off her body.

What the hell, they'd just have to get an eyeful. Maybe it would be an effective distraction, who knew?

Without missing a beat, she kept going and aimed the canister at the door of the suite. "Don't move or I'll shoot!" she shouted at the top of her lungs.

Darius swung around to face her, his hands up in the air as if she was talking to him. His mouth fell open as he caught sight of her. He shook his head and mouthed something, but she was already glaring at the intruder behind him.

Intruders...plural.

A small group of people crowded in the doorway. One of them held a cake. Another had balloons. There was a bottle of champagne in there somewhere. And a lot of shocked faces that belonged to members of her old law firm. Danisse from accounting. Chad, the frat boy intern. Jamieson, her immediate supervisor.

Darius, bless him, took only a split second to step between her and her former colleagues. Never before had she been quite so happy about how damn big he was.

Bluff. She still needed to bluff her way out of this, even though it wasn't quite the situation she'd thought she was facing.

"Hi everyone. Great to see you all. Ooh, is that cake?" she said cheerfully as she dropped the can of spray to her side and peered past Darius. "Aw, you guys shouldn't have. This is just so sweet! The last thing I expected. Literally."

Darius stepped toward her, filling her field of vision and shielding her from sight. "Why don't you let me take this," he murmured as he touched the hand holding the bear spray. "You're making people nervous. Me, in particular."

She let him claim the can. "I wasn't going to use it unless I had to," she whispered. "I'm not that reckless."

"No, I'd say you're the perfect amount of reckless." The amusement in his voice brought a smile to her own lips. He shepherded her toward the bathroom, still blocking everyone's view of her backside. "You thought I was in danger."

"Obviously."

"I'm deeply moved that you would try to save my life buck naked."

They reached the bathroom, which felt like a heavenly haven of safety.

As soon as she stepped inside, the aftermath of all that adrenaline hit her. She started to shake.

"My coworkers just saw me naked," she moaned. "I swear I've had nightmares *exactly like that.* Except usually there was a judge and a courtroom involved."

"Shhh." He wrapped his arms around her, the scent of his wool sweater blanketing her in comfort. It also reminded her that he'd had the good sense to throw on some clothes before confronting the world. "You have to remember something very important."

"What?" she moaned, resting her forehead on his broad chest.

"You don't work with them anymore."

She tilted her head to gaze up at him. The silvery amusement shining in his eyes brought a bubble of laughter to her own lips. "That's true. I work with Emma now and she's seen me naked. When I was a baby."

"My hockey team has seen me naked," he added helpfully.

"Yes, but they were naked too." Somehow it made a difference.

"Sweetheart?" He cupped his hand under her chin and caressed her face. "Everyone has seen naked people before. They'll get over it. Want to know what I won't get over?"

"What?"

"You and your hair all wet down your back and that fierce look on your face like you were ready to mow down anyone who got in your way."

"I thought they were going to hurt you."

He dipped his head and touched his lips to hers, a firm press of warm flesh that sent a sigh through her. Gently, he parted her lips to go deeper. She swayed against him, feeling desire stir again.

"Thank you," he murmured. "I know who to hire if I ever need a bodyguard."

She smiled against his lips. It was amazing how everything felt fine now. It didn't even bother her anymore that she'd flashed her old coworkers.

Darius reluctantly pulled away. "Now where do you safely stash that damn thing? And where are your clothes? Do you want me to tell them to leave?"

"Only if they leave the cake and champagne behind," she said cheekily as she kneeled down to search through her suitcase. "I think I've earned it."

She rummaged for an outfit to put on—the less revealing, the better. She'd put on enough of a show for one night.

"How did they even know I was here?" she wondered aloud. "Only the key players were supposed to know."

"I was asking them the same thing. Apparently Danisse is dating someone from billing at Cotton and Bryant. They were having lunch in his office and she caught sight of a hotel invoice and put it together. She feels terrible now, but she swears that no one else knows. To be safe, we should find somewhere else to stay tonight."

"Damn it." She pulled on some yoga pants and an extra-large, extra-baggy hoodie. "I was really looking forward to more time in that bed with you." With a wistful smile, she tugged her wet hair into a ponytail and straightened her shoulders. "Well, off to face the mockery."

He touched a hand to her shoulder, forcing her to pause on her way out the door. "You've got a brave heart, Kate. I won't forget how you jumped out like that."

That gentle compliment warmed her from the inside out.

When Darius spoke, she believed him. And she couldn't say that about very many people in this world.

BY THE TIME Kate's law firm crew left around one in the morning—after sharing so much gossip his head spun—they only had a few hours left before their flight. So they headed straight for the airport. Darius didn't relax until they were safely through security and waiting in the nearest first-class lounge for their flight.

Kate snoozed with her head on his shoulder, while he eyed everyone who walked through the door of the lounge. Years of overnight shifts had gotten him used to nights without sleep. He certainly wouldn't be able to close his eyes until he knew for sure that Kate was safe.

Maya was right. Kate had a knack for getting into trouble. At the same time, she possessed a fearlessness he respected.

He sorted through all the things he'd learned about her on this short trip. She'd emancipated herself from her lawless father at the age of seventeen. She'd taken charge of her own education and put herself through law school. Then she'd sacrificed her career in order to protect her father. She'd put herself at risk by agreeing to testify against the people still out to get her. And then she'd jumped out naked with a can of bear spray when she'd thought he was in danger.

She was really something else.

And he'd do whatever it took to get her back to Lost Harbor safely.

He'd also do whatever it took to get her into another bed. Say, in his apartment. Or hers. Or both. One after the other. Both in the same night. Whatever worked.

But when they got back to Lost Harbor, would things go back

to how they were before? Would it be as if this trip had never happened? Arguments over hot water and occasional hellos in the driveway?

And what did he really want from Catriona Robinson? His body was all-in. But his experience said "keep it simple."

His heart...

Lucky for him, that wasn't a factor. Not any more.

CHAPTER TWENTY

They didn't get back to Lost Harbor until midday, and Darius had to go straight to the firehouse when they landed. Kate gave him a yawn and a brief acquaintance-type hug before hopping into her car and dropping him off at the station. They'd both slept on the plane and neither was in the right state of mind to discuss anything beyond peanuts or pretzels.

Or maybe it had all been a crazy dream, the kind you could barely believe the next day.

The firehouse was nearly deserted when he got back. He'd gotten word that Nate and a crew were responding to a grease fire at the Nightly Catch. The quiet unnerved him after all the noise of the big city. Sunbeams floated through the stained glass lunette of a fire truck on the front door, and the distant whir of a power tool told him someone was working in the apparatus bay.

He sat behind his desk and stared blankly at his computer. It didn't seem quite real; none of this did. He should boot up and work through the backlog of emails that he'd ignored during the trip. But instead, images of Kate kept floating through his mind.

Kate stretched out naked in bed in that silk blouse and red

panties. Kate coming apart under his touch. Kate jumping out from the bathroom naked and brandishing bear spray.

He nearly jumped out of his own skin when Maya knocked on the doorjamb and poked her head into his office.

"Jesus, Maya. A little warning next time."

Frowning, she came into his office and plopped a folding chair next to his desk. "You seem a little jumpy, Chief. Why would I have to warn you before I knock on your office?"

Of course she didn't have to do that. He had an open-door policy—mostly because he didn't even have a door. It had come off its hinges during the previous chief's administration and never been replaced. On his first day as fire chief, as a joke, the volunteers had installed a beaded curtain instead of a door.

That had lasted about half a day, until he'd nearly gotten blinded by a bead to the eye.

"Sorry, I didn't get any sleep last night. The only reason I'm here is that Nate's out on a call. What's up?"

"How was your trip to LA?" she asked neutrally.

"Are you asking as a professional colleague or as Kate's friend?"

"Little of both. Mostly as Kate's friend. I know something's going on that she doesn't want me to know about."

"So you're doing an end run around her and asking me?" he said dryly. "Sorry, you know me better than that. Her business is her business."

"Unless it's the town's business." She fixed him with a strict stare. "If there's anything I should know for public safety purposes, you need to tell me."

He hesitated. He supposed it was possible that the Kramer minions could have tracked Kate to Lost Harbor. Ethan James had done it, after all.

"I agree, Chief. If anything like that comes up, I'll tell you."

He held her gaze in one of those stare-downs that neither of them ever won. He had patience on his side and Maya had badassery, and it worked out about even.

"Is that why you hauled your busy self all the way over to this side of the building? Is something up with our bond proposal?"

"No, it's something else."

"S.G.?"

"Nothing new there. I still have some inquiries out. But she seems fine where she is, so I'm not in a big rush to distract myself from town business."

"Good." He nodded and sat back, feeling exhaustion drag behind his eyes. "It might be more disruptive for her than anything else."

"That's what I'm thinking too. No, it's the fires we've been experiencing the last few weeks. A lot more than normal, right?"

That woke him up fast. "Yes. More frequent, but not damaging—so far. You got any theories?"

"It's not a theory, just something odd that I noticed. I've been keeping a spreadsheet of them. Logging each fire, location, damage, date, and so forth. I turned that data into a graph. Want to see?"

"Sure." He leaned his elbows on the desk and she whipped her iPad from under her arm. A colorful bar graph marched across the screen. He blinked at it; his eyes felt like sandpaper. "There's a gap there."

"Yup. A pretty noticeable gap."

"What does it correspond to? Long night, no sleep, no data comprehension."

"This gap represents the last few days. There was another fire this morning, that's this." She pointed to an orange bar labeled Nightly Catch. "The fire before that was here. The Dunfords' bear cache. On May sixth."

May sixth. That was the day before he and Kate had flown to

Los Angeles. He stared at the graph, double-checking the dates of each fire she'd logged.

"There were no fires while I was gone. I know, Nate told me. Two medical calls, a creek rescue, but no fires."

"Right. Not a single fire while you were gone."

"We've gone days without fires before this."

"Yes, but not so many days. If you include every fire and every nuisance call, the way I did here, the longest gap before this was only a day and a half."

His gaze flew to meet her steady brown eyes. "What are you saying? I didn't set those fucking fires."

Her expression didn't shift. "Didn't say that you did."

His brain clicked over to the next possibility.

"Are you saying Kate did? That's absurd, she wasn't even here when the first few broke out. Look, you've been tracking them since January, and—"

"Of course Kate didn't set any fires," she said irritably. "But the fact is that we don't know when the first *suspicious* fire broke out. This graph includes all the fires since the start of the year. I wanted a baseline to start with. The fires don't exactly match the time that Kate's been here, but they did tick way up over the past few weeks."

He dragged a hand through his hair. This, he didn't need right now. He needed a nap or a drink or a motorcycle ride. Not together, obviously.

He forced himself to focus on the data Maya was showing him. "You're saying the fires might be connected to Kate being here?"

"They did stop when she left."

"They also stopped when I left."

"True that. Something you want to tell me, Chief?"

"Yes, fighting fire in a town the size of a paper towel is boring, so I wanted to spice things up a bit," he snapped. "No, there's nothing to tell you. I have no idea what's going on here."

Except that maybe he did. Maybe it had something to do with Kate's enemies. But what? Why would anyone travel all the way to Lost Harbor and set random fires that didn't even do much damage? None of them were even related to her.

It didn't add up at all.

But it was worth mentioning to Kate. And worth urging her to tell Maya everything before the police chief made a bar graph out of her.

"I'll talk to her and see if she can think of anything that might help," he said finally.

"Good. Because an arson spree is a crime. So that's my territory."

He glared at her. "You want a turf war over a bunch of nuisance fires?"

"No. I'm just saying that *I* can talk to Kate in case you don't want to intermingle your professional and personal relationships." She lifted one eyebrow at him.

"Don't worry about our personal relationship."

A smile twitched at the corner of her mouth. "So you're saying you have one."

"I'm not saying shit other than I'll talk to Kate as part of my investigation."

She snorted and retrieved her iPad, then stood up. "I find out everything sooner or later anyway. But good luck fooling yourself."

"Thanks for putting that graph together," he called after her as she headed for the open doorway "Can you email it to me?"

"Sure thing, Chief."

"Thanks, Chief."

Darius rummaged for an aspirin bottle that he kept on hand for post-hockey aches and pains. Definitely called for right now.

After downing a couple with a swig from the least sketchy mug on his desk, he hauled himself to his feet. Time for a quick inventory of the firehouse, before Nate and the crew returned.

Quite a few strange things had occurred in this firehouse. Last year, one of the volunteer firefighters had gone off the deep end and tampered with Padric Jeffers' boat. He'd nearly killed Lost Harbor's biggest celebrity.

Then there was S.G. and her adventures. Not only had she hidden here for weeks, but the trapper had hunted her down and nearly kidnapped her in the apparatus bay.

Oh yes, the Lost Harbor Fire Department had no shortage of weirdness. If there was something extra strange behind these fires, it wouldn't surprise him.

CHAPTER TWENTY-ONE

After several hours of sleep to recover from the trip, Kate drove out to the farm to check on Emma and the peonies. Truth was, she'd missed both.

"Well," Emma said as soon as she caught sight of her. She was on her knees, weeding the *Festiva Maxima*. Little shoots of pushki were already poking through the Typar. "You look like you've been rode hard and put away wet."

"That's a horrible saying and I think you should remove it from your vocabulary."

"Eh, let an old lady say what she wants. Help me up." Kate held out a hand to help her to her feet. Emma rubbed her lower back as she straightened. "I'm glad you're back. Those kids have been driving me bonkers."

"Kids?"

"S.G. and her friend. Dylan, I think his name is. Always in that hoodie."

Right, the kid from the hockey rink. So much had happened since then, she'd forgotten that she'd given S.G. permission to bring her friend to the farm. He was living at Denaina's now;

she'd signed his paperwork. "I told S.G. it was okay. Is it not working out?"

"Oh, I guess it's fine. It's good to have the help. He's a hard enough worker, but he and S.G. go off together and talk about lord knows what. He's got a phone and you can't tear him away from that device."

"They're probably looking at TikToks or something. I'll talk to them. If we're paying them, they need to put their phones away and focus."

"Good, good. You tell 'em. Threaten to sue them if they misbehave."

She laughed and dropped a kiss on her grandmother's cheek. "I'm not going to sue them, sorry. My lawyer days are over, I keep telling you."

"Pffft." Emma let out a snort. "Where's Darius? I want to thank him for keeping you safe."

"Darius is here?" S.G. spoke from just behind her. Kate turned to see S.G. and her hoodie-wearing friend. Both wore mud boots and work gloves. She smiled at them, noting that the boy didn't return her smile. He was a good-looking kid, with a thatch of brown hair falling over his eyes and a tall frame he was still growing into.

"No, he's either at the firehouse or asleep. Are you looking for him? I can give him a message."

"No, it's okay." S.G. shook her head. "This is Dylan. He's my friend."

"Dylan. Good to hear you have a name." The boy didn't laugh at her joke, and S.G. glared at her. She made a mental note to be more sensitive with S.G. and her first crush. "Welcome to Petal to the Metal, Dylan. How's it working out so far?"

"Pretty good." His voice cracked when he spoke, landing in that uncomfortable realm between childhood and adulthood.

"Where are you from? S.G. says you're new at school."

"Fairbanks," he answered, his gaze sliding away from hers. Interesting. Kate got the distinct impression that he wasn't telling the truth. Oh well. It was none of her business.

"Is Darius your boyfriend now?" S.G. asked in her cut-to-the-chase way.

"Who told you that?" Kate wiped suddenly sweaty hands on her pants. Had word already spread around Lost Harbor about them—before there was even a real "them"?

"Nobody. But he's a really good person, isn't he?"

"Sure. He puts out fires and he's an excellent tenant. Why do you ask?"

S.G. shrugged.

Kate shot a quick glance at Dylan, who was staring down at the ground, probably ignoring the conversation. She couldn't figure him out; he seemed withdrawn and a little sad. But with her troubled teen years, she always gave teenagers the benefit of the doubt. It was such a bewildering time of life. Thank God she'd had Emma back then.

Turning to her grandmother, she asked, "So what are we working on today, Emma? What gloriously muddy task have you assigned to us? Weeding? Botrytis patrol? Maybe something relaxing like the website? It could use some updating."

"We gotta fix the old tool shed. It's turning into a toxic waste site. Next Wednesday is the day to bring all our old chemicals to the dump. Heavy metals day, they call it."

"Sounds like it's right up your alley. Petals to the Heavy Metal." She winked at the two kids. "Get it?"

Finally she got a reaction out of Dylan. A smile. An actual smile that traveled across his wary face and reached his eyes, like a light turned on in a basement room. He looked like a completely different kid when he smiled. A blue-eyed, happy kid.

It was such a dumb joke, too. She had to like someone who didn't mind a lame joke, no matter their age.

"Any dangerous chemicals in that shed?" she asked her grandmother. "We don't want to expose the kids to anything like that."

"No no, it's just fertilizer and paint. Copper to fight the slugs. Some pesticides. Come on, kids, I'll show you. Kate, bring the old Ford around and we'll load everything in there. It's the only truck with a canopy that doesn't leak."

She hustled the kids onto a path that led to the back of the property, while Kate headed for the motley assortment of vehicles parked willy-nilly along the front driveway. One of Emma's many abilities was fixing cars, although she refused to work on any rigs besides her own. She knew her own vehicles inside and out, but other people's confounded her.

Just one of the many things that made her adore her infuriating but fascinating grandmother.

The key was already in the ignition of the Ford, and it started up with only a bit of pumping of the gas pedal.

She drove down the gravel drive that led to the bottom of the property, where the two kids were already carrying cans of old paint out of an ancient shed. Thick moss covered its roof; a baby spruce tree had taken root there.

"Is this thing even salvageable?" she asked as she pulled on the work gloves S.G. handed her.

"Oh yes. I'm gonna teach these kids some basic carpentry while we fix it up."

"Fix it up for what?"

"Honeymoon suite." Emma plopped two crusted old cans into the bed of the Ford, while Kate goggled at her.

"Those are two words I never imagined I'd hear you say. *Honeymoon suite*?" Kate followed her grandmother inside the dank shed. It smelled of mold and manure. Not exactly romantic honeymoon material.

"Never say never, kiddo." Emma lifted her eyebrows at her

and pointed at a jumble of broken tools in the back of the shed. "All those need to go."

"Whose honeymoon? Is there something you're not telling us? Are you seeing someone, Emma?" She picked up an ancient rake with rusted tines and a broken handle. "I've seen some very attractive silver foxes around town, behind those long-ass beards."

"I'm never getting married again, but some of us are still young." Emma's knowing glance made Kate stop in her tracks.

"Okay, let's just clear this up once and for all. Even if Darius and I get something going, neither of us is looking at marriage. You know me, I'm as cynical as they come."

Emma snorted, as if none of those words meant anything to her. "You go ahead and try to fool yourself, if you want. You can't fool me. I'm a thousand years old."

"You're only eight-two, and you're in for a shit-ton of disappointment if you think Darius and I are headed for a honeymoon. I just don't want you crying in your oatmeal over us."

"You worry about yourself, not me." Emma scolded her. "And those revolting Pop-Tarts you call breakfast."

"I call them a pre-breakfast snack, and I could say the same to you." Still arguing, they carried armfuls of tools to the Ford, passing the two kids on their way. "Worry about your own honeymoon, not my hypothetical, never-gonna-happen one. Besides, Darius has already been married twice and he has nothing good to say about it. At all."

A clattering sound made her jump; Dylan had dropped one of the paint cans he was carrying. He looked stricken, almost pale.

"Don't worry, they like to bicker," S.G. reassured the boy. "It's okay." She bent to pick up the paint can for him.

Kate silently scolded herself. Why did her mouth always run away with her? She should set a better example for the next generation. "Just so you kids know, even though we do *occasion-*

ally argue, I would do anything in the world for this woman. And she would do the same for me."

"Except go on a honeymoon," Emma grumbled.

"True." Kate grinned and hugged her grandmother with her free arm. "I have my limits."

CHAPTER TWENTY-TWO

When Kate got back home, she found a note from Darius on her door.

We have to talk.

Worst phrase in the English language. All it did was inspire dread. Instantly in a bad mood, she crumpled the note and tossed it away. The time she'd spent with Darius in LA had sparked a fire in her—and left her wanting so much more. Was he about to put a stop to it before they went any further?

What else had she expected? She was the cynical one, after all. She was Team Sex, the one who didn't believe in relationships that went anywhere. She'd just lectured her grandmother about that very thing.

And yet...damn.

She reached the living room and glared at the Kama Sutra rug. "Don't tease me, you."

"Talking to the furniture again?" Darius' deep voice resonated across her skin, along her nerve endings.

She spun around and as soon as she met his silvery eyes, all her worries drained away. That was not the face of a man who wanted to slow things down. It was the face of a man who wanted to take her right then and there, up against a wall, on a rug, wherever, whenever.

"Hi." Already a little breathless. Great.

"You left the door open. You really shouldn't do that." He advanced toward her, a frown gathering on his forehead.

"So true. Any old riff-raff could just walk right in." She stood her ground as he reached her. Her pulse was already racing.

"Did you get my note? I have to talk to you." His expression said the opposite, that talking was the very last thing he wanted to do.

And there went her nipples. Already perking. Jeez. She had zero self-control around this man.

He stopped about six inches from her. She closed the gap so the front of her body brushed against his. A hot shudder of lust gripped her, so intense she clenched her fists to hold it back.

His eyes darkened to a deep charcoal. "You're making it hard."

"Hmm, you don't say."

She moved her hips from side to side in search of the bulge she could already imagine.

"That's not what I mean." He gave a soft groan. "And now you're making it even harder. Still not what I mean."

"And yet..." There it was, the swell of his erection against her lower belly. She traced its outline with eager fingers. So hard and large. Pure masculine heat.

He gripped her forearm and thrust her hand away. "Do me a favor. Clasp your hands behind your back so I can put two thoughts together."

Ahhh, so she was getting to him.

"Okay," she murmured, doing exactly as he'd requested. But maybe he hadn't thought it through, because with her hands interlaced behind her, her breasts thrust forward. She still wore the t-shirt she'd been working in at the farm. Not only did it have a deep V-neck, but she'd gotten mud on it, then splashed water on herself to clean it off. Basically she was a muddy mess, but that t-shirt clung to her boobs like nobody's business.

His expression shifted and his eyes dropped to her chest. *Okay then.* This was working.

"Fuck it. It can wait," he growled.

He crowded close to her and cupped a hand around the back of her neck. He used it to hold her still while he ravaged her mouth with deep, turbulent kisses. All she could do was brace her legs apart, as if she were riding swells in Misty Bay.

His scruff brushed against the skin of her cheek, adding another layer of stimulation. And then there was his scent, that deep, manly smell of wood and wool and soap. It sent her to a place of wild fantasies—naked skin in firelight, light and shadow playing over rippling muscles, silver eyes consuming her body. The way his strength surrounded her made everything else turn into vapor and disappear.

Next thing she knew, he was pulling away and claiming one of her hands to tug her toward the bedroom.

"I'd fuck you right there on that rug, but I don't know where that thing's been," he said roughly. God, she loved it when he got down and dirty like that.

"Bed works. I like beds." She sounded like Jane communicating with Tarzan. And that's how she felt, too. Primitive and carnal.

They practically ran into the bedroom. She hadn't set up the old ironwork bedframe yet. It leaned against the wall, waiting for her to get around to it. In the meantime, she'd been sleeping on the box spring and mattress.

None of that seemed to bother Darius. Breathing fast, he stopped next to the bed and ripped his shirt off. Two layers of shirts disappeared in one swift motion. He stood before her in all his muscled glory. The sight brought back so many memories from their night in the hotel that she literally licked her lips.

"Hello again," she murmured as she caressed the hard curves of his chest. A soft mat of hair darkened the area between his pectorals. She found his nipples poking between the curls, and felt them tighten as she brushed her fingers over them.

This time he didn't wait for her to take off her own shirt. He did the job himself. Underneath, she wore a sports bra that had also somehow gotten mud on it. "Do you know that every time I see mud I think of the first time we met?" His rumbling laughter added to the sensation created by his big hands as he worked her bra off her body.

When it was gone, he filled his hands with her bare breasts. "You have a little bit here too." He flicked a speck of mud from one nipple, causing a jolt just short of orgasmic.

"I should clean off..."

"I like you just the way you are. Nothing wrong with a little mud and dirt. You're hot no matter what, babe." He slid his hand over her ass, under her work trousers, under her panties. Jerked her against him. A gasp wrenched from her as their bodies joined. Her bare breasts against his naked chest...so good. So good.

He worked her against him with those strong hands of his—one on her ass, one still flicking her nipple—until she thought she might come from dry humping alone. It could happen so easily, just a little more pressure right there—but she didn't want that. She wanted all of him this time. She wanted every inch of his penis inside her.

She pulled away, their damp skin creating a popping sound as they separated. Her hands went to the waistband of his jeans and she slid the top button out of its hole. Down came the zipper, revealing the wide elastic of a pair of gray briefs.

And a thick mound of swollen flesh underneath.

To the sound of his hoarse breaths, she freed his cock from his briefs and hefted it in her hand. Reacquainted herself with its specific length and weight and texture. The dimensions of Darius. He had lots of dimensions, inner and outer, but right now she was most preoccupied with this one. His raging erection.

She sank to the mattress and put her lips to his tip. The heat of the skin there surprised her. Darius burned hot, with that big frame of his and those muscles carved out of living rock.

She opened her mouth and slid her tongue across the knobby head. Found smoothness and hard ridges, and soft veins that throbbed beneath her tongue. She lost herself in his flavor and texture, the tremor of his muscles, the sound of his ragged breathing. His thighs clenched the longer she tasted him, and she knew he must be barely hanging onto his control. That awareness added an extra layer of spice to the excitement of his cock in her mouth.

"Stop," he finally groaned. "For the love of God. Can't take any more."

Taking her time, she slid her mouth away from him. A spear of glistening flesh appeared before her. A thing of pure masculine beauty.

He lifted her up off the mattress and spun her around so her back leaned against his front. He plunged his hand between her legs and clamped it against her wet sex. She cried out—already turned on, that one touch nearly sent her over the edge. He spanned her breasts with one of his big hands as he stroked her with the other.

A second ago, he'd been at her mercy; now she was completely at his. She writhed against him as want and need coursed through her. The only thing that mattered was the electric contact of his flesh against hers.

"On the bed," he growled. Together, somehow, they collapsed onto the mattress. He tugged her pants off and pushed his own jeans down his powerful thighs. When he'd gotten rid of his pants, he turned his attention back to her. With a firm hand on each of her inner thighs, he spread her open.

And put his head between them and licked her, up and down. The pleasure felt like an electric shriek. Her back arched all on its own and she dug her fingers into his thick hair. His sensual lips parted her softness, kissed her most intimate self, explored, tasted, savored. Lashed her with one overwhelming sensation after another. The way he drove his tongue against her—no mercy, no hesitation—sent her onto a wild plane of pure sensation. She had no control there, all she could do was hang on and let Darius' magic mouth do whatever he wanted to her.

And then he was gone...and he was reaching for the pocket of his jeans. He slid a condom on that jutting cock and her heart was pounding and she couldn't wait...couldn't stand to live another second without feeling him inside her.

He moved on top of her and slid his belly against hers. "You good?" he murmured.

She nodded, almost frantic. "Do it. I'm good. We're good."

A slight smile flashed through the scruff already darkening his jawline. This man was one hundred percent testosterone, damn it.

Except he was so much more than that. He was gentle power, aching restraint, exquisite control as he eased his swollen erection inside her. She was so wet from all his suckling that he entered easily at first. The deeper he went, the more her channel contracted around him. Flutters of pleasure accompanied his slide, little promises of the ecstasy to come.

Her eyes drifted shut as he seated himself fully inside her. A sense of satisfaction came over her. Even if they did nothing else, they were joined together as intimately as two people could be. She felt the beauty of that down to her soul.

He slid his hand between them, to her clit. His big thumb

found a spot that sent searing pleasure to every one of her nerve endings. She cried out and trembled under his rubbing.

"I can't...Darius...I'm going to come...I can't..."

"Do it," he commanded. "Don't fucking hold back for anything. Just come."

She didn't know what he was doing anymore—she couldn't keep track. All she knew was that everywhere she needed it, there was pressure and friction and heat and wetness. There was a man growling in her ear, there was hot skin sliding against her, there was a huge cock moving inside her, filling her up—and that hand sending her higher and higher, up and up until she exploded into a sky full of fireworks.

He stayed with her, not letting up as the spasms ripped through her. Only when she'd started to float down from that other planet did he pump himself into her with wild, almost desperate thrusts. With her knees wrapped around him, her body arched, she welcomed every feverish bit of him.

CHAPTER TWENTY-THREE

Darius surfaced from a fog of afterglow to remember that he actually had a reason to be here that didn't involve sex.

With the two of them sprawled in a naked tangle on Kate's queen-size mattress, he settled his hand on her ass. Her curves settled so sweetly into his palm. She lay face down, her eyes half-closed, lips parted.

"You awake?" he said softly.

"Mmmm." If a sound could express pure satisfaction, that would be it. "Barely. Get it? Barely?" She gestured toward her naked form.

Trust Kate to crank out the bad jokes even on the verge of sleep.

"I didn't actually come over here to tumble you into bed."

"I know. I had to work hard for this. I think you owe me a thank you." One eyelid dropped closed in a sleepy wink.

"Thank you," he said without a second of hesitation. "Seriously."

She gave a soft chuckle. "Any time, big guy." She rolled onto her back and stretched her arms over her head. He visually traced the line of her body, from pointed toes to linked hands. She was a long, tall drink of something strong, Kate was. Something that went right to his head.

Then she sat up and wrapped her arms around her knees. All serious business.

"Hey, you're hiding all the naughty bits," he complained.

"We can't be naughty all night," she said reasonably. "There's something you want to talk about. Go ahead, I'm ready now. My brain cells have reassembled in their proper order."

He loved the idea that he'd helped scramble them in the first place. "Maya came to see me with some data analysis she did about the fires we've been having."

"Fires?"

"Backing up. Lost Harbor has been experiencing an abnormally high rate of nuisance fires. No one hurt, no real damage. But they're a problem because they could spread if we don't get to them in time and they're taking up fire department resources. After the first few, we began to wonder if they were deliberately set."

"You mean arson?"

"I mean arson."

She frowned in thought. "Isn't it pretty easy to tell if a fire is due to arson? I remember a case my law firm was involved with."

"It usually is, but so far there's been nothing especially obvious. The fires aren't big enough to be destructive, indicating that the firebug isn't using accelerant."

"If there's a firebug."

"Right. Anyway, our dedicated police chief, Maya, made a chart of all the fires that lays out the timing and she noticed something very strange and interesting."

"Well, they do say strange things happen around Lost Souls Wilderness," she quipped.

"Yes, they do. And it's a hundred percent true. But I'm not

willing to shrug off an arson spree. That would be a dereliction of my duty as fire chief."

She gave a delicious shiver. "I love when you use legal terms. So hot."

He laughed. "I'll have to remember that. Writ of habeas corpus. Appellate brief."

"Okay stop, you'll get me going again. Back to Maya's chart. What did she discover?"

"That the only extended gap in the fires happened when we were in Los Angeles."

It took a moment for that shocker to sink in. "*What?* Why? What does that mean?"

"I don't know. I wanted to talk to you about it." He held her gaze, hoping she'd jump to the same logical conclusion he had.

"Could be a coincidence."

"It's possible." He shrugged one shoulder, dismissing that idea. He didn't really believe in coincidences, not when it came to fires. "Can't assume that. I can rule out myself as the cause."

"And me." When he didn't answer, she scrambled onto her knees and swatted him hard on the arm. "Are you implying that you think *I* set those fires? Because I *failed* basic Girl Scout wilderness survival. I suck at starting fires."

"Of course I wasn't thinking that," he said patiently, while she glared at him. "Anyway, you have no motive."

"Oh, this just gets better and better. If I had a motive, I'd go around starting fires? Let me guess, you think I'm a petty criminal just like my father? Naughty Kate is at it again?"

"Jesus, Kate." He wrapped a hand around her waist, but she pulled away. "Do you really believe I'd think any of those things? I know you're not like your father. I know you didn't set any fires. I'm trying to be logical here. We have to rule out suspects and that means considering every possibility."

She stared at him, and the hurt in her eyes told him he'd touched a deep sore spot.

"Is there a chance the people who were threatening you in LA followed you here and are making trouble for the town?"

Shock flashed across her face. Her dark hair flowed around her shoulders in inky waves as she shook her head. "No. That makes no sense. Why would they set a bunch of random fires instead of coming after me?"

That was exactly the same thought he'd had. But maybe there was something he wasn't seeing.

"Is arson on their playlist?"

"Probably." She twisted her mouth to one side. He hated the fact that he'd upset her so much. He'd gone about this all wrong. Why hadn't he gotten it out of the way first, before having sex? Now she probably felt ambushed. "I don't know everything about them, but burning down homes and businesses is a pretty standard way of punishing people who don't do what they want."

"What about someone else connected to you? Disgruntled former client, that sort of thing?"

She nibbled at her thumbnail. "When did the fires start?"

"It's hard to pin down, since we don't know which ones are run-of-the-mill fires and which aren't. But probably sometime last month."

"So around the same time that I got to Lost Harbor."

"Roughly."

"Shit." She flung herself off the bed and stalked toward the bathroom. "I have to think about this, Darius."

"Hang on, honey. No one's blaming you." He started to get up, to follow her, but she shot a look over her shoulder that stopped him in his tracks.

"Just give me a minute," she said tightly. "Please."

He lay back and rubbed at his forehead while she shut herself in the bathroom. By now he knew Kate well enough to know what was going on. Her default mode, where she felt the safest, was self-reliance. Inside that bathroom, she was in the process of shutting out everyone else. She was trying to figure out what was "right" and how much blame she bore.

He cursed out loud—"damn it." He should have taken Maya up on her offer and let her do the dirty work. He'd introduced suspicion into his and Kate's relationship, and they might not recover from that.

He swung his legs over the side and sat with his feet on the floor. Dragging his hands through his hair, he tried to imagine his life without Kate in it. In such a short time, she'd completely transformed his existence. Lit it up like a comet hitting the atmosphere.

He'd thought his heart was done with this kind of thing. But right now it was on some kind of roller coaster ride out of his control.

The toilet flushed, the water in the sink ran, and then she came out of the bathroom, still naked.

But her expression had changed to one of determination. "I know what I have to do," she said firmly.

"What's that?"

She stepped to the edge of the mattress and lowered herself onto his lap.

Always unpredictable, his Kate. Maybe it would be all right. Maybe she wasn't bailing on them.

He circled his arms around her naked form as she spoke. "The fires must be connected to me somehow. You aren't the common denominator because you've been here for over a year. I am. The logical conclusion is that it's the Kramer crew, or like you said, maybe some other enemy I made in Los Angeles. So." She visibly steeled herself. "I need to leave."

"Fuck that." He scowled and tightened his arms around her, as if he could physically keep her right where she was. "You always want to solve everything on your own, but that's not the answer."

"So what is?"

"Find out who's doing it and stop them. That's my job. And Maya's."

"And I know you'll nail the bastards. I know that. But I don't want to put Lost Harbor in the crosshairs until you do." She sniffed, and he realized that she'd been crying in the bathroom. The skin around her eyes was ever so slightly puffy. "I know I joke about Lost Harbor a lot, the weather, the mud, whatever. But you have no idea what this place means to me. Emma was the only adult in my life I could ever rely on. She was the only one who always loved me, no matter how much trouble I caused. She was the only one who put any effort into teaching me about life. And it's not just her. Maya, Jessica, Toni, Nice Kate, the friends I hung out with in the summers. I love all of them. Some of my happiest memories are from the boardwalk. I refuse to do anything that's going to make trouble for Lost Harbor."

"Honey." He ran his hand down her back. Her smooth skin warmed under his stroking. His cock stirred; the inevitable result of a sexy naked woman on his lap. He tried to force his erection to subside before it got too obvious. "I think you're overreacting. We're talking about a few garden sheds and old boats. That's no reason for you to take off."

"So far," she pointed out. She shifted in his arms, so her butt nestled closer to his crotch.

Exactly the kind of move he didn't need. He clenched his jaw and thought about flat tires again.

Nope, flat tires didn't work anymore. They made him remember the first time he saw Kate. He needed a more extreme image, like a bucket of ice dumped over his head.

Okay, that did the job.

He cleared his throat and made his next point. "There's no

evidence of escalation. Besides, where would you go that's safer than here—in bed with the fire chief?"

He knew she was truly worried because she didn't crack some kind of joke in response.

"This isn't about *me* being safe," she said seriously. "It's about Lost Harbor being safe."

"Keeping Lost Harbor safe is my job." He brushed her hair back from her face. "And Maya's. She's your best friend, right? Maybe you should trust her. You should trust both of us."

A wry smile tugged at the corner of her mouth. "You don't know what you're asking."

"I do. I really do. I know trust doesn't come easy to you." He allowed his thumb to trace her kneecap. A subtle motion that she'd barely notice, and that would satisfy his need to touch her.

She tilted her head back and scanned his face with a curious frown. "I thought it was a pretty good solution. Now you're making me rethink. But if I'm the problem, why are you so anxious for me to stay?"

Good question, he realized. His reaction to her announcement had been a knee-jerk one—*don't leave.* What was that all about, besides the obvious?

"Well, there's the sex," he said lightly. "That's a good reason right there."

"All the great sex in the world isn't worth jeopardizing the town," she said dryly.

Great sex...he was happy to hear she saw it that way.

"Okay, here's a reason. I just got used to a new landlady. I don't want to break in another one."

"Oh ho." She twisted on his lap and pushed at his chest. He allowed himself to fall back onto the mattress, laughing. "You broke me in? Is that how you see it?"

"I'm here, aren't I? Not evicted."

"Yeah, well...that's for services rendered." She crawled on top of his body. "That hand railing went a *long* way. All that moose turd shoveling."

"A guy does what he can." He decided to let her take charge and folded his arms behind his head.

She straddled his hips with her warm thighs and squeezed. "You like me, despite all the trouble I cause," she teased. "Admit it. That's why you don't want me to leave."

She was right. But if he told her how much he liked her, she might flee from anything resembling a relationship. Damn, sometimes being with Kate was like getting close to a porcupine. He had to be cautious. Keep it light.

"A tap dancer might move in upstairs," he told her. "Can't take that chance. I'm used to you."

She squeezed her thighs again.

"S.G. would be sad if you left," he continued, gasping. "She's been through enough, poor kid."

Another squeeze, so hard he actually coughed.

"On the other hand, if you leave maybe my full-time hard-on will go down. Might be nice to get a break." He grinned at her as she clocked him in the chest. "Okay okay. I don't want you to leave because you make me laugh."

"Like this?" She tickled under his arm and made him lurch with laughter.

"Sure," he gasped. "Like that. God, I hate being tickled. When are you leaving again?"

"Ooh, you're in trouble now." She pounced on him like a tiger out for revenge. But he was prepared for that and managed to Jedi-move her so that she lay on top of him, on her back, her legs on either side of his.

"What...how did you..." she gasped. He didn't give her any time to complain, just slid one hand between her legs and clamped the other one over her breasts.

"Never mind how." He tugged her earlobe with his teeth, like some kind of wild beast paralyzing its prey. "It's just a demonstration."

"Of what?" she asked breathlessly.

He stroked the sweet juicy folds that were already getting slippery as silk. "The fact that I haven't done nearly all the things I want to do to you yet. And that's why you can't leave."

Her breath caught and she arched against him. Her backside pressed against the rigid length of his cock. "See, that's why I'm not leaving until *tomorrow*."

He found the kernel of her clit and pinched it between two fingers. The plump flesh pulsed in response.

She let out a low moan. "Think you can fit all those things into one night?"

"I can be naughty all night long, babe. All night long."

CHAPTER TWENTY-FOUR

Darius wasn't kidding about the all-night-long part. After he brought her to a wild orgasm with just his fingers, while she lay spread open, her back to his front, they took a break for a snack. Except that it wasn't really a break because somehow fudge sauce wound up on her nipples and he spent an insanely long time licking it off.

Then he hoisted her onto her kitchen countertop and spread her legs apart with those strong hands.

She was seriously getting addicted to the way he manhandled her.

He pulled her to the edge of the counter and made her pose like that, splayed open, while he took himself into his fist.

"You sure you don't...want me..." she panted.

"Not now. I just want to fucking look at you. You're so sexy like that. You're always sexy, but damn, woman."

She touched herself between her legs, both to tease him and because she was itching for more. And because the sight of his big hand wrapped around his penis and his powerful arms flexing with each stroke—it just sent her wild.

His eyes went dark as night as he watched her play with herself. When they were both right on the edge, he pulled on another condom, gripped her hips, and plunged inside her. He used his strength to move her hips to the angle that would pleasure her the most. Something brushed against her clit—maybe his thumb, maybe his groin, she didn't know what, but it sparked an electric arc of response.

Her body clenched around the iron rod of flesh working inside her. Shudders gripped her—so intense she knocked a stray apple off the counter. Something else fell too, maybe some silverware. She didn't know and she didn't care. The blinding waves of her orgasm blocked out everything except the pure pleasure he was igniting in her body.

Everything except the thrill of watching him come a few moments later. His deep groan brought her eyes open just in time to see every one of his defined muscles flex and tighten with his climax.

"Okay, okay, I need a real break now," she told him once she'd gotten her breath back.

He took a step away from her, his chest heaving. "No kidding. Damn. I need a nap now. You wore me out, lady."

"A nap sounds good, now that you mention it. I guess we're not kids anymore, huh?"

He helped her slide off the counter. "Nope. At least not if you ask my knees."

"How old are you, anyway?" she asked as she landed on the floor. He held her up as she got her feet under her; they'd almost gone to sleep during that epic orgasm. "Seems like something I should know already."

"I'm thirty-five."

She took him by the hand, grabbed a bag of corn chips, and headed for the bedroom. "Not too old to crawl under the covers and snack in bed, right?"

"Two of my favorite things in one place—snacks and a naked woman. Can't say no to that." He grinned at her, his eyes a silver haze of contentment.

She ushered him ahead of her so she could ogle the thick flex of his muscular ass. As much as she loved the idea of one last night of naughty fun, she knew it wasn't going to come close to satisfying her. The more time she spent with Darius, the more she wanted to spend.

If she really wanted to make this easy, she'd kick him out right now. Evict him from the upper floor, and from her life.

But she didn't want to. She'd given up her job, her condo, possibly her career, and definitely her LA life. The hell if she was ready to give up this amazing, delicious, sensuous, intimately wonderful connection. At least not yet.

IT WAS a good thing that Kate had slept in that morning. The hunger that had built up between her and Darius refused to be satisfied. She wanted to know every inch of him—in between the times when he was exploring every inch of her.

He wasn't just a big guy, he was inventive too. She figured that out when she found herself kneeling on the bed, facing him, with one leg propped on his shoulder as his cock found a spot deep inside her, a place that had never been touched.

After she shuddered to another climax, she collapsed back onto the bed. "Have you been studying my Kama Sutra rug, Darius?"

He rumbled with laughter. "No, but it's good to have research materials handy." He rolled off his condom. His penis was still hard, just barely starting to soften. She touched it tenderly.

"There goes condom number three," she joked as he climbed off the bed and disappeared into the bathroom.

"I might have to grab extra from downstairs," he called over the sound of running water.

When he came back out, the impact of his naked body hit her all over again. "Okay, I have a question, Darius Boone. You said you've been divorced twice. Why would any woman let you go? You just gave me three orgasms in half a night!"

With a slight groan, he stretched out next to her. Heat radiated from his big body, and she curled into a little ball by his side. Such a comforting position, as if nothing could hurt her here.

"If true love ain't real, at least we have orgasms," he drawled.

"True love. What's that?" She tangled her fingers in his mat of black chest hair. "I haven't believed in true love since my junior high boyfriend dumped me through his sister."

"How'd that work?"

"She sent me a text message saying he wanted to break up with me but was too scared to tell me himself."

"Now that's gutless."

"I thought so. I cried for a day then decided the whole 'love' thing was a load of crap." She said it as lightly as possible, but she could still remember the embarrassment of that moment.

"But back to you. So you told me about wife number one. Gillian. What about number two?"

"Amelie."

The way he said her name put her on red alert. Whoever Amelie was, she'd really hurt him. "Was she French?"

"Yes. She...well, she had some problems. She wanted me because..." His jaw flexed as he struggled to get the story out. "She wanted me to be rough with her, in bed. Rougher than I wanted to be. Not at the beginning, just later on. I got uncomfortable but she would just laugh when I tried to say so. I started sleeping at the firehouse whenever I could. I didn't want to have sex. Then one of my engineers got killed in a fire. It was a rough time for the department and I needed to be there for my crew mates. I had to grieve too, and she didn't like that."

"She didn't like that you were grieving for someone?" Kate had a hard time believing that anyone could be that callous.

He looked uncomfortable at that reaction. "She'd probably tell a different story. She'd say I neglected her in bed. *Don't be such a crybabeeee,* she'd say."

His French accent made her laugh. "It sounds like she wanted Strong Darius only. Not the rest of you."

"That's exactly it." He shot her a glance filled with surprise. "How'd you put your finger on it like that?"

She shrugged one shoulder as she played with his chest curls. "That's kind of the story of my life. I was always expected to just take care of myself. When I lived with my father, I made my own meals, we had no schedule, and I had to figure out my own rides to school. With my mom, her mood always depended on who she was dating and how it was going. If I had a problem, it was always less important than her life because she was the adult. So I always dealt with everything the best I could, and people started praising me for being so strong."

"Strength is a good quality. But it's not everything." His silver-blue eyes were filled with so much kindness that she melted a little inside. "And you're a lot more than your strength."

"You are too, Darius. A lot more. You're honest. That might be the most important one of all. Do you know how much honesty I've seen in my life? Very, very little, and about eighty percent of it came from Emma. You're also pretty sensitive. You're kind. You're very handy to have around. You pay your rent on time. You're extremely hot. You have a good sense of humor."

A smile dented his cheek. "Wait a minute now. This is so unlike you. Where's my fire-breathing Kate? Are you saying all these nice things because you think you're leaving tomorrow?"

"*Think* I'm leaving? I *am* leaving. We went over this already."

"Seems I have some more persuading to do." He rolled on top of her and spread her arms to each side. He tongued one nipple and just like that, desire came flooding through her. "You left out a few things on your list of my amazing qualities. You left out my stamina."

CHAPTER TWENTY-FIVE

Despite Darius' best efforts, eventually he and Kate wore each other out. She fell asleep in his arms, looking drained and satisfied and utterly content.

He was too—almost.

The thought of her leaving tomorrow didn't sit well with him. Not just because it felt so sudden. It also just felt wrong. Why should Kate allow these anonymous, cowardly losers to control her life? It was unfair that she should have to uproot herself all over again.

Especially when she was just starting to appreciate her roots here.

Also, selfishly, he didn't want her to leave. He liked having her around. His whole body perked up every time he caught sight of her, or even heard her footsteps upstairs. One glance from those fiery dark eyes and he came alive inside.

Did that mean he'd been dead inside all this time? Maybe not dead, but definitely slumbering. He'd closed himself off from love and relationships and everything related to them. Hibernating, like a bear waiting out a long winter. Well, now it was spring and damn it, the world was calling to him in the sexy form of Kate Robinson.

Who thought she was leaving tomorrow. Going off all by herself to fight her battles alone, as she always had.

And that was another thing. How could she stay safe out there on her own? Here, she had lots of backup. The goddamn police chief was her best friend. Her grandmother was a badass who owned a hunting rifle. And what about him? He'd just proven himself as a bodyguard. Wouldn't she be safer living upstairs from her personal security guard?

Wouldn't she be even safer sleeping in the same bed with him?

The arguments went round and round in his head as he drifted off to sleep. He dreamed that he was standing guard outside a bear's den. Inside, a mama bear playfully batted her little cub's ears while he squealed. As guardian of the cave, his job was to watch for threats, and he couldn't join in the fun. So he stared into the forest looking for armed strangers. It was such a lonely job, but in the dream he knew it was important.

When his phone rang, he struggled out of a deep sleep, half expecting to see that his hand had turned into a bear's paw.

Certainly his voice sounded like a bear's low growl when he answered. "Boone."

It was Nate Prudhoe. "Chief, there's a fire out at Emma Gordon's place. We're on the way, but I thought you might want to know since—"

He cut Nate off. "On my way."

Kate was already blinking her way out of sleep. "Where are you going?"

"There's a fire and they need me. Kate..." He hesitated for the merest moment, knowing how this would affect her. A fire like this was exactly what she'd wanted to prevent. She'd probably blame herself. But he couldn't shield her from it. "It's at your grandmother's place."

"*What?*" She scrambled off the bed, landing on her hands and knees on the floor. Frantic, she searched for her clothes. "I'm coming with you."

No point in arguing. "Let's go."

She threw her clothes on with impressive speed, and they ran down the outdoor stairs toward his rig. She jumped into the passenger side, and he backed out the driveway before she'd even closed the door.

"Did they say anything else? Is she okay? What about the high tunnels? Do you know what part's on fire? I'm gonna call her."

"No." He put his hand on her arm to stop her. "All she has is the land line. If you call her, she might try to answer it. We need her to stay out of the house."

"Right, right. Is there anyone else we can call? Nate or someone? I just want to know she's okay."

"Not Nate. Don't want to interrupt him. I'll call the dispatcher."

He dialed the personal number of the dispatcher he knew was on duty. He wouldn't normally do something like that, but he was afraid that Kate might burst with anxiety if she didn't get some information.

"Mandy, hi, it's Chief Boone. Sorry to bother you like this, but can you tell me anything more about the Gordon fire? I'm headed there now."

"Not much, Chief. Emma called it in. I told her to get out of the house and wait for us to get there. Knowing her, she's probably hosing the place down right about now."

"True that. Thanks Mandy. Good job." He hung up and relayed the news to Kate. "Emma called 9-1-1, which tells me she's okay."

"Oh thank God." Kate clutched at her heart. "I'd never forgive myself if—"

"Hey. Don't jump to any bad scenarios. Do what we do. Work the fire. Work the problem."

"Work the problem," she repeated. "Okay. Yes. Right now the problem is you're going so slow."

"I'm driving twenty miles over the limit. Just for you." He turned onto the spur road that ran along the bluff where Petal to the Metal was located. The clock on his dashboard said that it wasn't yet five in the morning, but the first hint of light glowed behind the mountains of Lost Souls Wilderness.

The dark waters of the bay reflected the oncoming sunrise in little ripples of gold. Such silent magnificence everywhere he looked. The quiet world waiting for dawn.

Kate was looking out the window too, but he doubted that she was seeing the beauty. She was probably too worried about her grandmother to appreciate the scenery.

But he was wrong.

"It's so beautiful here," she choked out. "I love this place so much. I shouldn't have come back here. I should have chosen some random industrial wasteland. I should have moved into a landfill or a junkyard, some place where a few extra fires don't matter."

He bit the side of his mouth to keep from laughing. Trust Kate to make her distress into something almost comical.

"Don't laugh! I'm serious. I came to the one place that I actually care about, and look what happened."

"Okay, sweetheart. Let it all out now. Because when we get there Emma is going to need you to be cool. Okay?" He reached across the bench seat and took her hand, offering strength with a quick squeeze.

"Yes. Yes. I will. Don't worry, I'm good under pressure. My law firm would confirm." She took a deep breath. "I got this."

"I know you do." His confident tone seemed to help, and she got herself together just as they turned down the long, winding drive that led to the peony farm.

Smoke was billowing from the back of the property, not the farmhouse.

"The house is okay." He scanned the property with his expert eyes. "So are the greenhouses. Looks like some kind of outbuilding. Just like the other fires, the firebug went for the least amount of damage. See? It's not so bad."

Kate leaned forward to peer through the windshield, then gave a sudden laugh. "Holy shit. It's the honeymoon suite."

"The what?"

"A shed Emma wanted to turn into...eh, never mind. It wasn't being used for anything except paint cans, and we just cleared out most of those. Of all the buildings on the property, it's the least valuable. No big loss at all. Thank God."

Just as the dispatcher had predicted, they spotted Emma Gordon wielding a hose. She wore a rubber apron and mud boots over her nightgown, and had wrapped a bandanna around her face to protect her from the smoke.

The crew was already working the fire from the alpha and beta side of the little shack. A nearby high tunnel and a truck loaded with trash were both at risk if the fire spread too far.

"Strange," Kate murmured as they neared the ladder truck.

"Strange that Emma would be out here with a hose? Not really."

"No, not that. It's Emma, what would you expect? No, it's the shed they chose. You can't even see it from the road. You'd have to pass the farmhouse to reach it, and Emma's geese would be all over anyone who tried. Geese are incredible guard dogs."

"So maybe they came from another direction. We can worry about that later." He jerked the truck to a stop and jumped out. A quick glance told him that Nate and the others had things under control, so he loped over to Emma.

"You can take a break, you know. They're on it."

"No, I can't," she said. He realized that she was trembling.

"It's okay. They've got this. You might even be able to rebuild this shed." He offered to take the hose from her, but she shook him off. "Don't be afraid."

"I'm not afraid," she said fiercely. In her tense posture, he saw the same fearlessness he'd witnessed in Kate. "I'm furious."

"I'd be, too. Kate feels terrible—"

"Kate? This has nothing to do with Kate!"

He stared down at the eighty-two-year-old in mud boots. "Are you saying you know who did this?"

"Yes, I know. I told them to stay in the Ford until you got here."

He swung toward the truck but couldn't see inside the windows. "Are they dangerous? Armed?"

She snorted. "Dangerous to themselves, that's it. Where's Kate?"

Kate was hurrying across the lawn as she zipped up her hoodie. "Emma, are you—"

"Follow me," she interrupted. Dragging the hose along with her, she marched over to the truck. A hunting rifle was propped against the truck.

"Emma!" Kate gasped. "You didn't—"

"It's not loaded, but they don't know that," Emma grumbled. With the rifle in one hand, hose in the other, she gestured for Darius to open the truck door.

Inside, he found two suspects huddling together. Two soaking-wet teenagers. S.G. and a boy he didn't recognize.

"What the hell?" His voice must have come out louder than he meant, because the two kids shrank back against the seat.

Kate peered over his arm. "S.G.? *Dylan*? You guys did this?"

"Yes, they did. I caught them in the act." Emma waved the hose at the kids, getting them even wetter in the process. "They snuck over from Denaina's property. That's why my geese didn't wake up. But I don't sleep much anymore and I saw them."

S.G. shot a look at the boy, Dylan. She seemed to be urging him to say something. But he set his jaw and refused.

"Who are you? Who are your parents? Why'd you do this?" Darius demanded.

The kid stared back with a mulish scowl. With his wet hair and soaked clothing, it was hard to tell much about him. He seemed to have brownish hair and bluish eyes and looked much like other kids in town.

Darius turned to S.G. instead. He knew her—or thought he had, up until now. "What's going on here? Why would you do something so stupid? Denaina has a zero-tolerance policy for this kind of shit. Do you want to get kicked out of Denaina's place?"

That was a little unfair, because Denaina loved S.G. and would probably be willing to give her some leeway because of her very strange history. But he intended to get the truth here, one way or another.

His strategy worked. S.G.'s pale eyes filled with panicked tears. "I didn't do it! I was trying to stop him. I saw him out the window at Denaina's. I got up and followed him. By the time I caught up he'd already started the fire."

He looked back at Dylan. "Is that true?"

Dylan glared at him, all sheer stubborn bravado. "I want to speak to a lawyer."

"I'm a lawyer," said Kate. "I'm not an Alaska lawyer, but I'm happy to advise you that your best chance here is to answer the question. All the questions. Like why you'd try to hurt the people who are employing you."

"I wasn't trying to—" Dylan stopped and folded his lips together.

Ah ha. That sounded like a confession to him. All they needed now was a motive. Why the hell was this strange kid running around Lost Harbor setting nuisance fires?

Darius exchanged a look with Kate. He lifted an eyebrow and jerked his head toward the house. She nodded slightly. Maybe it was all the time they'd spent in bed, but they seemed to understand each other perfectly.

Kate turned to the two shivering kids. "How about this? You're both wet and probably freezing your butts off. Let's go inside the house and warm up. You can sit by the fire and ... never mind, we'll skip the fire. But we can get out of this truck and have some food and then we'll try this again. Deal?"

CHAPTER TWENTY-SIX

Darius had to check on the firefighting crew, so Kate and Emma led the two teenagers into the farmhouse. Emma was still muttering furiously as she turned on the light in the mud room.

"Setting fire to my shed. What a stupid, stupid thing. What was the damn point?" As the kids crowded into the entry, she added, "Take off your shoes!"

Kate tugged her grandmother into the warm living room, ahead of the kids. "I want to hear what they have to say, okay?"

"So do I!"

"Just don't scold them the way you did me at that age. They're not used to you."

Emma scorched her with an indignant glare. "You didn't set my shed on fire."

"I could list twenty things I did that made you just as mad. I'm not saying they don't deserve punishment. Just give me a chance to talk to them first. We'll get more information that way."

A glance at the two kids put that in doubt. Looking anxious, S.G. perched on Emma's old corduroy-upholstered couch right away, but Dylan refused to join her. With his hands in the pockets of his hoodie, he gazed down at the old planked floor as if he wanted to strip the varnish from it with his eyes.

Kate decided not to give up her height advantage by sitting down. She took a position a few feet away from him, blocking the path to the mud room in case he tried to make a run for it. "Look, Dylan. This is just my friendly advice, but I promise you that stonewalling the legal system is not a good idea. If you were behind this fire, and the other ones, there's going to be a serious price to pay. Your best option is to be open and forthcoming."

He snuck a glance at S.G..

"You should just tell her," the girl urged him. Tears streaked her face through a layer of dirt and soot. "Tell her everything."

Dylan's shoulders hunched forward. Even though she was furious about Emma's shed, Kate's heart went out to him. She remembered exactly how it felt to do something stupid and get in trouble for it.

The question was, did he know it was stupid? Did he regret his actions?

He looked up long enough to meet Kate's eyes, then dropped his gaze down again. "If I tell you, will you be my lawyer?"

His voice wobbled as he made that request. He looked so young and out of his depth.

"Like I said, I'm not licensed here in Alaska. But I can help you find someone who is."

"You would?" Another crack in his bravado as he glanced up at her. "Why? I—I set fire to your grandma's shed."

Emma marched over to him like one of her strutting roosters. "Why would you do such a thing? There was nothing in it! You emptied it yourself!"

Dylan turned red and twisted his hands in his pockets. "I know that! That's how I knew it wouldn't be a big deal." He looked Kate's direction again. "Why would you help me?" he demanded.

Emma whirled on her too. "Why would you, Kate? After what he did!"

Kate stood her ground against her furious grandmother. "He's a minor and deserves representation. Besides, I know what it's like to be a kid on your own. It sucks." When Emma's expression relaxed, she turned back to Dylan. "Tell me more about your situation. Where are you from?"

"Can I wait until *he's* here?"

"He? You mean Darius?" That surprised her. As intimidating as Darius could be, why would the kid want to spill his guts in front of him? "You know he's the fire chief, right? He's not too happy with you right now."

"I know who he is."

Kate's eyebrows lifted. There was something in the tone of his voice that set off her legal Spidey senses. "Fine, we'll wait for Darius. Emma, want to make some tea or something?"

Her grandmother folded her arms across her chest. "I'm not making tea for the juvenile delinquent who burned my shed down."

"I'll fix it!" Dylan burst out. "I can work for free if you want. I can feed your chickens or whatever."

"You'll be feeding chickens until you're thirty to make up for it." Emma threw up her hands and headed in the direction of the kitchen.

"It's just a stupid shed!"

"Okay, okay." Kate came to Dylan's side and shepherded him toward the couch. "Good rule of thumb. Don't yell at the woman who could sue you for destruction of property."

He snapped his mouth shut and plopped down on the couch next to S.G..

"That's better." Kate let out a breath of relief. She wasn't used to dealing with minors. If only most clients did what she said so quickly. "Can you tell me why you came to Lost Harbor?"

He didn't answer, apparently determined to wait for Darius.

"Okay, let's try something else." She turned to S.G.. "How did you get to know Dylan? You don't have to share any of his personal details."

S.G. waited until Dylan gave her a go-ahead nod, then answered. "He's a runaway like me. We started talking at the high school pool. Anyone can swim there, and take a shower afterwards. I was curious about him because he was just like me when I first came here, afraid and lonely. So I followed him after swimming and found out that he was camping near the playground. No one else is camping yet, it's still too cold and muddy. No wonder he had to take so many showers."

A runaway. Well, that complicated things. Where were his parents? Who was responsible for him? Denaina had signed his work permission slip.

"You told us you were staying at Denaina's," she told him sternly. "Was that not true?"

"I am staying there. But..." He ducked his head. "She doesn't know it. I've been staying in the well house. It's heated and no one goes in there. Except S.G.."

Lovely. This just got more and more complicated. Would that be trespassing?

"Did you forge Denaina's signature when you applied for the job here?"

Neither of them answered that, which served as answer enough to her.

"Okey-doke. So far we have arson, destruction of property, forgery, and trespassing. Not to mention pissing off Emma Gordon, which ought to be a crime in and of itself. And then there's getting your friend into trouble."

Dylan threw S.G. an anguished glance. "I didn't mean to. You shouldn't have followed me, S.G.. Why are you so good at that?"

"Tracking wild game," the girl said matter-of-factly. "You have to be very very quiet. You're lucky I didn't have my bow and arrows with me."

Dylan's eyes widened.

"Welcome to Alaska, kid," Kate told him. "You're not from around here, are you?"

"I'm from Texas," he muttered. Finally, some information. Maybe S.G.'s offhanded comment about bows and arrows had distracted him.

"Texas is a very long way from Alaska. How'd you get here? That must have been quite a trip."

For the first time, he answered a question with something like eagerness. "It was great. Part of it was on the bus and part was hitchhiking. I used a fake ID at the border."

"Great. Let's add that to the list."

His face closed up again. "I know I'm in trouble. You don't have to keep telling me."

"Look, kid, if you're going to work with me, you'll have to get used to my sense of humor. It's how I deal with shit."

One corner of his mouth drew up, and she had an odd sense of familiarity. Maybe she was seeing her teenage self in him.

"That's cool. Me too."

Emma came back into the room with three mugs of tea, which she planted on the old captain's trunk that served as a coffee table. She looked marginally calmer than before.

"Kate, if you actually want to help this boy, you should take the Alaska bar exam like I keep telling you."

Kate had to laugh. Trust Emma to jump on any opportunity to encourage her to stay in Lost Harbor. "Nice try," she told her. "Right now, we're just talking."

"Better talk fast." Darius stood in the doorway, wiping his sooty hands on his pants. A smudge of ash darkened his cheek, adding to the effect of his overnight stubble. His expression was extremely forbidding. The atmosphere in the room instantly changed to one of dead seriousness. "You put my crew at risk with your stunts. Emma, too. Her shed, her chickens, her flowers, her livelihood. You want to talk now or after I call the police chief?"

Dylan's face shut down and he huddled deeper into his hoodie, like a turtle into its shell.

S.G. jumped to her feet. "Don't call Maya yet! Really. You have to wait until he explains."

Darius' eyebrows drew together in a fierce frown. "Why? He set a damn fire, S.G.. Maybe *all* the fires. Why shouldn't I call the police?" He paused for a beat, maybe waiting for Dylan to say something.

When he didn't, Darius pulled out his phone and scrolled through his numbers.

"Dylan!" S.G. cried. "Tell him."

No response from the boy.

Kate wondered if she should step in, but she held her tongue. Darius was playing the "bad cop" magnificently. Also, he had every right to be pissed off.

Darius hovered his thumb over his phone. Before he could press it, S.G. launched herself into the air to tackle him.

If Darius weren't such an oak tree of a man, he might have staggered. Instead, he caught her with one arm and quickly set her back on her feet.

"Don't!" S.G. cried again. "Please don't."

"Why not?" he demanded.

"Because you're Dylan's father!"

CHAPTER TWENTY-SEVEN

The phone slid from Darius' hand and hit the floor. He barely noticed. He stared at S.G. while her words seemed to bounce off a funhouse mirror. He must have misunderstood. Or she was making things up to keep him from calling Maya. But her wide eyes showed nothing but sincerity, and he'd never known S.G. to be deceptive.

Other than hiding out in his damn firehouse.

Since then, she'd been entirely honest.

Slowly, he swung toward the kid, Dylan. He hadn't paid much attention to him when he'd been sitting in the truck. A wet boy in a hoodie, that was the sum total of his observations.

The boy was staring down at the floor, as if he wanted to sink right through it. Under the weight of Darius' scrutiny, he slowly raised his head. And Darius saw in his eyes that it was true—or at least that he believed it to be true.

"Explain," he ordered the boy, causing him to flinch.

"Darius, lighten up," Kate said softly. She came next to him and touched his arm. "He came a long way. Seems he's from Texas."

He did a quick calculation. *Gillian.*

Holy fuck. It couldn't be. Could it? She'd wanted to have a child—they both did. If she'd gotten pregnant, why hadn't she told him?

"Is your mother—" He broke off because his voice was so hoarse he scared even himself.

"Gillian O'Connor," muttered Dylan.

He stared at the boy, noting the ski-jump nose that was just like Gillian's, and the rounded shape of his face—a male version of Gillian's. No doubt in his mind; this was Gillian's son. But was Dylan *his* son?

"Who's the O'Connor?"

"O'Connor is my stepfather's last name. Buck O'Connor."

"O'Connor...." That rang a bell. The memory came swimming back. "Her boss. The owner of the restaurant chain she worked at."

"Yeah. He's a big shot, all right." His bitter tone made Darius do a double take. "I knew he wasn't my real father. He didn't really bother to pretend after I was about six."

Pretend. His alleged son had been raised by someone who *hadn't bothered to pretend* he was a real father. Darius flexed his fists, ready to rip something apart with his bare hands. Like the cast-iron wood stove or the sheetrock in the walls. Something big. But nothing was as big as this.

"How do you know..." He cleared his throat, not quite sure how to ask the next question.

"That you're my father? My mom told me when I was ten. She said she thought someone who owned a restaurant would be a better father because you were still in school. I guess they were having..." He shrugged, letting the sentence trail off.

An affair. He'd known about that part. He'd gotten over the cheating part of the story many years ago. Hiding his son, however...that went way, way beyond anything he could accept. "Where is she now? Why are you here?"

"Mom..." Dylan chewed at his lower lip, suddenly looking much younger than—wait, how old was he? He must be...Darius did the math. Fifteen? "Mom died six months ago."

A murmur of shock and sympathy swept the little group. S.G. sat back on the couch and scooted closer to him. He caught a glimpse of Kate's dark eyes shining with sympathy.

But Darius couldn't feel anything, at least not yet. The hits were coming too fast, one after the other.

A son. Raised by someone else. And now Gillian was gone. Really gone, not just gone from his life.

A hole opened up in the pit of his stomach. "How?" he managed.

"Cancer. Cancer sucks," he said fiercely. "I fucking hate it."

With that one outburst, Darius got an inkling of what this kid had been going through. "I'm sorry. Gillian and I have been out of each other's lives for a very long time, but I loved her. You've... uh, been through a lot."

But Dylan hunched back into his shell, AKA his hoodie, and shrugged. "Everyone has their shit. Before she died she told me where to find you. I have all the paperwork and everything."

Kate spoke up gently. "I take it you stayed with your stepfather after your mother died?"

"Yeah."

"Does he know you're here?"

"Maybe."

Okay then. Back to monosyllables. The boy looked so miserable, slouched on the couch, the weight of the world bearing down on him, that Darius couldn't take it. He stepped to the couch and crouched before him so he could connect with him at eye level. "Listen. I promise you that I didn't know you existed until just now. Gillian never told me. I never suspected. Never had a reason to."

Dylan didn't show any obvious reaction, but Darius knew he heard every word.

"I'm happy you found me. I want to know—" He broke off, because the idea of getting to know his own teenage son was too overwhelming right now. One step at a time. "There's a lot that I want to know. But the first thing is whether Buck O'Connor is looking for you. Does he know that you're here?"

"I left a note that I was going to find my real father. He knows who you are, so I guess he just doesn't really care. He's probably relieved that I'm gone."

"Okay. Well, just in case, we're going to have to get ahold of him."

Dylan shrugged, as if it didn't matter to him one way or the other.

"My other question is, why'd you set those fires?" Even though he tried hard to keep his tone gentle, an edge of outrage entered his voice. Fire wasn't something to mess around with. The idea that his *own son* had been setting fires around *his town*...it stuck in his craw.

"I don't know." Dylan finally looked up, revealing an expression of honest confusion. "I guess I was just mad."

"At me?"

"No. I don't know. I guess. You have a good life. You're all happy and shit. You have a hot girlfriend. It's like my mom and me never existed." The hurt words burst out of him, seeming to surprise even himself. "I didn't want to hurt anything. And I didn't, not really. So what if a bunch of junk got burned up? I just wanted to mess with you. Like, why should everything be good for you and everything sucks for me?"

"Okay. I guess I can see the logic. Sort of." He glanced back at Kate, who offered a mystified shrug but no advice.

Great. Where was the guidebook for how to deal with an angry teenage son you never knew existed? An angry teenage *runaway* son. An angry teenage runaway *firebug* son.

A son. He had a son. This complete stranger of a kid was his blood. He could barely comprehend it.

But one thing he knew for sure was that this boy needed him. He was all alone in Alaska, in trouble with the law. He needed adult supervision.

"I want you to come stay with me." His brusque statement made Dylan's head whip up. "You can stay on the couch."

"But I set all those fires."

"And you're going to have to answer for that. But right now, that's not the point. You're my son and I want you to stay with me. You came all this way for a reason, right?"

"I guess so," he muttered. Darius put a hand on his shoulder, feeling the young bones under the thick hoodie. What had those bones been like when he was a little boy, or a toddler, or a baby? The thought twisted his heart, but he couldn't let his own emotions get in the way here. The important thing was Dylan.

"Then it's settled." He squeezed lightly and caught a tiny nod from the boy. Darius rose to his feet and looked down at S.G.. She was practically plastered to Dylan's side. "S.G., did you know anything about the fires before tonight?"

She shook her head quickly. "He didn't tell me that part. He just told me he was here to find you. I couldn't tell you before because it wasn't my secret. I mean, I did tell you eventually but that's because Dylan was being so stupid and stubborn."

He gave a wry chuckle. "Maybe it runs in the family."

Even though Dylan's head was still lowered, Darius caught the slightest hint of a smile from him.

Emma cleared her throat loudly. "I'm going to bed. I never did like soap operas, and now I know why. I'd like my house to myself now, if you all don't mind. Be nice if someone can feed my chickens on the way out." She marched out of the room.

Kate beckoned to the kids. "Come on, let's give her some space. Dylan, you got your first chicken-feeding payback opportunity. I'll show you the drill." As the kids got to their feet, she added, "By the way, Darius, I've already offered Dylan my legal expertise. I can't represent him, but I can help out in any other way that you need."

"Thank you. I appreciate that."

"Oh, it's not for you. It's for him. I know how it feels to be a kid alone in the big wide world."

"He's not alone," Darius corrected her. "Not anymore."

A strange look came across her face, a very un-Kate-like expression of pure tenderness.

As Dylan gained his feet, his hood fell away from his face. For the first time, Darius got a chance to really scrutinize him. His resemblance to Gillian really was striking. Even his eyes were the same summer blue.

Kate looked back and forth between the two of them. "You know, I thought Dylan looked familiar, but I couldn't place him. He looks just like you."

Darius shook his head. "He looks like his mother. Spitting image. Same coloring, same features."

"Maybe so, but he also looks like you." She gestured at Dylan's chin. "It's all in the chin. The stubbornness. His smile is like yours too. I've only seen it once, but it did ring a little bell."

Looking fed up with their inspection, Dylan pulled his hood back up. "Are you guys done arguing?"

"She's arguing," Darius corrected him. "I don't argue."

"Of course you do." Kate shook her head at him. "You just don't like to call it that because I usually win the arguments."

"Oh, is that how you see it? Interesting."

"Are you guys arguing about arguing now?" Dylan asked.

They both looked at him, and burst out laughing. "Busted," Kate said cheerfully. "Let's get going. We can argue on the way home."

Home. The word suddenly felt so much more complicated. Home already had an upstairs landlady who rocked his world. Now it was getting a strange kid who'd just blown up that world.

THE WHOLE SITUATION would have been so much more awkward without Kate around. After they said goodbye to S.G., the three of them drove home in Darius' truck. Kate peppered Dylan with questions about Texas and what music he liked, what he did for fun, what he liked in school. Basic stuff. It gave Darius a chance to know more about him, without the burden of figuring out what to ask.

When they got back to Fairview Court, he panicked. It was almost six in the morning and they all needed some sleep—but Kate had her own bed to retreat to. That meant he'd be all alone with his brand-new son.

Kate gave them both a sleepy smile and a wave goodbye as she headed for the outdoor stairway.

He longed to kiss her goodnight. Or good morning, actually. Or maybe give her a "thank you for everything" kiss. Or an "I want to throw you down on a bed next chance I get" kiss.

But Dylan's presence made him think twice about any kind of kiss. Was it appropriate? Would it upset the boy? Fuck, this was confusing.

He skipped the kiss and beckoned Dylan toward the downstairs entry. "I'll call you tomorrow, Kate."

That sounded more formal than he'd planned. She paused on the staircase and gave him a curious look over her shoulder. "Okay. Let me know if you need anything. Either of you."

She hurried the rest of the way up the stairs. Darius had the strangest feeling that she was receding out of his reach, like a wave on the shore.

But why? The fires had been solved. There was no need for her to leave anymore.

He shook it off and ushered Dylan into the apartment. "The couch is there." He pointed toward the very obvious couch in the middle of the living room. "Bathroom's back there. I'll get you a sleeping bag. We can pick your things up from Denaina's tomorrow. Do you have much stuff?"

"Backpack. Sleeping bag. Not much."

Darius nodded and went into his bedroom closet to search for a sleeping bag. His heart was hammering and he felt almost feverish. *He had a son.* A nearly grown son. What were you supposed to do with a son that was almost grown up already?

"When's your birthday?" he asked as he came out with a North Face bag and one of his spare pillows. "I figure you're about fifteen, yeah?"

"I'll be sixteen on August third."

"August." He didn't want to do the math, but he couldn't help it. If he'd been born in August, Gillian had been three months pregnant when she'd left him.

But what was the point in rehashing the past? Gillian was gone. Dylan was here now. That was what mattered.

He tossed the pillow to the boy. "You should get some sleep. I have to be at the station by nine. Do you know how to make yourself breakfast?"

Dylan caught it against his chest and smiled. And suddenly, Darius saw exactly what Kate had been talking about. That smile was like looking in a mirror. Or maybe a time machine, before he started growing so much five o'clock shadow.

"I can make huevos rancheros like you wouldn't believe," he said. "Mom taught me."

"All right then. Look forward to that." He hovered in the hallway that led to his bedroom. What was he supposed to say now? Where was Kate with all her words when he needed her?

He cleared his throat. Logistics. Those were always a good topic. "There's an extra key under the mat. But this is Lost Harbor and there's not much to worry about."

"Except fires," said Dylan. His tone of voice was so extra dry that it took Darius a moment to see he was joking.

"Yeah. I guess so. And for the record?" He paused to get *his* tone just right. "I don't joke about fires. Ever."

Dylan's smile disappeared. "Sorry, Mr. —" He stopped dead. "I mean, Fire Chief. Sir. I mean...what should I call you?"

Wow. Good question. Nothing in the realm of "dad" or "father." That would just be weird. What would Kate suggest?

He could picture her laughing answer. *Big Guy is taken, that's what I call you. How about just your name? Why is this complicated?*

"You can just call me Darius."

The kid nodded and unrolled the sleeping bag onto the couch. Darius escaped into his bedroom and closed the door behind him, with a feeling of shutting out the entire big scary world Kate had mentioned.

His phone dinged. Text from Kate.

You guys doing okay?

Fuck if I know, he answered.

You got this. Get some sleep.

But what do I do with him? He fired off a string of texts. *I missed the playing with Legos phase. The playing catch phase. I missed all the phases.*

Just be yourself.

That sounded like a bad idea. His grumpy ass had no business taking on a troubled, grieving kid. But what else could he do?

Good luck. Don't worry. Conking out now. Been a long day.

No shit. Not just long, but with some unbelievable ups and downs. His world had completely changed since their time together in her bed. And now that he had a boy on his hands, when was the next time he'd find his way up to her place?

Not long at all, if you counted dreams.

He fell asleep almost instantly, and his brief hours of sleep were filled with Kate. Naked Kate, laughing Kate, arguing Kate, kind Kate. Smart Kate, with her good advice. Lusty Kate. The more Kate, the merrier.

He woke up...happy. Not scared, just happy.

He had a son.

That truth sank through him like a blast of sunshine after a long winter. *He had a son.* Something he'd basically given up on—a family—had magically appeared in his life.

The answer to last night's worries was simple, after all. He'd do anything his son needed. End of story.

CHAPTER TWENTY-EIGHT

Kate's offer of help was accepted the very next day. Darius had a training he couldn't miss.

"Can you go with Dylan to his meeting with Maya? The news is already all over town and I just got a call from her. She wants to see him immediately. He could use your legal...presence. I'd really appreciate it."

How could she say "no" to that deep voice on the phone?

"After all the times you helped me? Of course."

"I'll make it up to you." She shivered at the promise in his voice.

Around noon, she led Dylan into Maya's office at the fire and police building. Two folding chairs awaited them, along with an extremely stern police chief.

"So." Maya planted her elbows on the desk and fixed Dylan with her classic Officer Badger stare. "You're the one responsible for Lost Harbor's first arson spree."

He gulped. "I'm real sorry, ma'am." When he was nervous, his Texas drawl became even more obvious. "I wasn't trying to hurt anybody. It was just old stuff I didn't think would matter."

"You never know what's going to matter to someone."

He hung his head and stared at the floor. He must be having flashbacks to all the lectures he'd gotten last night.

Kate came to his rescue.

"Chief Badger, Dylan O'Connor is a minor and extremely remorseful over his actions. While they were of course reprehensible, he is willing and ready to make recompense for them in any way you deem acceptable."

Maya blinked at her. "Hello, lawyer."

"Hello, Chief." Kate bit back a smile. Maya had never seen her in full legal mode. Lawyer versus police chief—definitely a shift from the days of hanging out on the boardwalk in their swimsuits.

"Are you representing this boy?"

"Not officially. I'm here on behalf of Darius. He's unable to be here so I volunteered to speak for him."

"So it's true what I hear, that Dylan is...?" Maya drew out the question for Kate to answer.

"Dylan is Darius' newly discovered son. He claims full responsibility for Dylan. If you decide to charge him with something, Darius will support it. But he's hoping we can work out something short of charging him with a crime."

A twinge of irritation crossed Maya's smooth brown face. "You know what would be great? If people who didn't want to be charged with crimes didn't commit crimes."

"Yes. That would obviously be preferable."

"Are you going to send me back, ma'am?" Dylan burst out.

"I don't know what I'm going to do with you yet."

"Then let us handle it." Kate leaned forward eagerly. "I was going to suggest some form of community service related to fire mitigation. Dylan has already offered free labor to Emma. If he does the same to everyone whose property he damaged, that seems much more productive than sending him to court. He is truly remorseful. His actions were born out of anger and grief over the loss of his mother. It's not something that's going to continue. He poses no danger to this community."

"And you can guarantee that? Or Darius can?"

"*I* guarantee it," Dylan said eagerly. "A hundred percent."

"And Darius will back that up," Kate added. "Financially, legally, in whatever way you can think of."

"Pretty unusual for a fire chief to vouch for a firebug," Maya said dryly. "I'm not sure how well that's going to go over around here."

"Everything about this situation is unusual. But they say that strange things happen around Lost Souls Wilderness, so..."

"Not what that saying means. Not even close." Maya shut that approach down pretty quick. Just as if she were in court, Kate switched gears.

It was fun to use her legal muscles again, she had to admit.

"Dylan understands that if there's any more trouble, he won't be able to stay here. Right, Dylan?"

"Yes, ma'am. Ma'ams."

His "ma'am" didn't seem to soften Maya much. She leaned back in her chair and steepled her fingers together. "I'm still trying to understand why you did something so boneheaded, Dylan. Were you trying to get Darius' attention?"

He twisted his mouth to one side. "I guess. Maybe. Why does it matter? I'm not going to do it anymore."

"See, that's the thing. How do I know that? If you were trying to get his attention, well, now you have it. Mission accomplished. On the other hand, if you were trying to be the opposite of everything Darius is, how do I know you won't keep on being the opposite?"

Dylan stared at her blankly. "Huh?"

"It's a rebellion thing. He puts out fires, you were setting fires. Look at Kate, here. Her father is...okay, I'll skip the details, but

Kate rebelled by becoming a lawyer. So if you're on a rebellion trip, I look at Darius and I see an upstanding guy, someone I know will do the right thing, someone strong, both physically and mentally, highly respected and kind. Kate, anything to add to that description?"

She could think of many things, but none of them were appropriate at the moment. "I agree with all of the above. You could include stubborn, though maybe patient would be better."

"Patient. Good enough." Maya turned back to Dylan. "My point is, that's who Darius is. That's someone you can be proud to call your father. But if you're set on going the opposite direction—"

"I'm not," Dylan said quickly. "I was just really messed up."

"Will you agree to see a therapist?"

Dylan made a face, but Kate dropped her hand onto his shoulder and spoke in his stead. "You bet. I'll make sure of it."

Maya looked from one to the other of them. She clicked off items on her fingers. "Therapist. Darius takes responsibility. Zero leeway for errors. Are we all understood?"

"Yes." Dylan and Kate both nodded, then he added a quick, "Thank you, Officer."

"It's police chief, actually." But Maya's expression finally softened into a wink. "You should get your terminology right. You're lucky you have such good advocates speaking up for you. Don't mess this up, kid."

"I won't. I promise."

Kate nudged him to his feet, figuring they should leave while they were ahead.

"And don't expect everyone to be this forgiving," Maya warned him. "Kate, got an extra second?"

Kate nodded. "Wait outside for a sec, Dylan." She closed the door and faced her old friend. "You have more questions?"

"Yeah. I do." An unfamiliar expression of hurt came over

Maya's face. "I'm used to you being in the middle of trouble. I'm not used to being the last to hear about it."

"We just found out last—" She stopped as she realized what Maya was referring to. Not Dylan's mess...her own. She squeezed her eyes shut. Time for her to face her friend. "Did Emma fill you in?"

"While you were gone. She was worried."

Kate tilted her head back with a groan. "I should have told you everything. I was just...embarrassed."

"Embarrassed?"

"My father's always been a grifter, but not some hardcore criminal. And I defended him. Well, I represented him. You're a police officer, you protect and serve, and you're great at it. And meanwhile I'm..." She shuddered to demonstrate her own disgust at herself. "Repping a lifelong scam artist."

"He's your father."

"I don't need reminding." Kate still couldn't manage to meet Maya's eyes.

"I'd probably do anything for my dad too."

"That's different. Harris is a prince among parents. He's a gem."

Maya got to her feet and came around her desk. "Kate, you're not your father. Would your father quit his job to protect you?"

Kate screwed up her face, trying to imagine such a scenario. "He wouldn't even stay in the same town so I could finish out a school year."

"Exactly. You're one of the best, most loyal people I know. You always act like you're some bad seed. I was there for Naughty Kate. You were never bad. You sure as jeebus aren't bad now. Ever think maybe you should stop seeing yourself that way?"

Finally Kate allowed herself to look her friend in the eye. The easy acceptance she saw there made her want to cry. Of all the people she'd ever known, Maya was one of those she respected the most. They used to have so much fun together, laughing until they cried. Her biggest teenage regrets were the times she'd gotten Maya into trouble with her father.

"Would I be best friends with a bad seed?" Maya demanded.

"Very unlikely," Kate agreed with a smile. "If you were, you'd straighten her out before she got out of high school."

"Oh no, that wasn't me." Maya shook her head firmly. "You did that, Kate. Stop beating yourself up. And start confiding in your goddamn friends. Trust us."

Kate tapped a finger on her chin. "Funny, Darius said almost exactly the same thing. Except he wasn't dressed when—"

"Okay, you don't have to confide *that* much."

AS THEY WALKED through the corridor after she'd left Maya's office, Dylan let out a breath of relief. "Whoa. She's such a badass."

"That she is. But she has a fun side too. She's one of my best friends. Do you want to see where Darius works? The fire department is in the other wing of this building."

He made an uneasy face. "I don't think so. The other firemen..."

They reached the exit and pushed out into the sunshine. A yellow fire engine filled one side of the lot, drying in the open air. It gleamed in the bright midday light.

"That's the one that came to the farm last night," Dylan said.

"Is it?" The fire engines all looked the same to her.

He bit his lower lip, looking even younger than fifteen. "It was terrible, what I did. S.G. thinks I should do something to say I'm sorry. She offered me her knife to carve something but I don't know how."

"That doesn't sound like a good idea," Kate said quickly. The last thing she wanted was Dylan in possession of a weapon when he was already on thin ice. "What else could you make? Or do?"

"I'm pretty good at cooking. I used to work at my stepdad's restaurant."

"Well, one thing I know for sure is that firefighters love to eat. What else?"

"I play guitar."

"Really? Did you know that Darius is a fantastic bass player?"

"He is?" His pale face lit up until he looked almost like a regular excited kid.

"Oh yeah. And let me tell you, there's nothing quite as attractive to the girls as a guy playing music. Just something to think about."

"I don't want a girlfriend. My life is very complicated right now."

His serious tone nearly made her burst out laughing. That line could have come straight from the mouth of a twice-divorced fire chief.

Maybe it was another thing that ran in the family.

But she knew Darius better now, and she understood that his wariness came from being a romantic at heart. A wounded romantic.

She was the jaded one who'd never really allowed herself to get close to someone.

But now she was getting drawn in, bit by bit, day by day. Body part by body part. First all her naughty bits had fallen under Darius' spell. Now her *brain* was tied up with Darius and his new son.

What if her heart came next? Would that really be so bad?

CHAPTER TWENTY-NINE

Darius quickly fell into a routine with Dylan. The boy would sleep in and make his own breakfast. Then he'd walk to the firehouse and put in some time doing community service with the crew. When that was completed, Darius would drive him to Petal to the Metal, where he did whatever Emma required.

Often he would spot Kate at the peony farm, and they'd have a quick conversation along the lines of:

"Can I come up tonight?"

"I'll leave the deadbolt off. Key's under the mat."

In the evenings, Darius would make dinner with Dylan—they both liked to cook. Sometimes Kate would come downstairs to eat with them. Later, after Dylan had fallen asleep on the couch, Darius would slip out the door and tiptoe up the stairs to Kate's. And they'd spend the next few hours devouring each other and talking late into the night.

They talked about everything—his fears about suddenly being a father; her bad-girl teenager years; his love for the blues and especially Muddy Waters; the frustration and entertainment of being the daughter of Frank Robinson; why he'd become a fireman—with no family in the works, he'd channeled his protective nature into firefighting; what she missed about LA—mostly it seemed to come down to brunch, for some reason.

He hadn't felt this close to anyone for a very long time. It helped to share his worries about Dylan—how to take care of him, how to get the town to accept him after what he'd done, how to connect with him.

As for Kate, she finally seemed to completely trust him. She no longer talked about leaving, and he liked that. A lot.

Tonight, sleepy-eyed, she opened the door for him wearing the sexiest little sleep tank and shorts he'd ever seen.

He slipped inside and slid his hand onto her ass. Those shorts were just too tempting. Her skin warmed through the thin fabric.

All day long, as he and his crew sat through a session on preparing for biohazard emergencies, he'd looked forward to this moment.

Her smooth curves settled under his hands as if some cosmic sculptor had created her ass and his hands as one perfect work of art. "God, I missed you."

Against his chest, her body vibrated with laughter. "You saw me at lunchtime."

"That was hours ago. Let me feel that skin. I need my hands on you. I need to feel you." His voice was low and urgent. Sometimes his need for Kate shocked him, but he blocked out the alarm bells.

He didn't care if this was risky, or if he was sliding down a slippery slope into a different kind of relationship. Right now he wanted her and he needed her and she wasn't objecting. Not at all.

She hooked one leg around the back of his thigh. He felt the radiant heat of her pussy press against him. With a chest-deep groan, he gripped her ass cheek and rotated her against him.

Her nipples hardened under that skimpy little top. He looked down and saw the dark peaks push against the nearly see-through cotton. Her top clung so erotically to the full mounds of her breasts that the saliva dried up in his mouth.

He cupped them in his hands, with the feeling that he was filling himself up with everything he needed. Touch, release, glory, hope. And sexy, sensual woman.

She moaned as he skimmed his thumbs across her nipples. The material of the shirt offered extra friction that made her shudder, so he left it right where it was, at least for now. With thumbs and forefingers, he pinched those plump points of flesh into hot hard peaks. She arched her back so her top rode up and exposed a pale flash of skin. Her head fell back, offering him absolute and total access to her body.

Ah God, what a sight. Under his own sleepwear, his cock was already rock hard and pushing against her belly. She twisted her body back and forth against his, caressing him with the bare skin of her stomach.

He wanted to come all over her, right this second. But he also wanted to claim her from the inside. *Yes, inside. Now.* He spun her around and planted her hands against the wall.

"I want to see your ass in those little shorts," he muttered as he kneed her legs apart.

Breathing fast, she rested her forehead against the wall. The submissive position made his brain sing with lust. The way her ass quivered under the micro shorts nearly undid him. Beyond the hem, he could see the shadow of her pussy, a glint of wetness.

He slid his fingers inside and found the crease between her legs and the drenched bit of fabric that formed the crotch of the shorts. He used it the way he'd used her top, sliding it back across her clit to stimulate and madden her.

With a low cry, she arched her hips back in eager invitation. *Take me. Take me hard.*

Abso-fucking-lutely. Just as soon as he'd finished driving her mad with lust. He reached around her, under her shirt, and found the nipples he'd already teased. Still erect, still swollen, still eager for his touch. She jolted as he spanned his hand across them, nipple to nipple.

"God, Darius." Her groan tore right from her core. Her body trembled and shook. Her ass nestled right between his thighs, such a wicked temptation. With the hand that wasn't on her nipples, he toyed with her clit. Each pulse and swell sent a shot of adrenaline through him. He slid a finger inside her, glorying in the wet heat he discovered. He brought it out to smear across her clit as he rubbed.

She buried a shriek in the crook of her arm.

"I got you, baby. I got you," he told her roughly.

He reached into his pocket and pulled out the condom he'd stashed there. With his teeth, he tore it open, keeping one hand clamped on her pussy. The old one-handed condom roll.

When he was completely sheathed, he set both hands on her hips and tilted her ass toward him. He pulled down her shorts and let his hands linger on the bare, pale skin of her ass. God, she was something. The light and shadows playing across the globes of her ass, and the valley between, were sheer erotic beauty. She should have posed for that damn Kama Sutra rug.

He slid a finger along the seam of her sex, capturing a trickle of moisture and the pulse of her excitement. His cock jumped in response to the incredible silky heat. Inside. He needed to be inside.

He guided himself to her entrance and paused there, giving her a chance to adjust her position. She widened her legs, tilted her hips. "Come on," she urged him in a voice like a hit of adrenaline. "Fuck me."

Damn.

He thrust inside, hard enough to make her jolt, but easy

enough to make her sigh. "Oh yes, that's amazing, Darius. Oh my God. Right there."

He found an angle that hit a spot he knew she liked—he'd catalogued it the other night. He added pressure on her lower belly with his right hand. *There.* That was the spot. Pinned between his cock and a hard hand. *Thrust. Thrust again.* Grit his teeth against the crazy pleasure that tried to capsize him before they reached their peak. Thrust again. Nibble her earlobe. Growl random words in her ear. *Fucking hot. Come, baby. Come hard. I can do this all night, honey. And I will. I'll fuck you so long and hard we won't leave this house for a week.*

When she finally exploded, she let out a cry of ecstasy that she forgot to muffle. She quickly bit it off into a series of whimpers as her body pulsed around him. Her tight muscular channel gripped him hard, demanding everything from him.

And he gave it to her. Every bit of him. The orgasm detonated through him with blinding force. He clamped his jaw shut against the shout that tried to burst from his chest. *Holy hell,* he wanted to yell. *Holy frickin' hell.*

When they came back to themselves, he drew up her shorts and rolled the condom off his penis. "Stay right where you are," he whispered in her ear. She spread her arms wide against the wall and leaned against it.

"You melted all my bones. I'm stuck here." She looked so adorably sleepy that he grinned. He ducked into the bathroom and disposed of the condom. He looked at himself in the mirror and almost didn't recognize the crazy-eyed, wildly satisfied man he saw there. When was the last time he'd looked that alive? That *happy* to be alive?

Probably around the time that Dylan was being conceived.

He came back to the hallway and heard a soft snore from Kate's limp form. Had she actually fallen asleep with her face against a wall? That would take a special talent. Along with all her other special talents.

Gently, he peeled her off the wall and tucked an arm under her knees. He lifted her off her feet and strode toward her bedroom.

"I wasn't actually snoring," she murmured against his chest. "That was a joke."

"It was a cute one. Very cute. But I'm still carrying you to bed."

"You just really like carrying me to beds. Admit it." Her sleepy demand made him smile.

"I have no problem admitting that. I'll carry you to bed any time you want."

"Works for me."

He tumbled her onto the mattress where they'd spent so many blissful hours. She reached for him, beckoning, so he stretched out next to her.

"I should probably get back. Early morning tomorrow."

"Just snuggle with me for a minute," she murmured.

He cupped his body around hers, like a bear protecting a cub. She wriggled her body to get into the perfect comfy position. "How are you so warm and snuggly-riffic?"

"Snuggly-riffic?"

"Mmm, hmm. Snuggly-riffic," she repeated. "Cuddle-tastic. You're even better than a weighted blanket."

He chuckled deeply. "Never heard that before. I hear good things about weighted blankets."

"Yeah, well, they can't fuck like you do. They can't make me feel the things you do. No one makes me feel the things you do. No one ever has."

In the hush of the night, those quiet words held nothing but blunt truth. The kind of truth Kate might not be willing to share if she wasn't half-asleep.

In the morning, would she even remember that she'd said them? Would he?

Hell yes, he would. He wasn't likely to ever forget those words in Kate's husky voice.

"Same," he said gruffly. He could say more than that, but he didn't have her way with words. Hell, she'd just invented some new ones off the top of her head. He liked to demonstrate rather than explain, and as far as he was concerned, he'd shown her exactly how he felt—with his body.

Maybe in time he'd say more. He was patient.

He heard another soft snore, and smiled to himself. Good thing he hadn't taxed his brain to come up with the perfect words. They would have been wasted on her sleeping ears.

He nestled closer to her. He should probably go back downstairs. If he fell asleep here, he'd never want to leave.

The next day was a Saturday, and he didn't have to work. For once, he wanted to be around when Dylan woke up. Make him breakfast, hear how things were going with his community service.

Maybe give him a hockey lesson. Hockey skills would go a long way toward making the Lost Harbor kids accept him.

Despite his best intentions, sleep dragged down his eyelids. He was almost entirely under when Kate spoke again.

"I almost forgot." She sounded drunk with sleep. "My old firm called and offered me my job back. Imagine that."

He waited for more, his breath caught in his chest. Was she leaving? Heading back to the Kingdom of Cities? Why wouldn't she? She'd always had one foot out the door.

Another snore told him he wasn't getting an answer tonight. *Well, hell.*

He slid out of her bed and dressed, then padded down the outdoor stairs into the dawning blue of the next day.

CHAPTER THIRTY

The Olde Salt Saloon always smelled as if they served turpentine and varnish on tap. With a garnish of sea kelp and a whiff of stale beer. It had always smelled that way, as far as Kate could remember.

She and Maya and another friend, Toni, had talked their way into the Olde Salt when they were sixteen and just wanted to see what all the fuss was about. Maya had walked out in disgust. Kate had struck up an entertaining conversation with a deckhand from Dutch Harbor. And Toni—for some strange reason—had decided she wanted to bartend there some day.

"Hola, stranger." She poured Kate a shot of something amber and unnamed from a flask. "Haven't seen you in a hundred years."

"I've been living that ancient curse, may you live in interesting times."

"Tell me all. The real story, not the gossip I pick up from the motley crew here." She wrinkled her forehead at the weathered and whiskered fishermen slouched at the bar. You could always tell a fisherman because they never quite lost that faraway horizon gaze—and they often had a stray fish scale or a bloodstain somewhere on their clothing.

"I want to hear the gossip first." Kate tossed back the shot, which was strong enough to be either varnish or turpentine, but was probably some kind of whiskey. "It's only fair."

"Oh no, the gossip is just plain unbelievable." Toni grabbed the bottle and scooted farther down the bar, out of earshot of the others. "I'm off the clock," she called to the fishermen. "You're on the honor system."

Kate followed her into the dark shadows at the far end of the bar. It was mid-afternoon and outside the sun was blazing. Not California blazing—it was still only around fifty degrees. But warm and very welcome. Even so, here in the Olde Salt it could have been a winter night. The Olde Salt knew no seasons.

"Does that actually work? The honor system?"

"Yes, because they know I'll kick their asses if they abuse it. Or at least ban them from the Olde Salt, which would be like death to these guys." She splashed another shot into the glass. Toni was a badass in her own right. She'd studied martial arts and had once broken up a bar brawl involving three competing oil tanker crews. Maya might know everyone in Lost Harbor, but Toni knew all their darkest secrets.

She also knew to keep them to herself, which was why people confided in her. That, and because they were drunk.

Kate took a sip and made a face. "What is this?"

"Truth serum. Now spill, Naughty Kate. Are you really sleeping with the super-hot fire chief?"

Kate spluttered the rest of her mouthful of "truth serum" into a napkin and decided to bluff it out. "Seriously? *Seriously? That's* what people are saying?"

"Okay, so that one's obviously true."

So much for bluffing.

Just then, Jessica slid onto the stool next to Kate. Her bright smile and auburn ponytail could have been a sunbeam lighting up the dark bar. "What's obviously true? If we're talking about Kate and Darius, someone needs to fill me in."

"Oh cripes." Kate dropped her forehead onto her folded forearms. "This is why I like cities. No one knows who you are or gives a crap about you."

"Oh, don't be such a baby. Woman up. Who cares what people say?" Toni gestured at the degenerate group farther down the bar. "Just look at them."

It wasn't so much that she cared what people said about her. She'd given up on that long ago. It was the idea that she and Darius hadn't been existing in their own personal universe all by themselves. Other people had noticed. "I'm just not used to it, I guess," she muttered into her forearms. "I like my privacy."

Jessica gave her shoulder a comforting squeeze. "Then maybe you shouldn't have hooked up with the intriguing and wildly attractive new fire chief. Just food for thought. But I suppose it's too late now, right? It's pretty hot and heavy, or so I hear from my morning muffin customers."

Kate made a face at her. "You're just as bad as Toni. Something I never thought I'd say."

Toni laughed as she added another finger of whisky to Kate's glass. "So just how hot and heavy is it? That's what we really want to know. No one can hear. It's just us. Your summer sisterhood."

Finally, Kate straightened up. "Very hot. Very heavy." A dreamy smile spread across her face. "So very hot and heavy. Quite down and dirty too. Some wild and crazy thrown in."

"Wow." Jessica sighed and gestured for the bottle. Toni handed it to her and she took a long guzzle. "Gosh, that's vile."

"Yup. Have some more."

"Okay." She took another sip. With a revolted face, she pushed the bottle back to Toni. "You should pour that into a burn barrel and start a bonfire." She turned back to Kate. "You have all the luck. You waltz into Lost Harbor and snag the hottest new guy in town. I've been hearing some crazy things at the bakery."

"Me too," said Toni. "I keep telling people they shouldn't spread such ridiculous rumors, but you know how people are. What have you heard, Jess?"

"Someone said Darius just found out he has a son he never knew about."

"Yup, heard that one."

They both looked at Kate. "That's true," she admitted.

"Whoa." Toni's green eyes widened. "But it can't possibly be true that his son has been setting all the fires around here."

Kate glanced around the Olde Salt making sure they couldn't be overheard. "That part's true too, but please don't say anything."

"Oof." Jessica winced. "Well, that's certainly an awkward situation for a fire chief."

"Dylan is...a little troubled. He's had a rough time. Mother, stepfather...anyway, I shouldn't say anything more. The situation is being handled. Dylan—that's Darius' son—has been doing community service at the firehouse." She shouldn't even say that much. But she trusted her friends. "Anything else in the rumor mill? Are we up to speed now?"

Jessica rested her elbow on the bar and propped her head on her hand. "Here's one. Is it true you might be going back to LA?"

"*What?*" This time she was genuinely blown away. She'd just barely gotten the offer a few days ago. "People know about that? How is that possible?"

Jessica laughed and put a comforting hand on her arm. "Don't worry, no one else knows about that one. I was setting up a flower delivery schedule with Emma and she seemed very upset. I asked her what was wrong and got an earful."

"Whew." Kate let out a breath of relief. "I was starting to

wonder if there was a surveillance camera in my house. It's true, my old law firm invited me to come back."

She still savored every second of that phone call, which she'd memorized word for word. *"We were highly impressed with your testimony in the Kramer case and have come to see that you behaved ethically under the circumstances. We'd like you to consider coming back to work for us. Take a few days to decide."*

After she'd finished dancing across her Kama Sutra carpet hooting with triumph, the other side of the equation set in.

Darius. She wasn't ready to leave Darius.

"I haven't decided yet," she told her friends.

Toni cocked her head and folded her arms across her chest. "I know you, Kate. You're trying to be logical about it. What are the pros and cons?"

"The pros are that I'd get my old life back. I'd have to find a new place to live and buy a new car, but at least I'd be practicing law again. The cons are..." She hesitated. The biggest one—besides leaving Darius—was that she still wasn't sure LA was safe for her. But her friends didn't know about that part. "I'd miss the peony harvest, and I promised Emma I would help. But with S.G. and Dylan and a few other helpers, she can manage without me."

"She'd miss you," said Jessica softly.

Her heart twisted with regret. "She would. And I'd miss her. I'd miss you guys too. But I can always come visit, so that doesn't seem like a big deal." She made a weighing gesture with her two hands, with one hand coming way up, the other all the way under the bar. "High-paying legal job versus part-time peony farmer. Honestly, logically, there's not much to debate here."

"No no." Jessica waved both her hands, as if wiping away those words. "This isn't a situation for logic. It's about gut instinct. What is your heart telling you? Not your brain."

"My heart is too busy pumping blood through my body to have an opinion," Kate said dryly.

"Do you want me to consult my pendulum for you?" Jessica offered. "I get very reliable guidance from it."

Toni snorted and gave an epic eye roll. "Don't get her started on her pendulum, Kate. Just let me ask you this. Do you want to be a peony farmer for the rest of your life?"

"No, but—"

"That's not the right question." Jessica interrupted with a frown for Toni. "You know that saying, 'Even if I could go back, I wouldn't belong there anymore'? Everything you said was about 'getting your old life back.' But is that really what you want? If you ask me, you're not the same Kate Robinson anymore."

"It's only been a couple of months."

"Time is irrelevant. It's more about the soul growth you've gone through. "

Toni wagged a finger at Jessica. "How many times do I have to tell you the Olde Salt is a no-soul-growth zone? I'll pour tequila on that shit."

"Someday, Toni Tequila, you're going to come begging to consult my pendulum," said Jessica, tossing her head so her long auburn hair caught the dim light. "That will be one of the happiest days of my life."

Kate burst out laughing. "I love you guys, but this is a decision I have to make by myself."

"Of course you do," Jessica said soothingly. "We're just here for support."

"And shots," added Toni, picking up the bottle.

"Oh, I'm done." Kate covered her glass with her hand. "Any more and I'll be singing sea shanties to a spider, the way Old Crow used to."

They launched into stories from their summer boardwalk days, but in the back of her mind, Kate was still sorting through pros and cons and gut instincts.

After they'd all said goodbye, Kate took a walk down one of

the ramps that led to the boat slips. The vessels ranged from vast iron-sided fishing tenders to one-person wooden skiffs, with a few speedboats and sailboats mixed in. There were even a number of houseboats releasing puffs of smoke from their smokestacks.

The float rose and fell with the ocean, as if it was breathing deep and slow. She found its motion highly soothing. It lulled all the thoughts that had been swarming her brain since she'd gotten the call from her law firm. None of that mattered right now.

All that mattered was the scent of salt and tar that rose from the harbor. The overhead caw of a seabird. The excited laugh of a child wrapped tight in an orange life preserver onboard a water taxi. The breath of the wind against her cheek, with that edge of cold from passing across the glaciers of Lost Souls Wilderness.

A seagull lighted on a post up ahead and settled its wings into place. It gazed down at her with a tilt of its head.

"Sorry, I have no food." She spread her hands apart. "I'm just passing through."

It cocked his head the other direction, still looking at her.

"But if you need legal advice, I'm here for you," she added.

With a noisy flap of its wings, it launched into the air, wheeled around and headed across the harbor.

"I really know how to clear a room," she murmured under her breath. The seagull joined a flock of other gulls who were circling a fishing boat just gliding into the harbor. Funny how they had their own community up there in the sky. A society of seagulls, mostly oblivious to the society of people down below in Lost Harbor—unless they could provide food, of course.

Speaking of community, in some ways, Lost Harbor was the only one she had. With her chaotic childhood, she'd never felt connected to any place except this one. When her life had gotten turned upside down, she'd fled back here, because where else would she go? Lost Harbor had always been a haven for her.

But now that she had a job waiting for her in LA, she wasn't sure she wanted to leave. Even if she could guarantee her own safety, there was something else she kept thinking about—Dylan and S.G., and how she could use her legal skills here to advocate for kids like them, kids who didn't have adults looking out for them.

She would really love that kind of work. And she could do it here. She could study her ass off for yet another bar exam. Once she'd passed the Alaska bar, she could set up a law office here in Lost Harbor. What's-his-name was retiring, after all. There was always a need for lawyers, even in a little town like this.

The best part was, she wouldn't have to say goodbye to Darius before she was ready. When she'd told him about the job offer, he hadn't reacted. He hadn't asked her to stay. Why would he? They'd never talked about the nature of their relationship.

If she stayed here, they wouldn't have to. She wouldn't even have to tell him she'd rejected the job offer. She wouldn't have to make a big deal out of it. They could just...keep going. Keep spending nights together. Keep having amazing sex. Keep getting closer. Keep avoiding any mention of deeper emotions. Nothing would have to change.

Perfect for a Team Sex non-romantic like her.

She laughed out loud and danced down the float. Maybe it was the influence of Toni's weird shots, or maybe it was the relief of making a decision. She wasn't ready to go back to LA and that was the end of that.

Even if she took Darius out of the equation, she wasn't ready. Emma needed her. As much as her feisty grandmother didn't want to admit it, she couldn't handle the entire harvest by herself, even with her helpers. Summer was almost here and Kate didn't want to miss a minute of it.

She pulled out her phone to communicate her decision to her law firm before she could spend any more time agonizing about it.

CHAPTER THIRTY-ONE

"This is a hockey stick. That's a puck. The net's thataway. You hit the puck with the stick into the net, no matter who tries to stop you, and that's all you need to know about hockey." Darius handed the stick to Dylan. The boy was gingerly testing the ice with the new hockey skates Darius had bought for him.

They'd finally made it to the Lost Harbor ice rink for Dylan's first hockey lesson. Darius had started to suspect that his son was avoiding the rink, but how could that be possible? What could be more fun than hockey?

"You skipped the part where I get good at skating," Dylan grumbled.

"I'm surprised your mom didn't teach you. She and I used to skate at a rink in El Paso. She was great on skates. She used to dream about being a figure skater."

"I didn't know that." Dylan slipped and clutched at the boards. "Sorry."

"It's okay. Take your time. Get your skates under you, as they say. I'm gonna go say hi to some folks."

Dylan nodded, his attention on the patch of ice right before him. Darius struck out across the rink to join Nate and Zander and a few others from the amateur team.

Maybe he was rushing it with this hockey thing, but he was just so eager to find a surefire way to bond with the kid.

"How's it going, Dad?" Nate asked as Darius swirled to a stop next to them.

"Not too bad." He glanced back at Dylan and winced as the boy wobbled again. "Skating might not be our thing. But we're getting on okay. I want to get him into school, but it's too late for this year. I need to line up a summer tutor so he can catch up."

Zander paused in the midst of wrapping tape around his wrist. "So he's staying on through the summer?"

"Maybe. I'm working it out with his stepfather back in Texas. Buck's glad to have Dylan off his hands, at least for now."

"And he wants to stay? He doesn't miss his friends?" Nate asked.

Darius didn't know the answer to that. Should he? Why didn't Dylan talk about that stuff? "He doesn't say much about what he wants. Zander, you know about boys. How can I get him to talk to me?"

Zander was raising his two younger brothers. Now that he'd gotten engaged to Gretel Morrison, he had help; but for years he'd been on his own.

Zander mulled that over as he tugged on his gloves. "You could bring him up to our place sometime. We just set up a basketball net. Sometimes things slip out."

Darius smiled gratefully at the younger man. Zander was an ex-Marine and still had that posture that screamed military. He had a lot of respect for what the guy had done, leaving his career and taking on the care of his brothers. "We'll do that. I'll talk to Dylan about it. You guys are right, he could use some friends."

Nate tap-tapped his stick on the ice in one of his warmup

exercises. "I know S.G. likes him. A lot. I believe it's a first-crush kind of situation."

"No doubt. I don't ask about that."

Nate gestured for him to take a position a few yards away, and they began passing the puck back and forth. "Darius, I gotta warn you about something. I've overheard some talk at the firehouse. A few of the volunteers aren't happy about...well, about Dylan."

"What do you mean?" Darius slapped the puck back to Nate, who had to scramble backwards to stop it.

"They feel like he's getting off easy with just community service. He admits that he set all those fires. We were lucky no one got hurt."

Darius' stomach clenched with tension. He didn't give a crap about people's opinions about himself. But when it came to Dylan—that was different.

"He's a minor. He's doing community service and restitution. Hasn't missed a day. What do they think should happen?"

"I'm just letting you know that I've heard some whispering. That's it. Don't jump down my throat."

Darius shook off his anger. Nate was right. He shouldn't shoot the messenger here.

A crash from the other side of the rink made them all turn around. Dylan was sprawled face down on the ice as a younger boy skated away from him. Darius recognized him as the son of one of the volunteer firefighters. That kid was an ace hockey player who played on the peewee team. He was too skilled to have tripped Dylan by accident.

"Hey!" Darius skated across the ice toward Dylan and crouched next to him. "You okay?"

"Yeah." He planted his hands on the ice and pushed himself up. Darius took his hands and gently turned them palms up.

They were scraped and bloodied. "Whose genius idea was it to ride on top of a pair of knife blades?"

Darius helped him to his feet. "Did that boy trip you? What happened?"

Dylan refused to answer, which Darius took as a "yes."

"I'll talk to his father. That's not okay."

"No!" Dylan shook Darius' hand off his shoulder. "Don't. It's a scrape. It's no big deal. I just need to get these stupid-ass skates off my feet."

He managed to skate toward the gate well enough, and stomped off the ice.

Darius planted his hands on his hips and circled the ice to cool himself down. Maybe it was an accident. Maybe the kid hadn't intended to trip anyone.

But he had to face facts. Even before Nate had mentioned the "whispers," he'd noticed something was off. There was a coolness in the way the crew treated him. Nothing blatant, nothing disobedient. Nothing that would require disciplinary action. But noticeable.

Maya had warned him the town might take a while to forgive Dylan. But how could he just stand by and watch his son get shunned?

He mentioned the problem to Kate while they were snuggled in each other's arms that night.

Things had been a little strange between him and Kate since she'd dropped her bombshell about her old law firm wanting her back. He hadn't pushed her about it.

He didn't want her to leave, but how could he ask her to stay? *Please, Kate, I wish you'd stick around for the great sex and the fucking confusing new parenthood scene. Sounds fun, right? Even more fun than being a hotshot lawyer with a fancy car?Yeah, thought so.*

Instead of some bullshit like that, he'd decided to wait and see what she decided. If he had to deal with her leaving, he would. But he wasn't going to do that until he absolutely had to.

In the meantime, he kept sneaking upstairs every chance he got.

"Kate, you still awake?"

"Mmm-hmmm. Sort of." He loved the way she looked when she was half asleep after one of their intense lovemaking sessions. Stretched next to him with her dark hair in an inky fan across the pillow, her curvy limbs relaxed and content.

"You've been coming to Lost Harbor for a long time. Do you think people are going to get past what Dylan did?"

One shoulder moved in a shrug. "Like, what people? There are some grudge-holders around here. Some of the fishermen's feuds have been going on for decades. But Dylan's just a kid. Who holds a grudge against a kid?"

"That's true." He rolled onto his back and stared up at the ceiling. Dylan was still a minor, a few months from turning sixteen. But with that attitude of his, he wasn't making many friends beyond S.G.. "The thing is, he isn't from here. No one knows him. All they know about him is that he set some junky sheds on fire."

"I got into tons of trouble around here when I was an angry kid. I smoked weed under the boardwalk. I shoplifted. I snuck into the Olde Salt. I spray-painted an octopus on the boardwalk."

"An octopus?"

"I had a thing about octopuses. I used to cry when people ordered calamari because squid are related to octopuses. Anyway, the point is, I got into plenty of trouble when I was his age. I was forgiven. No one even remembers that stuff anymore except for Maya. She's still mad about all the times she covered for me."

"The town forgave you because Emma's your grandmother."

"Probably."

"Dylan doesn't have an Emma. All he has is me. And I'm

pretty new around here myself. I thought I was in good standing with this town. But my own crew is giving me the side-eye."

Kate sleepily patted his chest. He covered her hand with his, trapping its warmth against his heart. "Give it time. Lost Harbor's a small town and people are protective. But they love you here. You're the hottie fire chief."

He snorted and traced her fingers with his. "Never heard that one before."

"It's more of a behind-the-back thing. Anyway, don't worry about Dylan. It's just going to take a little time."

He fell silent for a moment, turning her words over in his mind. "Maybe, but is that fair to Dylan?" He spoke almost to himself more than to her. "He's been through so much. I'm not excusing his actions, but I have to take some responsibility for them because I'm his father and I wasn't there for him."

A snore interrupted him. Apparently he'd put Kate to sleep with his middle-of-the-night worries. He kept talking anyway, because it felt good to get it all out there.

"Dylan must have grown up wondering about his real father and what kind of person I am. I bet he thought all kinds of shit about me because Gillian chose Buck O'Connor over me. Who knows what she told him? He doesn't talk about that. And then she died and he was alone with a stepfather who never really cared about him. The amount of grit it took to travel by himself all the way to Lost Harbor, Alaska, it's pretty fucking incredible. I owe him, Kate. I owe him the best I can give him at this point in his life, now that I've found him. Is it fair to make him live surrounded by people who think the worst of him?"

He didn't need an answer from Kate to know what his own heart was telling him.

Now that he knew about Dylan, he had to make him top priority. He had to do his absolute best for the boy—whatever that was.

A COUPLE OF DAYS LATER, Dylan came home with a bruise on his jaw. He slumped onto the couch and refused to say what had happened.

Darius experienced a wave of so much fury that he stuck his head in the freezer to cool off while he grabbed an ice pack. Sure, he'd gotten plenty of bruises in his life. But his son? This confusing troubled thin teenager who had found a place in his heart so quickly?

He couldn't bear it. He'd seen enough. The idea that had been percolating through his thoughts ever since the incident at the hockey ring suddenly seemed like the only option.

Darius retrieved the ice pack and brought it to Dylan to hold against the bruise.

"Dylan, I have an idea."

"What?" he asked indifferently. Sullen, as if nothing was really going to make a difference in his life.

"What do you think about moving to Texas?"

"*What?*"

Finally, he got the boy's attention. All his indifference disappeared as he sat bolt upright on the couch. "What are you talking about?"

"I'm talking about us moving to Texas."

"But—you live here. You're the fire chief."

"Yeah, well, it's not like I'm a statue. I can move."

"To Texas?"

"I am from Texas, after all." He gave his son a wry frown. "That's where you came to exist."

Dylan adjusted the ice pack, which had gotten dislodged by his sudden movement. "You're going to quit your job?"

"Yeah. I'm going to quit my job. I'll find another one in Texas. People do that all the time, you know. I've only had this job for a year or so. Nate's ready, he can handle it. Or the town will do a search for someone from outside. The point is, I'm going to Texas, and I want you to come with me. I want you to live with me. We'd have to work it out with Buck, of course. You have what, one more year of high school?"

"Two, after this year."

"Right." God, he should know that. He *did* know that. He'd just forgotten. He had to do better about staying on top of the details of Dylan's life. Dentist appointments and hockey games, that sort of thing. Except maybe not hockey. Baseball, football, whatever. This was going to be his life now. Taking the best care possible of this grieving boy. "Don't you want to be back in Texas for those two years instead of in a strange town with kids you don't know?"

"I guess."

"You didn't intend to move to Alaska, right? You came to find me. What was your plan after that?"

"I didn't really have one. I didn't think—" A strange expression came across the boy's face. "You'd really do that? Move to Texas on my account?"

"Yes," Darius answered simply, arms folded across his chest. "I would. I will. Right away. They don't even need much notice at the firehouse. Nate can step in today if needed."

"I thought you liked it here."

"I do. But Texas...my family's there. They'd love to get to know you. Gillian's family, too. I bet they'd be happier if you were closer."

Try as he might, he couldn't get a read on Dylan's reaction to this plan.

"I've been thinking about it the past few days. Seems to make sense. At first I thought you should stay the summer. But when I saw you with that bruise, I changed my mind."

Dylan looked away, toying with the ice pack. "That doesn't matter."

"It does to me." His firm tone seemed to take the boy by surprise.

He stayed quiet for a moment, thinking his own mysterious thoughts. Maybe one day his son would share things with him; Darius would keep working on that. The kid needed to express himself instead of doing shit like starting fires.

"But what about Kate?" he finally asked.

The boy had put his finger on the one single biggest flaw in this proposal. Leaving Kate would be excruciatingly hard. But she'd made it clear that this wasn't anything serious for her. It was a fun sex-drenched diversion. She enjoyed him, but she didn't *need* him. This grieving, troubled son of his did.

"Kate's got her own thing going on. She's probably moving back to LA."

"Really? S.G. didn't tell me. Neither did Emma. I was working at the farm yesterday and they didn't say anything."

"They probably don't know yet. Kate's been pretty quiet about it, so don't say anything to them."

"Okay."

"Anyway, it's not serious between us. We're both adults and we didn't go into this looking for romance."

Even though that was true, it didn't feel like the whole truth. Things had changed for him and it was going to hurt like hell to say goodbye. She had no idea how much it would hurt, and he didn't plan to tell her. If he'd fallen in love with her, that was his own damn fault.

No ifs about it. He *had* fallen in love with her. But he'd take that secret with him back to Texas.

"Maybe she could come with us," Dylan said, surprising him.

"You like Kate, huh?"

"Yeah. She's kind of my lawyer. She never looks at me all judgy like some people do."

Another testimonial to the amazingness of Kate. "She's pretty damn cool. But like I said, she's doing her own thing. She's a California girl. You should hear her go on about brunch."

He stepped closer to Dylan and dropped a hand on his shoulder. "Anyway, this decision is about you. You and me."

Dylan looked up with one of his sudden, rare smiles. "I still can't believe you'd move for me."

The stunned wonder in his voice made Darius want to hit something. Had the boy been an afterthought his whole life? Hadn't anyone ever put him first?

He remembered some of the things Kate had said about her childhood, and suddenly understood why she and Dylan had hit it off so well. She understood Dylan in a way he probably never would.

"Believe it, kid." He hesitated, searching for the right words. "I'm late to this father thing, so I have to make up for it. And I'm going to. From now on, I'm a father first, before anything else. Understand?" He didn't want to get sappy, but he needed Dylan to know he was serious.

Dylan nodded, his wide eyes glued to Darius' face.

Darius squeezed his shoulder again, then added lightly, "We might want to find another sport besides hockey, though."

"Yeah." Dylan pulled away the ice pack and handed it back to him. "Or maybe we can skip the sports. Kate said you're a good bass player. I was learning guitar before Mom died, but I didn't bring it with me. Maybe..."

"Say no more." Darius pulled out his phone and punched in the name of Lost Harbor's only music store. "We'll find you a guitar. We can have a jam session with Harris Badger, he's a kickass fiddle player. He and I play backup for Gretel sometimes—"

He broke off as it occurred to him that there would be no more Lost Harbor jam sessions for him. No more Lost Harbor Puffins, either. No more bantering with the local police chief. No more town council meetings. No more hanging out at Gretel's Cafe or the Olde Salt. No more Lost Harbor at all.

And worst of all, exponentially worse, unimaginably worse—no more Kate.

CHAPTER THIRTY-TWO

Whistling, Kate reached into the back of the Ford truck for one of the new raspberry canes that Emma had ordered. Since peonies bloomed year after year—sometimes as long as seventy years—no more new bushes were needed. To scratch her planting itch, her adventurous grandma had decided to try some raspberries. It was a bright sunshiny day and they'd be better off under cover, out of the brilliant sun, until they could be planted.

It was a time-sensitive task, and Emma was in town at a doctor's appointment, and neither S.G. nor Dylan was available. Perfect timing for Darius to show up and lend a hand.

But as soon as she caught sight of his sober expression, she knew something was wrong. He didn't have to say those lovely words, "We need to talk." They were written all over his face.

And then other words were coming from his mouth, but the world had turned strange and surreal and she barely took them in.

Moving to Texas. With Dylan. Leaving in a few days.

A few days.

Leaving.

Leaving her. As if their relationship meant nothing. As if *she* meant nothing.

"Wow, big news," she managed. On autopilot, she lifted a burlap-wrapped cane from the bed of the truck and set it into the red wheelbarrow.

"We just decided this morning. I wanted to tell you right away."

She barely heard him. This feeling—this horrible helpless rejected feeling—it was so familiar. She'd grown up with it and she knew exactly how to handle it.

Make it not matter.

She and Darius had no commitment to each other. They'd never spoken about a future together. They were both jaded grownups who knew the drill. It didn't matter if he left. *But it hurts.*

Make it not matter.

She could do this. Cool under pressure, that was her. *Bluff your way through. Fake it until you make it.*

"S.G.'s going to miss Dylan," she said. Her voice sounded strange to her own ears, but hopefully not to his.

Darius studied her for a moment, while she schooled her expression as if she were facing a Superior Court judge. *Show nothing. No weakness. No vulnerability.*

"We're hoping she can visit." Stepping to her side, Darius grabbed two of the raspberry canes, one under each arm, and loaded them into the wheelbarrow.

Oh sure. Visit. S.G. could visit. That's who they were worried about.

Feeling almost savage, Kate stalked back to the truck. "Sounds fun. I'm sure she'd love to see another part of the country. Especially one that's so different from Alaska. I doubt she's ever experienced temperatures above seventy. Should be quite the adventure—" She broke off as Darius put a hand on her arm and spun her around. "Hey!"

"Are you upset, Kate?" The softness in his deep voice nearly made her snap.

"Upset? Why would I be upset? I'm sure S.G. would love that."

Something flinched across his face, and she realized that some of her inner fury was leaking out.

"Maybe you could come with her." A tentative suggestion, nothing more.

"Maybe. Like a chaperone or something. She certainly can't travel by herself, she's never been on an airplane. I'll consider that." His touch on her arm felt like torture, all that warmth and strength that would never be hers again.

She freed her arm and returned to unloading the truck.

"Kate..."

"Yes, Darius?"

"It's not...it has nothing to do with...that is..." He dragged one hand through his thick hair, leaving a smudge of potting soil on his forehead.

She could guess what he was trying to say, but she refused to help him out. If he was going to spring this on her, the least he could do was express it in his own words.

"I have to do what seems best for Dylan."

"Of course you do." Her fierceness seemed to take him by surprise.

"Then you aren't...are you...okay with this?"

"Of course I am."

Of course she wasn't. *He was leaving,* without any warning at all. Just—up and leaving. After she'd let down all her protective shields and given him her trust. She never did that. *She knew better.*

On the other hand, the logical side of her agreed with his

decision. He'd just become a father without any warning at all. He was trying to readjust his life to that new reality. He wanted to do his best for the son he'd just discovered. He was trying to do the right thing, and that was Darius in a nutshell.

And she loved him for it. Loved him so much it hurt.

And hated him for it too, because *he was leaving.*

Grow up. She busied herself with a raspberry cane, her face shielded by the burlap sack. *This is how things go. We're not committed to each other. I don't know how he feels about me. I don't know how I feel about him.*

No, that was a lie. She knew exactly how she felt about him. She loved him. She loved him wildly and passionately. And most of all, she deeply, deeply respected him.

Which meant that she shouldn't make "doing the right thing" difficult for him. Using every speck of her willpower and self-composure, she forced her lips into a smile and straightened up to face him.

"I truly respect your decision, Darius. You're a good man. You're a good father. You're putting Dylan first and I completely support that. Without hesitation."

He absorbed her words, holding her gaze with a searching intensity that made her nervous. She didn't want him to see what was going on behind her calm facade. She didn't want him to second-guess his decision.

"You don't have to worry about me," she said brusquely. "I'm a big girl and we always knew this was just a..." She ran out of words at that point. "Thing," she ended weakly.

"Kate, it was never just a 'thing' to me." His deep voice, the voice that had offered her so much kindness and strength, so many hot, sexy growls, made this infinitely harder. She couldn't bear it. She had to put a stop to this.

"Well, it was to me. A fun thing. A very fun, sexy thing. But we've never talked about anything more than that. So please, like

I said, don't worry about me. We're good, you and me. It's all good."

His eyebrows drew together over his silvery eyes. Had she hurt him with her cavalier attitude? Could he tell it was completely fake?

The wheelbarrow couldn't hold any more raspberries, so she bent down to grab the handles. "When are you leaving, exactly?"

"As soon as we can. We're going to rent a van and drive the Al-Can Highway. I figure there's no better way to get to know each other than a road trip."

Next couple of days? So soon? With a sense of panic, she adjusted her grip on the wheelbarrow. This was happening so fast. Her heart couldn't keep up.

Her well-honed bravado skills came to her rescue. "Wow. You must be a speedy packer. It took me a week to leave LA."

He cleared his throat and tucked his hands in his back pockets. "I was thinking that we should spend as much time together as possible until I leave. You could stay with us. We could plan your first visit to Texas and—"

"No." That would be flat-out unbearable.

He gazed at her steadily, his gray eyes capturing hers.

"Let's not drag this out." She made an instant decision that felt like a lifeline. "I'm going to stay here on the farm and help Emma get these raspberries in. You guys take your time packing and planning your trip. There's no need for me to hang around for that."

She lifted the handles of the wheelbarrow and steered it down the path toward the high tunnel.

"Kate!" He strode after her, but she didn't turn around. "Please. Don't walk away. Let's—"

"Let's let it go." She paused the wheelbarrow and twisted to face him. "That's life in the big city. It's been a fun ride, Darius.

Let's not make it more than that. Let's move on down the road, okay?"

His eyes flared with emotion, but just then his phone rang. He glanced at it and swore. "Gotta take this."

"Goodbye, Darius. Have a great trip with Dylan."

She pushed forward, right into a patch of mud. The wheelbarrow's front tire slowed in the muck, but she shoved furiously through it.

The last thing she needed was a reenactment of their first meeting. She might completely lose it if that happened.

She made it through the mud with only a brief wobble. When she reached the high tunnel, she trundled the wheelbarrow through the opening in the plastic and fastened it behind her. If only she could deadbolt the plastic flap and pile furniture against it. She needed to be alone right now. Away from any temptation to show Darius how she really felt. Which was —heartbroken.

Darius had broken her heart.

She hadn't thought it was possible. She'd believed that all the tenderness had been drained from her heart by the time she filed for emancipation. Definitely by the time she got through law school. Most certainly by the time her father ruined her career.

But oh, how wrong she'd been. She'd fallen so hard and deep for Darius Boone that she had no idea how to get her heart back.

CHAPTER THIRTY-THREE

Three days after that maddening conversation with Kate, Darius completed the speediest packing job in history. He'd accomplished it by donating all his furniture to the Lost Harbor thrift store. The rest of his personal belongings he'd crammed into boxes and loaded into an RV called the "Sun Seeker."

He and Dylan had bought the Sun Seeker on Craigslist from a widower who had no use for it anymore. The two of them had driven it home and parked it in Kate's space in the driveway, then cleaned it from top to bottom.

Kate wasn't using her spot, after all. In fact, Kate hadn't come to the duplex once during their entire three-day packing spree.

She was moving on. Just like that.

He was trying to do the same thing. The long list of things to deal with before they hit the road helped. Every moment was occupied with meetings with the city council, the mayor, Nate Prudhoe, his crew, his hockey team, his music buddies.

Everyone expressed shock or distress over his decision, and most urged him to reconsider. It touched him that the town had accepted him so completely.

Only Harris Badger seemed unworried by this sudden move. "Eh, you'll be back," he said with a shrug. "I thought about leaving once. It didn't sit right, and I turned around when I reached Tok. We'll be seeing you again."

Darius shrugged and gave the man a hug anyway.

Saying goodbye to S.G. was the hardest part of all—not including Kate, obviously. That goodbye had been a total disaster. S.G.'s wasn't much better.

He took her to the Burger Queen drive-through, her favorite place for cheeseburgers. But she flat-out refused to accept that they were leaving.

"Dylan doesn't want to go," she kept saying. "He likes it here."

"I think he likes *you*, S.G.. Not the town."

She blinked her wide eyes at him as two spots of pink colored her cheeks.

"That's why we're hoping that you'll come to Texas for a visit."

But she was shaking her head with a panicked no. "I can't leave here. I don't want to leave here. I live here now and I can't leave." She put her burger down on the dashboard. "You can't make me, can you?"

"S.G., of course not. It's just an invitation." Slowly, her fear drained away and she picked up her cheeseburger again. "You really love Lost Harbor, don't you? You feel safe here."

"I don't ever want to leave," she said firmly.

He could understand that. Lost Harbor was the only safe haven she'd known after running away from that trapper. He could understand her attachment to the charming little spot clinging to the edge of the wilderness.

He loved it too. But what he wanted—or needed—didn't matter right now. Dylan was all that mattered.

As far as he could tell, Dylan was fully onboard with the road trip and the move back to Texas. He threw himself into every step of the process, from packing to acquiring road trip snacks.

Every night, after the busyness of the day, Darius lay in bed and thought about Kate. Where she was, what she was doing, what she was wearing, what she was thinking. He'd wake up in the middle of the night with the intense urge to text her, to beg her to see him one more time. To let him kiss her one more time.

Was this really the end? Was it really so easy for her to dismiss him from her life?

What if he opened his heart and told her just how deep his feelings for her went? What if he told her he...loved her?

But how fair was that when he'd made the decision to leave? And when he'd committed to putting Dylan first, no matter what he himself wanted?

So he turned his phone off and pulled a pillow over his head, knowing how absurd that was.

Sure, hide from his feelings for Kate. That would work.

BY THE TIME Departure Day arrived, he'd had three nights of rotten sleep. His eyes were gritty with fatigue as he packed up his bedding. The bed and mattress were staying put, to be picked up later by the thrift store.

Same with the couch, where Dylan slept. Except that it was empty. All of Dylan's things had already been packed in his backpack, which was propped against the couch.

He was probably saying one last goodbye to S.G., or having one last quad shot at Gretel's Cafe.

Darius carried the box containing his bedding and Dylan's backpack out to the RV. The Sun Seeker had a little kitchenette and a coffeemaker, along with the groceries they'd packed. But instead of wasting their road trip supplies, he decided to mosey down to Gretel's and join Dylan.

As he strolled the peaceful streets, he took deep breaths of the fresh Alaska air, so different from Texas humidity. If only he could bottle this up and take a whiff when he needed it. He nodded to a few people working in their front yards as he passed. Everywhere he looked, daffodils were blooming like splashes of earthbound sunshine.

Was Kate planting those raspberry canes? Was her hair falling out of its ponytail? Did she have mud on her shirt? Was she thinking about him?

Stop it.

No one at Gretel's had seen Dylan. He ordered a large coffee to go and quickly walked home, hoping the boy had reappeared. No sign of him at home either. His phone wasn't receiving texts, but that wasn't unusual. He had sketchy service from some company in Texas.

The upstairs apartment? Unlikely, but just in case, he jogged up the outdoor staircase and tapped on the door. No answer. He checked for the key that Kate used to leave under the mat, but it was gone.

Shoving aside all the hot memories of the time he'd spent behind that door, he ran back down the stairs.

Next theory: maybe Dylan was with S.G.. S.G.'s phone didn't pick up either, so he called Denaina, who called for S.G. to come to the phone.

S.G. came on the line, a little breathless. "I was learning how to jump rope. Did you ever try that?"

"Oh yeah. That's good exercise. Hey, have you seen Dylan?"

"No." Sadness filled her voice. "He said goodbye yesterday. I cried last night."

"I know what you mean. Okay, kiddo, if you see him, tell him to call me immediately."

"I will."

Shit. What now? This was starting to get strange. Dylan knew the plan to leave early. Should he reach out to Maya?

No, it was too soon to consider him officially "missing."

But he could call the firehouse. Between the fifteen of them, the volunteer firefighters had connections in all parts of the community.

He dialed Nate Prudhoe's number and explained the situation.

"We're on it," Nate said right away. "I'll get the word out to everyone. We have eyeballs everywhere in this town. We'll find him."

Darius hesitated to ask his next question. "I know he's not the most popular kid on the block—"

"Forget about that," Nate said forcefully. "He's a kid in Lost Harbor and that makes him our responsibility. Besides, he's been doing a good job with his community service. Putting up with a ration of shit, too. People are noticing. Don't worry, Darius. We got this. You do your thing. Have you called Petal to the Metal? He could be out there."

"Thanks, Nate. I'll do that. Let me know the second—"

"Of course." Already calling out instructions to someone, Nate hung up the phone.

Darius reached the driveway of the duplex, with the Sun Seeker poised for departure. The thought of the entire volunteer fire department fanning out to find Dylan moved him deeply.

What if he was wrong about the town? What if they would come to accept his son, with all his flaws and bad acts?

Never mind that, first he had to find the kid. Next step, Petal to the Metal.

Steeling himself, he called the farm's landline. Kate answered. The sound of her voice made his gut twist.

"Hi Kate, it's Darius. Have you or Emma seen Dylan today?"

"It's eight thirty in the morning." Judging by the extra huskiness in her voice, she hadn't slept well either.

"Yeah. Can't find him. Sorry to bother you, I'm sure he'll turn up."

"Wait." A rustling sound came from the other end of the line, then she spoke again. "Sorry, I had the cable wrapped around me. Landlines are such ancient relics, you know? So what's going on? You think Dylan's missing?"

He almost smiled at the image of her wrapped in the phone line—except he was too worried to actually smile. "Yes," he said simply.

"You're worried?"

He couldn't lie. "Yes. We were scheduled to leave this morning and—"

"Where are you?"

"Fairview Court, but—"

"I'm on my way."

Before he could object, tell her there was no need, she hung up.

Wild joy flooded through him. Kate was coming. He was going to lay eyes on her again. She was going to be next to him, at his side, lending her smarts and her fire and her spirit to the situation and that meant...it meant everything.

He checked inside the Sun Seeker again, but found no sign that Dylan had been in there. A quick run-through of his apartment offered no clues either. Every moment that passed, his fear ratcheted up.

It was the tail end of bear season, after all. Dylan could have had a run-in with a grizzly. He could be in the woods somewhere, bleeding out, in shock, with no service, or unconscious. Maybe he'd run into a porcupine and had quills stuck everywhere. Maybe—

Kate pulled up outside the house in Emma's old Saab and

flew out of the car. The sight of her tall form, with all that long dark hair and her worried bright eyes, sent a jolt of longing right down to his bones. She wore blue jeans and a gray knit top that clung to her curves.

God, how he wanted her. Still, even after she'd dismissed their relationship as a fun "thing."

"Any luck?" she asked, skidding to a stop next to him.

"No. It's the strangest thing. We were supposed to leave this morning, but when I woke up he was gone. His stuff was all packed up and ready to go. He just...vanished."

He filled her in on all the steps he'd taken to find the boy.

Kate listened closely, nodding at each point. "Okay, let's go through this logically. You said he was gone when you woke up. Did anything unusual happen overnight?"

"I didn't sleep well," he admitted. "Haven't for a few days."

She made a face at that. He noticed that she too had dark circles under her eyes. His guess was right; she hadn't been sleeping either.

"I finally fell asleep around three-thirty, I think. Slept hard after that." He frowned as something came back to him. "There might have been a noise. I woke up a little, then figured it was a dream."

"What sort of noise?"

He shrugged. "A thump, maybe? Not clear."

"What was the dream you were having?"

In bits and snatches, it came back to him. "Someone was falling down the stairs and I was trying to catch them. You. You were falling down the stairs. I tried to catch you but you kept slipping through my arms."

Her eyes widened and for a moment she looked as though she might cry. Then she took a step back and folded her arms across her chest. "Maybe you heard something on the stairs. Have you looked upstairs in my place?"

"I tapped on the door, but I don't have the key. I didn't get any answer when I knocked."

"I'll just run up and check inside. It'll just take a second, I'll be right back."

His phone rang; Nate calling. "Okay. I'll see what Nate has to say."

She ran up the blue-painted stairs and slipped through her door.

After she disappeared, he felt strange, as if he'd looked at the sun too long. And now all the light in the world had vanished.

CHAPTER THIRTY-FOUR

The second Kate stepped inside her door, a hand came over her mouth and someone manhandled her inside and shut the door behind her.

Terror froze her in place, her LA nightmares finally coming true. They'd finally snagged her, just when she'd stopped worrying.

"Damn, you're a troublesome bitch," the man growled in her ear. "Do you know how long I've been waiting up here for you to show up?"

She twisted in his grip and managed to peer up at him. He looked familiar, but she couldn't place him.

But the fact that she knew him from somewhere took some of the fear away. She tried to bite his hand, but he shifted to covering her mouth with his elbow.

"I have the kid tied up in the living room, so don't get any fucked-up ideas. Do what I say or I'll hurt him."

He dragged her into the living room. She tried to make as much noise as she could with her feet, just in case Darius could hear from outside.

Which of course he couldn't.

Dylan lay on his side on the rug, his hands tied behind his back, duct tape over his mouth. His eyes met Kate's, and he shook his head a little. He looked calm enough, though pale.

The man drew a gun from the back of his pants and pointed it at Dylan.

"You gonna be quiet now? If you are, I'll let you loose. If not, this kid's going to get it."

She nodded quickly, and he released her.

A knock sounded on the door. "Kate? Did you find him?" called Darius.

The man flicked the safety off the gun, which was still aimed at Dylan.

Damn it. If only she could yell for help, but she couldn't take a chance on Dylan getting hurt.

"Say he's not here. Say you'll be out in a while. Exactly those words. Nothing fancy."

She repeated his words exactly as commanded.

When Darius spoke again, she heard the coolness in his voice. He obviously thought she was abandoning the search. "All right then. Catch you later."

His footsteps sounded on the outdoor stairs, and then he was gone. Along with any chance of outside help. She was on her own, with Dylan's safety at stake.

She turned to the intruder. Salt-and-pepper hair, roughly good-looking features, avaricious eyes. He clicked the safety back on, but didn't put the gun away.

"Who are you?" she demanded. "What do you—" Suddenly she recognized him. "You work for my father. You're his servant. The one with the costume."

"I wouldn't put it exactly that way, but yeah, I work with your father."

"God, I should have figured. One of his criminal buddies?

You just made things so much worse for yourself. Assaulting a minor. Kidnapping. Assaulting *me*."

In his smooth smirk, she recognized the smile of a con man. "Guess that makes your job that much harder."

"My job? What are you talking about?" She gestured toward Dylan. "Obviously this has nothing to do with him. Just let the boy go and we can talk about what you want."

"The boy got himself into this. He came after me when he should have minded his business. Didn't even have his phone with him. Now he's my insurance policy. He's going to stay right where he is until we're outta here."

We? Why did this man keep talking as if they were in this together?

"This is absurd. If my dad wanted something why didn't he just call me?" A possible answer occurred to her. "They're monitoring his communications. So he sent you."

"Stop talking like he's in charge. He's not."

"Does he know you're here?"

"Look, I'm not here to hurt you."

Since he didn't answer her question directly, she had to figure her father knew. And man, did that sting. Even if this intruder didn't want to "hurt" her—he'd already done it.

"Why are you here?"

"You gave us no choice. We need more legal help."

God, it was like being caught in quicksand and never being able to get out. This was the feeling that had driven her to emancipate herself, to go to law school, to change her path. Was it all hopeless? Every step she'd taken in life, erased?

She folded her arms across her chest. "I already told Frank I was done. No more legal help."

"It's not for him. He's all set, not like the rest of us. You'll get plenty out of the deal. Big bucks. Clients out your ass. I'm first, though."

"You can't make me represent you guys. That's...coercion."

"That's real life. You don't have a choice." He indicated Dylan with his gun again.

He wouldn't really hurt Dylan, would he? Frank wouldn't do something like that, but she didn't know this guy. She couldn't take a chance.

She quickly ran through her options. No weapon. Dylan in danger. Her only advantage seemed to be that this man needed her alive. Needed her legal skills.

"What's your name?" she asked him. "If I'm going to represent you, I'll need that info."

"Steve."

Steve. It seemed like such an innocuous name for a hostage-taking criminal.

"Okay, Steve. Speaking as your potential lawyer, you need to let this boy go. You made a big mistake grabbing him. Everyone's looking for him. The entire town of Lost Harbor is searching. His father is pacing the driveway out there, worried out of his mind. Did you know his father is the fire chief?"

"I know, I know," Steve grumbled. "He told me. He wasn't part of the plan, but now he is."

"This so-called plan of yours, walk me through it?"

The word "so-called" made him give her the side-eye. "We're going to leave together and you're going to tell everyone your father is sick and needs you. As soon as we're on a plane back to civilization, you're going to call someone and tell them about this kid."

"They'll arrest you at the airport."

"At least I'll have my lawyer with me." He offered that obnoxious con-man smirk again. "Take this." He slid a dollar bill into her pocket. The contact made her skin crawl. "Can't tell on me now, can you? Client privilege."

Kate grimaced in disgust as the dollar bill crinkled in her pocket. "Did you see that on some TV show?"

"You trying to insult my intelligence?"

"The last time I saw you, you were wearing a bell boy uniform, so excuse me if I'm not sold on your scheme here."

Fury twisted his face and for a terrifying moment she thought she'd gone too far. He still had a gun. He could still hurt Dylan. Or herself.

"But you got lucky," she said quickly. "I'm actually Dylan's lawyer too. We can work out a deal with him so he doesn't file charges. Right, Dylan?"

From his spot on the rug, Dylan nodded his head. Steve walked toward him and stood over his prone body, his back to the sliding door that led to the deck with its spectacular view of Misty Bay. The bright sun blazed through the glass, making her blink.

And then something caught her eye. A figure rose slowly into view from below.

Darius. Crouched in some kind of big bucket at the end of a crane—like the kind on a fire engine.

CHAPTER THIRTY-FIVE

As Darius gained enough height to see through the glass, Kate watched him assess the situation. His face hardened and he tapped something into his phone. Then he met her eyes and put a finger to his lips. *Keep quiet.* She got that message loud and clear. Then he gestured toward Steve and made a talking gesture with his hand.

Talk. Keep him distracted.

She swung her gaze back to Steve. He was no longer looking at Dylan. His attention was now focused on the rug.

Talk about the perfect distraction.

"Pretty naughty rug, isn't it?" She laughed lightly. "It was a present from my grandmother. I claim no responsibility for it. I hope you don't find it too embarrassing."

He squinted at the naked entwined figures. "What am I looking at here?"

"I believe it's a threesome," she told him. "Best I can make out. And that over there..." She pointed to a voluptuous woman adorning the far corner of the carpet. "I think that's a self-pleasuring situation."

With an amused cackle, he scanned the rug. He stepped closer to it, searching greedily for more poses. She shot a quick warning glance at Dylan to make sure he didn't do anything reckless while Darius was executing whatever his plan was.

She barely dared to glance toward the deck for fear she'd give herself away. Out of the corner of her eye, she saw Darius swing himself out of the bucket onto the deck. Immediately it lowered back down and he stepped to the side of the glass door, out of sight. Then she saw his hand reach for the lock, holding some kind of jimmying tool.

Keep talking. She needed to cover any sounds he might make while he tried to pry open the door. Well, if there was one thing she knew how to do, it was spill a bunch of words.

"This rug is based on the Kama Sutra, as a matter of fact. Have you ever heard of it? It's an ancient Sanskrit text from India devoted to sexual and emotional fulfillment. I looked it up after my grandmother gave it to me. There's a lot more to it than sex, but that's the part most people think of. I guess you can see why."

He was riveted by the play of figures on the rug.

"You really should have picked a more appropriate place to put this poor kid. He's a minor, you know. Hmm, I wonder if this would count as corrupting a minor? I'll have to look into that. It could add extra charges, so we'll have to come up with a strategy for that. Obviously, it helps that you didn't know about the rug. Who could predict something like that? Oh, here's something about our lawyer-client relationship. You're going to have to tell me everything so I can represent you properly. Everything about my father, your connection with him, how you got here, how you got into my apartment, so on and so forth. The more I know, the more I can help you."

The door slid open enough for Darius to slip through. Still holding the tool, he advanced toward Steve with murder in his eyes. Even though Steve had a gun and Darius only a jimmy, with that look Kate gave the advantage to the infuriated fire chief.

Steve wheeled around. He must have caught a glimpse of Darius' reflection or a shift in the light. With a vicious snarl, he charged toward Darius, lifting his gun arm as he went.

"Gun!" Kate shouted to warn Darius. She couldn't see where it was at the moment, but she knew Steve still had it.

Her heart nearly stopped as the two men lunged at each other. Any second, the gun would go off, Darius would spin back, wounded, dead...

In the midst of his headlong dive into battle, Steve suddenly stumbled. He lurched to the side. Fighting to regain his balance, he staggered a step, then lost control and crashed onto the floor. On top of Dylan's bound feet.

Amazingly, Dylan had managed to scoot down the rug and trip up Steve before he could get off a shot.

Darius pounced on Steve and slammed his gun-bearing hand to the floor. The gun skittered away. Kate chased after it and kicked it into the corner. She wanted nothing to do with the thing. Too many people in close quarters.

Instead she dropped down next to Dylan and carefully took the duct tape off his mouth. "Are you okay?"

He nodded and wetted his lips. "Hands?" he croaked.

She examined his wrists, which were wrapped in several layers of tape. His hands were going to be harder to free.

In the meantime, Darius turned Steve onto his stomach and tied his wrists behind his back using his own roll of duct tape.

"Don't move a muscle." His lethal tone left no doubt about his seriousness.

Steve didn't say a word, which was so unlike him. Kate realized he'd been knocked out at some point. Maybe by his fall, maybe by Darius.

Leaving Steve where he was, Darius crouched across from

her, at Dylan's other side. Even from there, she felt the vibrating tension in his body. His eyes were absolutely wild. Filled with passion and fury and words about to burst out of him.

"I got this." He drew out a Leatherman and sliced through the duct tape wrapped around Dylan's wrists and ankles. "Are you all right, Dylan?"

"Yeah."

Darius held his wrists, stroking gently to bring the blood back into them. "You tripped the motherfucker."

"He was about to shoot you."

"You did good. Real good. And you, Kate. Nice job on keeping him busy."

"You can thank Emma and her rug for that." Her voice sounded funny because all she could think about was how beautiful Darius was, how strong and wonderful and stern and caring and how she couldn't bear to say goodbye to him ever again. "Besides, you're the one who saved us. How did you know to come in here?"

"You just didn't sound like yourself," he said simply, lifting his gaze to hold hers. The intensity in it made her breath catch. "I know all your voices. I knew something was wrong."

Tears sprang to her eyes. The aftermath of being grabbed and threatened at gunpoint and fearful for Dylan—it all snowballed and she wanted to throw herself at him and cry on his shoulder.

But she couldn't do that. He was leaving Lost Harbor.

"I need to use the bathroom," Dylan said. "He wouldn't let me take a leak the entire time."

"Yeah. Of course." Darius helped him stand up. Dylan limped off toward the bathroom as Kate and Darius watched his every move.

"I hope he's—" Kate began anxiously.

Darius cut her off by cupping her face in his hand. "He's okay. But I'm not."

Oh my God. Had Steve gotten him after all? Frantic, she patted his chest, his arms, anywhere that he might be wounded. "Are you hurt?"

"No, but I'll die if I don't say this. I love you, Kate. It's not over for me. It'll never be over." Pure emotion, open and raw, blazed from his gray eyes. This was a Darius she'd glimpsed, but never seen in his full glory. Loving, powerful, caring, opening himself up to her—he took her breath away. "We can figure this out. I'll do whatever it takes. I'll fly back and forth. Spend summers here. I don't care. Anything except walk away from you. I thought I could, that I wasn't a romantic kid anymore, but I was wrong. I mean, I'm not a kid—I'm a man, with a man's heart. And it's yours."

She let out a sob of sheer astonishment. "It is?"

"When I saw you arguing with that asshole, like you were made of pure fire trying to keep Dylan safe, I wanted to throw myself through the glass for you. I want you. I love you. I'm yours, if you want me."

She threw herself into his arms, which he opened just in time. Being held by him again flooded her with transcendent joy. "I love you too, Darius. I'm not used to loving anyone, it's so confusing. I couldn't believe you wanted to just leave. You didn't even ask me if I wanted to come with you!"

"I didn't dare. I have Dylan with me now, and it all seemed too much to ask of you. But I should have. God, I should have. I should have told you how I felt." Holding her tightly, he moved his hands in delicious circles on her back. "I'm sorry I ever made you think I could live without you. You're my Kate. You're my everything, my light, my joy, my fire."

The tears were flowing down her face now. "How'd you get so good with words?" she wailed.

"I guess you're rubbing off on me." His chest shook with a deep chuckle. "Or maybe you just inspire me."

The sound of Dylan's footfalls made them pull apart. The boy looked from one to the other of them, hands on his hips. "I saw that."

Darius cleared his throat. "Yeah. We should talk."

Dylan put up a hand to forestall him. "I already know. You and Kate love each other and want to be together."

They glanced at each other and Kate twined her hand in his for support. Was this going to be difficult? She thought she had a good relationship with Dylan, but he was still mourning his mother. Maybe he didn't want an interloper around while he got to know his father.

"Yes," Darius said seriously. "All that is true. But that's about as far as we got. We're not making any plans without you—"

The boy interrupted him. "Can we forget this stupid Texas idea and just stay here?"

Darius' jaw fell open. "You don't want to go to Texas?"

"No way. I like it here. It's a fresh start. Or it will be, after people get used to me. That's what Maya says."

Darius nodded slowly, as if he was afraid to hope it was all going to work out. "I'll have to see if I can get my job back."

"They'd better not turn down the hottie fire chief." Kate squeezed his hand.

He raised an eyebrow at her. "There's another problem. We'll have to work it out with the landlady."

"I was thinking maybe I could have the upstairs, like it could be my bedroom." Dylan grinned, suddenly looking like an ordinary, carefree teenager. "That's why I came up here before. I woke up early and I went upstairs so I could imagine living there. It looked like someone had messed with the door. I shouldn't have gone in, that was stupid."

"You were really brave, Dylan," Kate told him. "Brave and a little reckless."

"Maybe it runs in the family." Dylan smirked.

Darius settled his arm over Kate's shoulders. The strength and love flowing through it turned her heart into a glowing ball of joy. "We'll think about your idea. Now how about you go tell the crew we're all fine and we have a suspect in custody? Kate and I will be right behind you."

"Sure thing, Dad." He headed for the door.

The look in Darius' eyes at the sound of that word sent a new wave of emotion through Kate's heart.

He spun her against him and cupped her face in both his big hands. For a moment they gazed at each other, joined in silent union, suspended in time.

Then he touched her mouth with his and she lost herself in a kiss she wanted to never end. This right here, her and Darius, this was the rock on which her life would rest from now until forever.

The sound of applause from outside made them break apart again.

"Dad?" Dylan called from the outdoor staircase. "You should see this. Look out front."

Still hand in hand, she and Darius slid open the glass door and stepped onto the front deck. The entire volunteer fire department had gathered outside. Various official and personal vehicles were parked along the street. They were cheering Dylan as he limped down the stairs.

"I texted Nate about Dylan being held hostage and saving the day by tripping the dude," Darius murmured. "Guess word must have spread."

Someone spotted them on the deck, and everyone's attention turned their direction. More applause, along with whistles and cat calls as people noticed they were holding hands.

Laughing, they both bowed to the crowd. "Thanks for all the help!" Darius called down to his crew. "Nate, we need to talk."

Nate laughed. "Job's yours again, Chief. No questions asked."

Whoops and cheers went up from the crowd. Kate threw

dramatic air kisses, as if they were royals on a palace balcony. Lord and Lady Armor-All, perhaps.

Darius drew her close and whispered in her ear, "Are you sure you want to stay in this crazy town?"

"With you? Absolutely."

CHAPTER THIRTY-SIX

The entire world looked different now that he and Kate were together—for real, and for good. Even in the always dingy Moose is Loose Saloon, colors were brighter, sounds were jazzier, his bass practically played itself. Darius grinned as he thrummed the strings to match the pace set by the drummer. He finally had his black hat back, and he had Kate, and Dylan, and that meant that every little thing was right with the world.

He knew the very moment that Kate blew in like a spark on the wind, eyes bright and smile naughty. She blew him a kiss that sizzled onto his skin.

He shot her a look of pure locked-and-loaded lust.

She found the table he'd saved for her near the stage. Maya joined her, wearing an off-hours outfit of slinky black velvet. They chatted intensely, heads together, as the band finished out the song.

The set ended and the singer called for a break. Darius wiped off his face and sauntered to the table to join his love and his colleague.

He and Kate indulged themselves in a long, passionate kiss that nearly knocked off his hat, while Maya looked at the ceiling and whistled a tune.

"You two done yet?"

"Sorry," said Darius, not feeling sorry at all. "Carry on. What'd I interrupt?"

"I was just filling in Kate on the perp. It turns out there's already a warrant out for his arrest in Cali. So I sent him back."

Kate pretended to glare at her friend. "As his lawyer, I should have been informed—" She broke off with a laugh. "God, I'm not even going to joke about it. Did I tell you that I cancelled my California bar membership so I can never get sucked into their games again?"

"Yeah, and I heard you're going for the Alaska bar," Maya said. "Think you remember how to study?"

"Oh, it's much easier this time." She smiled blissfully at Darius. "Someone keeps bringing me snacks and backrubs."

"Spare me the sappy visuals," Maya grumbled and turned to Darius. "I got a message that you wanted to talk to me about something."

"It's S.G.. She came to me with a request."

Kate jumped in. "She saw how happy Dylan is now that he found his real father."

"So Dylan's doing well?"

"*So* well. No more fights with other kids. He's taking summer classes to catch up. He's doing great." Kate glowed as she recounted Dylan's achievements; Darius loved the fact that she now considered his son part of her own family.

He took Kate's hand and ran his thumb across her palm as he addressed Maya. "S.G. came to me asking if there's a way to find her family. I explained that we don't even know if they're alive, but she wants to find them anyway. I told her it's not my department but that I'd talk to you. Any chance you can help her out?"

Maya's warm brown eyes gleamed. "Would she be okay answering questions about her childhood? I've been checking a few things out, but I didn't want to go too far unless she was ready. You sure she's up for this?"

"It was her idea."

"Good. Okay, tell her I'll arrange a meeting soon." Maya already had her phone out and was tapping something with her thumbs. "This is pretty exciting, actually. I've been hoping she'd want to explore her background. You know what, guys? I think I might head back and put my notes in order."

"You sure?" asked Kate. "There's a hottie over there watching you."

Maya barely glanced toward the blond man in the Henley a few tables over. She paused briefly, then shook her head. "Damn. But no. What's a man compared to a hot investigation?" She stood up and pushed back her chair. "You can catch a ride with Darius, right, Kate?"

"Don't worry about me. I hear they have cabins out back." She leaned against Darius' shoulder and he wrapped his arm around her. It felt like...perfection.

"Well, don't burn them down," Maya quipped as she left.

"No promises." Darius growled and hovered his mouth over Kate's. "I have big plans for tonight."

"You do?" Her dark eyes teased him and her curving lips drew him in for an irresistible kiss.

Oh yes, he had very big plans. For tonight, and all the nights that came after.

Very big, very naughty plans.

THANK you so much for reading! Coming next is Love At First Light, out in late summer. You can find all the Lost Harbor books here. Want to be the first to hear about new books, sales, and exclusive giveaways? Join Jennifer's mailing list and receive a free story as a welcome gift.

ABOUT THE AUTHOR

Jennifer Bernard is a *USA Today* bestselling author of contemporary romance. Her books have been called "an irresistible reading experience" full of "quick wit and sizzling love scenes." A graduate of Harvard and former news promo producer, she left big city life in Los Angeles for true love in Alaska, where she now lives with her husband and stepdaughters. She still hasn't adjusted to the cold, so most often she can be found cuddling with her laptop and a cup of tea. No stranger to book success, she also writes erotic novellas under a naughty secret name that she's happy to share with the curious. You can learn more about Jennifer and her books at JenniferBernard.net. Make sure to sign up for her newsletter for new releases, fresh exclusive content, sales alerts and giveaways.

Connect with Jennifer online:
JenniferBernard.net
Jen@JenniferBernard.net

ALSO BY JENNIFER BERNARD

Lost Harbor, Alaska

Mine Until Moonrise

Yours Since Yesterday ~ Book 2

Seduced by Snowfall ~ Book 3

Wicked in Winter ~ Book 4

The Rockwell Legacy

The Rebel ~ Book 1

The Rogue ~ Book 2

The Renegade ~ Book 3

The Runaway ~ Book 4

The Rock ~ Book 5

Jupiter Point ~ The Hotshots

Set the Night on Fire ~ Book 1

Burn So Bright ~ Book 2

Into the Flames ~ Book 3

Setting Off Sparks ~ Book 4

Jupiter Point ~ The Knight Brothers

Hot Pursuit ~ Book 5

Coming In Hot ~ Book 6

Hot and Bothered ~ Book 7

Too Hot to Handle ~ Book 8

One Hot Night ~ Book 9

Seeing Stars ~ Series Prequel

The Bachelor Firemen of San Gabriel Series

Love Between the Bases Series

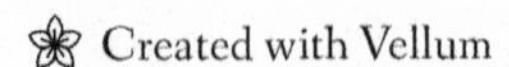
Created with Vellum

Made in the USA
Monee, IL
16 December 2020

53791275R00184